Over the Edge

Meredith Wild

WATERHOUSE PRESS

Over the Edge

For Team Wild,
for loving saucy stories as much as I do!

CHAPTER ONE

OLIVIA

The blackish walls of the underground tunnel blurred on either side of the train. The pungency of too many bodies crushed into one space mixed with the unnatural scent of the subway—something mechanical and gaseous at once.

On the other end of the car, a group of teenagers in school uniforms chatted loudly. A few middle-aged men in suits held onto the vertical poles and stared at their phones. A woman with long salt-and-pepper hair looked tired and worn, like she'd been on the train all night. We were a potpourri of culture and humanity, stuck in this stifling metal car.

I flinched when a warm hand touched mine. Beside me, a little girl no more than five years old gently traced her fingertip along the platinum charm that adorned my wrist. The Tiffany bracelet had been a gift from my parents.

"That's so pretty." She glanced up at me with mesmerizing brown eyes that widened when she smiled.

"Thanks," I said, returning her sweet smile.

She was striking for being so young. A true beauty. But as I looked closer, she had dirt under her fingernails, and her clothes were browning at the hems. Beside her sat a woman I guessed was her mother. Lines of age and experience spider-webbed her tanned skin. She glanced between her daughter and me before speaking to her in a language I didn't know, a series of reprimanding sounds and inflections. The girl's hand fell away quickly, and she cast her gaze to the floor.

No one ever said it, but I oozed privilege. I knew it. My upbringing clung to me everywhere I went. The truth of it made New York City the best and worst place for me to call home. Every day, extreme wealth met extreme poverty on the streets of this city. I'd been trying to work the middle ground, but I'd only ever known one life.

I exited at my stop and left the bustling station for the busy street. I exhaled the community air I'd spent the past ten minutes breathing. The early morning breeze was cool through my light shirt. I tried to tighten my blazer around me, except it was fashioned not to button in the front.

I turned the corner, and the building was already in sight. Only a block from the subway stop, the prime real estate would be home to our new fitness center—the project my brothers and I had been planning for months.

My brothers, Cameron and Darren, had informed me that walls would be going up this week. Construction sites weren't really my forte, but having been involved in the design and layout of our second location, I wanted to get a quick look at how the renovation was coming along.

I paused before the entrance. A temporary sign was bolted above the doorway that read, *Future Home of Bridge Fitness, A Donovan Property.* A swell of pride filled me when I thought about everything my brothers had accomplished with this venture, without the financial backing of our parents. Cameron and Darren were making it on their own, even if our family's wealth had provided every excuse not to.

One step inside, and a different kind of pride stiffened

my spine. The walls were going up indeed. Just beyond the entrance, a line of evenly spaced studs divided the entryway from the rest of the gym. I'd spent hours poring over blueprints with the architect, and that wall was *not* supposed to be there. Nonetheless, a worker was hammering nail after nail into the structure.

"This wall doesn't belong here," I said, pointing toward the offending two-by-fours.

The worker turned to me and then gestured to the other side of the room where two men were talking. "The boss is over there if you want to talk to him about it."

Without a second's delay, I approached the men. "Excuse me," I said firmly, barely able to harness my irritation.

Both turned toward me. The older one had gray hair buzzed close to his scalp and soft brown eyes. The younger man stilled when he saw me. His blue-eyed gaze made a slow circuit up and down my body. I shifted my blazer again. Unfortunately, the morning chill had turned my nipples into tiny popsicles, and anyone with two eyes could see that now.

I cleared my throat and prepared to rip him a new one. "We have a problem."

"What's the problem, miss?" The older man frowned.

"For starters, that's supposed to be a glass wall. You need to tell him to stop. You're wasting manpower and materials. This isn't what the plans call for."

The younger man spoke up. "And who are you?"

I cocked my head when his eyes narrowed slightly. The intense blue bored into me with an intensity that sent a shiver over my skin.

"I'm Olivia Bridge." I didn't bother shaking his hand. Hopefully the name rang a bell.

I straightened my spine, though I couldn't compete with the height of the broad-shouldered man in front of me. From the neck up, he was fashion catalogue material. Chiseled cheekbones and a strong jaw, dirty-blond hair that fell haphazardly across his forehead, and full, refined lips.

But this guy was a construction worker. Not my type. *At all.* His plain white T-shirt hinted at the muscular body beneath the cotton. His blue jeans fit well, snug around his thighs and bulging where his hands filled his pockets and in one more noticeable place. I averted my eyes quickly, noting the white dust that marked the denim at the knees.

I silently reproached myself for checking him out. He obviously had no class since his gaze hadn't left my breasts in the span of ten seconds.

I cleared my throat, regaining his attention. "This is *my* project. I worked on this design."

His unaffected expression seemed to reinforce my anger with every passing second.

I rolled my eyes with a sigh. "Maybe you're not the one to talk to. Who's in charge here?"

The corner of his mouth lifted, and his careful stare shifted to the older gentleman. "Tom, you want to deal with this?" He gestured along the length of me, as if *I* were the problem that needed to be dealt with. "I'm going to check out the progress upstairs."

"Sure thing." Tom rubbed his forehead as he guided me away. "So *this* is the wall you're talking about?"

"Yes, this was meant to be glass. All the way across. We want people to walk in and see the facility and everything we offer, not drywall. You need to take these studs out immediately."

"Okay." He frowned. "There must have been a change in

the plans."

I lifted my brows. "You have a blueprint. Why would you change the plans?"

"This is a structural wall here, so I'm guessing instead of putting in reinforcements, Will modified the plans."

"Why would he do that?"

He let out a soft chuckle. "Well, it's a lot cheaper, for one."

I frowned. "I don't care how much it costs." My voice went up an octave. "This isn't what we agreed on."

He sighed. "I guess I'll have to run it by Will."

"Who's Will? I thought you were the boss."

He laughed and rubbed his forehead again. "No, I'm just the GC. Will Donovan's the boss. You just met him. He owns the building, so whatever he says goes."

"Oh."

Shit. The man I'd mistaken for an exceptionally good-looking laborer was Will Donovan, the investor and real estate developer whom my brothers spoke of frequently. I'd never met him, but I knew enough about him to know I'd probably pissed him off. Too bad for him. I wasn't going to stop until I got my way.

I put my hand on my hip and took a quick scan around the empty shell of a room. I should let this go, but I couldn't. Cameron and Darren—all of us—had worked too hard to start cutting corners now. "I guess you'd better reintroduce me to Will."

"This way," he said with a grimace before leading me through a long unfinished hallway and upstairs to the second floor.

Will was leaning over a kitchen island, looking at blueprints that nearly covered the whole surface. He straightened when we entered. A quick glance passed between him and Tom, and I couldn't tell if Will was amused or on edge. His height and the confidence in his stride as he approached gave me pause though.

"Miss Bridge. You're back."

"I am," I said simply, curbing my tone now that I knew whom I was talking to.

He nodded toward Tom. "You can get back to work. I'll take care of this." He glanced back to me. "What can I do for you?"

"Tom explained the structural situation, but I'm concerned because this is not the design that we approved."

"Cameron has given me creative control." He crossed his arms, and the motion showcased his firm muscled arms. A mild distraction as I processed those last words.

"He has." A statement. More like a statement filled with disbelief. Cameron couldn't have done that. "I don't understand."

"Part of my investment is in the build-out. If I need to make adjustments to keep us on budget, I will."

"You're compromising our design and our brand. How do you expect us to pay you back when you're ruining our design?"

"I think you're being a little dramatic over a wall, Miss Bridge."

I glanced around the open floor plan and quickly moved past him. I stopped when I stood under a wide arch that provided an opulent threshold between the kitchen and the living room of what I assumed would ultimately be a luxury condominium.

I turned toward him and pointed to the arch. "Was this a structural wall?"

"Yes."

"And I take it you were able to resolve that?"

The corner of his lips lifted a fraction. "Obviously."

"To preserve the view?" I lifted my brow in challenge.

"That's a multimillion-dollar view, Miss Bridge. So is the room next to it. Needless to say, the budget allows for these things."

"Our fitness centers aren't sweaty gyms for jocks. They are visually appealing. They welcome members and inspire healthy lifestyles. We want patrons to walk through the front door and experience that."

"Have dinner with me."

My lips parted, but no words came. I wasn't expecting that major shift in the conversation. "Excuse me?"

He cocked his jaw, and his tongue poked against his cheek, as if he were considering something. "We can go over the plans. I appreciate your passion for aesthetic. I'm sure we can find some common ground."

"We can find common ground right here. I'm telling you—"

"I'm your only investor on this project, and you're challenging my choices. So you can continue pissing me off, or we can have dinner and discuss this further."

Blood rose to my cheeks as he walked toward me. Those slow confident strides were becoming more and more distracting. He paused when he was only a foot from me. His energy and dominance nearly set me back a step, but I held my ground.

"Maybe I should just talk to Cameron about this," I said, but the veiled threat came out shakier than I had wanted it to.

"Let me know how that goes," he said flatly.

I lifted my chin, weighing his last sentence. One carefully

worded call to Cameron, and Will could make sure I wouldn't step foot in here again until the ribbon-cutting. I was protective over the design, but I knew Cameron wouldn't do anything to compromise the timeline. And if getting my way cost me a night otherwise spent with reruns, fine. Obviously the current route wasn't getting me far.

"And the wall?" I crossed my arms as frustration and intrigue fought for control over my emotions.

Amusement glittered in his eyes. Maybe from my persistence. Maybe because he knew I was about to agree to his invitation.

"I'll tell Tom to stop construction on it for now. Stand me up, and I'll have drywall on it by morning."

I ground my teeth, biting down on all the expletives I wanted to hurl at him. "Fine."

He smiled, revealing a perfect set of straight white teeth. "I'll have a car pick you up at eight."

WILL

I had a weakness for rich girls. Maybe because I'd spent roughly half my life figuring out new and creative ways to get them to fall on their backs for me. But more than that, I enjoyed their layers. Or lack thereof, depending on the girl. I played a game with myself, trying to peg what their fathers did, what borough they lived in, what schools they went to. Out loud I pretended to care about any of it as a means to getting them to betray their careful upbringing and let me fuck them filthy.

Over time I'd discovered that under every rich girl I met, there was a dirty girl waiting for the right guy to invite them out to play. That was me. I was that guy.

I'd intended to pick Olivia Bridge up from her Brooklyn brownstone and eye-fuck her all the way to dinner. A prelude of the filthy things I planned to do to her—with her permission, of course. But my father had called me again, so she was riding alone, and I was stuck in my condo pacing through a conversation I didn't want to have. I'd dodged my father's calls all week, but I couldn't avoid him forever.

"How have you been? I haven't heard from you in a while." Forced affection strained his words.

I rolled my eyes and held back an audible sigh. Bill Donovan rarely wasted time with formalities, which told me that he was getting desperate for my ear.

"Cut to the chase, Dad. What do you want?"

He was silent a moment. "I want to talk to you about contingencies if this investigation escalates."

I shook my head, angry all over again for the mess he'd gotten himself into. A mess that was quickly bleeding into my own affairs, despite the years I'd spent ensuring our businesses intersected as rarely as possible.

"Do you think it will?"

His voice was quiet and low. "I can't say. We have the best legal money can buy, but if there's an indictment, we're finished."

The investigation into his and his business partners' shady dealings funneling millions through a local charity had been going on for months. There had been whispers, but so far no charges had come down on them. If they did and he was found guilty, he'd be looking at restitution and the possibility of doing time at one of those resorts in upstate New York they called "jail" for white-collar folks like him and his cohorts.

Worse, the damage to his reputation in the financial world

would be irreparable.

"It was an arts charity for underprivileged youth, for Christ's sake. You couldn't have picked someone else to scam out of their money?"

He made an unintelligible sound on the other end of the phone. "I didn't call to talk about that, Will. If any of us are charged, the business will suffer. All the investors will walk. I need you back in the ring until the situation stabilizes."

He'd been trying to pull me into the hedge fund he ran with David Reilly since its inception earlier in the year. I'd entertained a few cocktails and lunches with investors, but I wasn't interested in that world. I had my own projects to nurse.

"Don't you pay people to run your businesses? You don't need me."

"You're the only one I trust. Especially under the current circumstances. Beyond that, it's your money too."

"I don't care about the money."

"You think you don't care because you've never had to live a day of your life without it. I made damn sure of that." His words whipped through the phone, sharp with truth and weighted with years of tireless effort that went into building a lifetime of wealth.

Our relationship had always been matter of fact. The facts about the tried-and-true path to success. The facts about money and business. The facts about women, which in reality were his slanted personal opinions about the finer sex and their usefulness when it came to satisfying one's personal sexual appetites. He was all fact and no feeling, and that's how I'd been raised.

According to his law, I should drop him like a bad fucking habit and move on with my life. I searched for empathy, but

I could only muster mild concern and a massive dose of irritation that he'd been irresponsible enough to possibly get caught. Now I was at risk of being ensnared in his affairs when I was firmly committed to my own. The last thing I wanted to do was inherit his problems, or his hedge fund.

"I don't want to get involved in this," I finally said.

"The things that went down with the Youth Arts Initiative are a separate matter. The money in the fund is clean. You have my word. I can get back on track after all this, but not without your help. Just meet with me. I can lay it all out for you, and you can see what's at stake."

I hesitated. He was in deep shit, and as much as I disagreed with his ethics, he was my father and I could at least hear him out—even if I wasn't willing to stick my neck out to protect his money. *Our* money, considering I was his only heir and he'd rather burn every dollar than give a penny more to my mother.

"I'm in the middle of a major renovation. I don't have a lot of time right now."

"I'll swing by the site this week. Won't take long."

I didn't want him anywhere near my project. "I'd rather you didn't. Let's meet for lunch. I'll text you when and where."

"Okay. Thank you."

The hint of vulnerability in his voice scared me more than anything. Desperation where there'd been only righteous, fearless dedication to his work.

I hung up and stared at the skyline through my window. Another million-dollar view. I had plenty, and my father was right. I'd never known a life without the security of wealth—wealth that he'd amassed by any cutthroat means possible, it would seem. I'd taken my share and played with it in my real estate ventures. But I'd never take his path—moving money between accounts and countries and investments. Options and futures and formulas that only made sense to money-chasers like my father.

And when I finally decided to sit down with him, that's exactly what he was going to try to sell me. A life I'd never wanted.

I glanced at my watch and moved for the door. I was late, pissed off, and all I wanted was to take those frustrations out on the beautiful brat that was Olivia Bridge.

CHAPTER TWO

WILL

The maître d' led me to a private table for two in the back of Artu, the upscale restaurant I'd chosen for our dinner tonight. Olivia leaned back in her chair, staring at the brightly lit screen of her phone. Her legs were crossed at the knee under a black-and-white lace pencil skirt that hugged her hips and thighs. Her simple black top was tasteful and revealing at once. I guessed that every piece of her outfit tonight had been carefully chosen to appear professional, except those five-inch black heels that I wanted on either side of my ears.

As I approached, her smile was tight and her shoulders stiffened. "You came. And to think you were worried about me standing *you* up."

She was upset. I held my tongue a moment because that little temper of hers was proving to be a weakness for me. I couldn't wait to fuck the haughty right out of her. Blood flowed south when I thought about the lovely line of her body bending for me, arching under a screaming orgasm as I pounded my way toward my own.

I sat down across from her and exhaled air meant for words I couldn't say just yet. She wasn't a bimbo at a bar. She was highly educated, armed with high standards and a sharp tongue. I had to deal with those circumstances delicately to get what I wanted, not to mention mitigate any potential fallout with her brothers after she heard my proposition.

"I had to take an important call." I draped my napkin over my lap. "Have you been here before?"

"A couple times," she said flatly. She did her best to ignore me by studying the menu.

After a moment, the waiter came and took our orders. When he disappeared, the silence between us felt electric with possibilities. I raked her in, making up for the lost time.

"You look lovely, Olivia."

She tucked a sleek strand of dark-brown hair behind her ear. She was fidgety, avoiding my eyes, silently telling me that she wasn't immune to my blatant appraisal of her. "So you wanted to discuss the plans?"

"I'd like to get to know you first," I murmured.

She took a deep breath and folded her hands together in front of her. "You know my brothers well enough. Why are you suddenly so interested in me?"

"When I see something I want, I don't waste time going after it. I'm a little impulsive that way."

"And what exactly do you want from me?"

I exhaled softly. I wanted so many things...so many delicious and depraved things. I leaned forward and took her hand gently, bringing it across the table toward me. Her lips parted and her chest moved under a shaky breath. Soft olive skin slid like silk under my touch. Circling her wrist, I let the cool metal of her bracelet rest in my palm. A small charm hung from it. A crown with diamonds decorating the tips.

"This is pretty."

"It was from my parents. A graduation gift."

My wheels began turning. I already knew so much about

Olivia, the game almost wasn't fair. Still, I couldn't help myself.

"Vassar?"

"Smith."

I lifted my eyebrows in surprise. "Top tier, all girls. Interesting. Must be where you got that sharp tongue."

She laughed and pulled her hand back. "Four years without a bunch of elite chauvinists marching all over my words were refreshing, for sure."

"Women's studies?"

"Studio art. How about you? Oh, let me guess..." She pursed her lips like she was calculating. "Brown." Her eyes lit up as she said it.

I was silent, momentarily unwilling to admit she was right and in disbelief that she seemed to be enjoying a game I had invented a long time ago for my own smug entertainment.

"Why Brown?"

"Ivy league, because your family could obviously afford it. But trendy and progressive, because you don't really fit the mold."

"Is that so?"

"I don't know a lot of guys with your resources who are getting dirty on construction sites."

I laughed out loud. "Ah, right. Good thing Tom introduced us properly. No way I was getting a date with you until you could establish my tax bracket."

She rolled her eyes, and I couldn't hide the grin splitting my face. Getting under a girl's skin shouldn't be this much fun.

"I'd guess what your father does, but I obviously already know."

"Same," she said with a tight smile.

Her quick reply knocked the wind out of me a little. My

first instinct was always to defend my father to outsiders, but what he'd done was reprehensible. Didn't change the fact that we were flesh and blood, though.

"There it is. I was waiting for that."

A flash of remorse flickered in her cool blue eyes, like she wanted to apologize but had too much pride. I didn't need her apologies or her sympathy.

Under normal circumstances, I might be concerned about our family's connection. Our fathers had both spent time on Wall Street and no doubt shared several business connections. But I cared less about her parents learning of the proposition I was about to make than how my father's stained reputation could become an impediment to getting her under me.

I sipped my wine and watched her do the same, enjoying the way her full lips met the delicate rim of the glass. Then her tongue swiping over her lips.

"You're single," I said. *She'd fucking better be.*

"At the moment."

"That's good news for me, but why?"

She lifted an eyebrow.

"Beautiful, the best education money can buy, wealthy family. You should be married off by now. Or am I missing something?"

She looked thoughtfully at her wineglass, twirling it by the base. "Not that it's any of your business, but I only moved to the city a year ago, and I'm still getting settled. Getting 'married off' isn't exactly a priority for me. Right now, the only thing I care about is helping Cameron and Darren get through this expansion. I've devoted myself to the project, and now you're messing it up."

I drummed my fingers on the tablecloth. "Is this about the

wall?"

"This is about the wall and every other *adjustment* you plan to make that compromises our vision."

"What if I said you could have creative control on the renovation from here forward?"

She blinked. "I thought you were on a budget."

I shrugged and pursed my lips. "Convince me not to be."

She swallowed, a new light in her eyes. "Well, there are certain aesthetics that will set us apart from everyone else—"

"Convince me tonight. At my place."

She shook her head slightly. "What are you saying?"

"I think you know exactly what I'm saying. I'd like to get to know you better. Quite a bit better, in fact."

She stared silently, her soft lips parted. "You obviously don't know anything about me if you expect me to sleep with you after a little dinner and wine."

"I may know you better than you know yourself."

She let out a short laugh. "I highly doubt it."

I riled at the challenge, and after her little comment about my dad, I felt compelled to set her straight.

"You reek of privilege, Olivia. You pretend to be independent, but you still use your parents' credit cards. Nothing drives you more than social expectation and a looming fear of failure. You're naturally stunning, but that look of effortless beauty probably costs your parents a fortune. You're high maintenance. From your designer hair cut down to your manicured little toes. I'd be willing to bet you hit the spa once a month to wax your pretty little cunt too, not because you're getting laid but because being unkempt goes against your debutante religion."

"Fuck you," she snapped.

The murmur of conversation around us died down for a moment, but I didn't bother checking to see which of our table neighbors we were offending. Instead, I exhaled a frustrated groan because I'd hit a nerve. And because now I couldn't think about anything except her smooth pussy in my mouth.

"I'd love to, princess. When's the last time someone took you to bed and fucked you properly?"

I half expected her to storm out on me. I'd offended her in multiple ways, and we hadn't even hit the main course. But the determination in her eyes told another story. That spark of fire spoke of a willingness to hold her ground, or more, to fight back and win.

Her cheeks were pink, and her hand trembled when she went for her wineglass again. If not for her age, I'd have wondered if she was a virgin. Either way, I guessed she was way overdue in the intimacy department.

She swallowed and set her glass down hard. "You're a pig."

I smiled. On to the next round.

"I do enjoy the filthy arts. I think you might, too. What do you say, Olivia? We can enjoy a little rendezvous here and there, and in return, I'll let you spend my cash like Monopoly money on the renovation. Keep your brothers happy. Keep me happy. And then I'll keep you happy."

She lifted her chin. "You can't buy me."

"I'm well aware of that. But this isn't about the money. It's about you getting what you want. And me getting what I want."

She crossed her arms tightly but didn't say anything more. Poor little rich girl betraying her sensibilities. If the attraction was real, she could seduce herself with the prospect, her sensibilities be damned.

I leaned in and gazed intently at her. "Let me be clear,

Olivia. I'm not a guy you date, and I'm nowhere near husband material. I'm the one you mess around with until the right guy comes along—one your parents will approve of. But I'm rich and well connected enough for you to be seen with, and you'll find out soon that when it comes to delivering orgasms, I'm rather dedicated to my craft. Once you say yes to me, you'll be too busy coming to worry about your pride."

Her cheeks flushed a deeper pink, setting off the dazzling blue of her eyes. "You're cocky, too. You forgot that."

I smirked, and the waiter took that opportune moment to bring our meals. She lifted her knife and fork and speared them into her steak without a word. I dismantled my sea bass with a little less vigor, occasionally glancing up at her, trying to read her. I wanted to ask her more about herself, but I also enjoyed the way my proposition and her consideration of it hung between us. A little awkward, but heavy and sexual too.

I took my last bite and dropped my napkin on the table. The food was delicious and the company was fine, but I wasn't nearly satisfied. I wanted Olivia Bridge naked, under me.

"You're considering my offer. Tell me what's holding you back. What are you thinking?"

Her cool gaze flickered to mine. "Are you asking for an answer or a confession? My thoughts are none of your business."

I shrugged slightly. "I'm curious."

"So am I."

OLIVIA

"I'd love nothing more than to indulge that curiosity, Olivia." Will's words were low, confident, and laced with dark promises.

I would have paid to disintegrate into the floor without another word. I was being reckless. Brazen. Inappropriate. No more inappropriate than Will, but now I was inching my way to his level. I was letting him get into my head.

My negotiation skills might have been lacking, but I wasn't naïve. When a man invited a woman to dinner—a confident, gorgeous, and decidedly single man like Will Donovan—chances were high that he factored in the possibility of sex. He knew it, and I knew it. And now I'd basically shown him all my cards.

Going into this dinner, I'd had no intentions of sleeping with Will. That didn't keep the delicious fantasy from poking its way into my thoughts, however. I *was* curious. Physically, I was attracted to him, but I was also drawn to his confidence and that edge that made him different from other prospects. I wanted to peel him back the way he was intent on peeling me back. But I had a feeling he was a lot better at it and that I was woefully out of my depth.

The waiter cleared our plates and brought dessert menus. I tried to ignore Will and the silent push and pull that seemed to exist between us even when no words were being spoken. I studied the menu, attempting to buy myself time to get my head together.

The truth was I hadn't been with anyone since I'd left my father's private investment firm nearly a year ago, and that experience had been less than pleasant. After enough wine to dull my reservations, I'd let my father's newly appointed vice president at the firm take me to bed. The sex had been quick and passionless, but he was moving up fast in the company, so he was the one my parents were relentlessly pushing me toward. I wasn't sure, ultimately, if I'd given in for him or for them.

The next day, I'd called Cameron and made the decision to leave my job there and move to the city.

Now I was sitting across from a man who sizzled with sex appeal and was all but guaranteeing physical pleasure. Plus, no strings beyond the added bonus of getting to have a voice in the renovation of my family's next investment? He was challenging my sense of propriety, but he was also painting a picture that ran in stark contrast to anything I'd experienced.

After a few minutes, I finally looked up to meet Will's imploring gaze. "Are we getting dessert?"

"We can. Unless you've decided to come home with me."

"I'll have the cheesecake," I said quickly, dropping the menu between us.

He licked his bottom lip with a cocky smile. "Sounds delicious."

Dessert came and went, but I was too preoccupied with Will's dangerous energy and his proposal to savor much of anything. We left the restaurant, and the car that had collected me earlier idled by the curb. Will's hand rested lightly on my lower back. That small touch held the promise of so many more, heightening the physical ache that had been creeping up on me since we'd met. The ache made me want to give Will an answer that seemed unthinkable.

I moved quickly toward the car, needing to create space between us. But before I could slip away, he caught my wrist and spun me to face him. With a soft push against the car, Will had our bodies nearly touching.

"Will—" I gasped.

His heated gaze lowered to my lips. "If you won't give me

an answer tonight, how about a kiss?"

"No." My voice was soft and uncertain.

"Dare I ask why?" He leaned in but didn't make contact. His breath puffed softly against my cheek. His cool and woodsy scent drifted over me, making an indelible imprint on my senses.

The manageable measure of desire that had burned through my veins over dinner was spiking. A potent heat licked over my skin and settled between my legs. I swallowed hard, trying to find my strength. "Because if I kiss you, I may as well give you my answer now."

"I fail to see the problem," he murmured.

I placed a firm hand on his chest. "I think before I act, and you aren't giving me time to think."

He moved back slowly. Tension lined his shoulders and crept up to his jaw, as if he were restraining himself. "Then think. But I want an answer by tomorrow."

"You'll have an answer when I give you one."

He tapped his watch twice. "Clock is ticking. Need to close up that wall for the next inspection."

I opened my mouth to speak, but before I could throw any more sass at him, he guided me into the car and tapped the roof to signal the driver to go.

As Will's driver put the vehicle into motion, I relaxed against the cool leather and closed my eyes. I should have felt relief, but instead I was unsettled, stirred up with more emotions than I knew what to do with. All this and he'd barely touched me.

The prospect of letting him get any closer was frightening, and all too tempting.

★ ★ ★

"So where'd you go last night?"

"Huh?" I knit my brows together and glanced up from the haphazard sketches in front of me.

Maya, my very pregnant sister-in-law, joined me in her living room with a bowl of oatmeal in hand. "I saw you take off in a car last night. Hot date?"

She wiggled her eyebrows, and I tried not to laugh. Cameron emerged from the kitchen, the scowl noticeable on his face.

My smile faded. "More of a business meeting."

"With?" Maya sank into the couch adjacent to me, rested the bowl on her belly, and took a spoonful to her mouth.

"Will Donovan. I met him at the new location yesterday. He wanted to discuss...some design direction with me."

I felt guilty for lying, but if Cameron knew, his reaction would be murderous.

"And how did that go?" Cameron's deep voice filled the room, his overprotectiveness not to be missed.

"Fine. I noticed some of the build-out wasn't going to plan. I voiced my concerns, and he's agreed to give me creative control." *As long as I agree to sleep with him.*

I wanted to flog myself for even considering it, but I'd woken up with Will's proposition as prominent in my mind as it had been when I'd driven away from him last night.

I'd cycled through all the emotions. Fury that he'd be so bold to think I'd ever consider it. Frustration that bringing up his bad behavior to my brothers would only hurt the project that we'd all invested so much into. And finally, a spark of intrigue at what such a misadventure could be like.

He frowned, and for a second, I worried he could see the truth written on my features.

"He picked you up in a private car to give you creative control over his investment?"

"Something like that," I said, my voice light.

"So what did you think about him?" Maya asked.

I shrugged. "He's okay. Kind of cocky." *And rude. And incredibly sexy.*

Maya snorted. "Typical finance guy."

"He's a real estate developer. And typical or not, he's the one who's putting his money on the line," Cameron said.

He was right, and I probably should have cared more about Will's very important investment. But in this moment, I was more concerned about the way my body paid attention when he was near. His easy and confident way irritated me as much as it aroused me.

"He was making changes to the plans," I said, without looking at my brother directly.

"If it's a problem, I can step in, Liv. This needs to stay on schedule."

"I'm aware of that. So is Will. Trust me," I said, hoping to reassure him.

His expression remained taut. "Okay. Well, keep me in the loop." He softened when he leaned down to kiss Maya. "I have to head to the gym and take care of some things. You okay?"

"I'm good." She smiled, her brown eyes glittering when they met his concerned expression.

He gently rested his hand on the swell of her belly. "Call if you need anything. Anything, okay?"

"I promise. I will. Now go to work, and I'll try not to go into labor while you're gone."

He kissed her again and left us.

When the door clicked shut behind him, Maya blew out an audible breath. "Sorry. He's gone into big-brother-overprotective-daddy mode lately."

"I know. He's always been like that. Probably will only get worse now."

She put her bowl to the side and folded her legs up on the couch. "So tell me what really happened with Will."

I widened my eyes a fraction. "Nothing. That's pretty much it."

She canted her head. "Don't bullshit me, Liv. I've seen Will. He's a dream. Any sparks?"

I shrugged because I didn't know what to say. Sparks had flown, along with an indecent proposal and some very inappropriate banter. I couldn't risk telling Maya because it might get back to Cameron. I trusted her, but he was her husband and their confidences came first.

"He's definitely not husband material," I said, using Will's own words.

She fiddled with the tail on her long blond braid. "I don't think many single guys are. But you have to start dating at some point. You can't stay cloistered in your apartment downstairs forever."

I let out a short laugh. "I'm sure the last thing Cam wants is for me to start bringing dates home."

"He'd get over it. Eventually."

I shook my head, because he wouldn't.

Between Cameron and Darren hovering constantly, I could hardly give a guy a second glance at the gym, let alone my number. Even if I did, the prospect of entertaining any kind of normal dating relationship opened up another world of problems. My parents' world, specifically. I'd seen what they'd put Cameron and Darren through with their romantic relationships, but I wasn't like my brothers. They were fiercely independent, strong-willed in the face of our parents' judgments.

Frank and Diane Bridge weren't letting me slip away into the arms of just any man without one hell of a fight. They'd all but promised me this. I wasn't in the mood for that fight.

"I have plenty of time to date. I want to focus on the business right now."

"Listen, Cameron is going to have his hands full when the baby comes. Between that and work, he probably wouldn't notice if you shaved your head. Promise me you'll try to get out there a little more. I'd offer to be your wing woman, but you know." She gestured to her very pregnant state with a silly smile.

I laughed. "I'm not in any rush, but I'll give it some thought, okay?"

Oddly, I couldn't envision jumping into the dating scene, but I could imagine taking Will up on his ridiculous offer.

Being with him could be safe because he wasn't a prospect. Neither of us wanted a relationship, and he wasn't someone I'd have to measure up against my parents' or anyone else's standards. Truth was, this arrangement could be perfect.

Or it could be a complete disaster.

"What are you working on?" Maya pulled me from my tumultuous thoughts and pointed toward my notebook.

"Just sketching some things out for the baby's room."

Maya had enlisted my art major skills to paint a mural for my nephew's nursery, but I'd yet to begin.

"You should start soon. My due date is a few weeks away,

but I have no idea when this little guy will decide to show up."

"I know. I want it to be perfect though." I'd gone through a dozen drafts, but nothing felt good enough.

"Anything painted with love by his auntie will be perfect. Just go for it. Have fun with it." She smiled warmly, but her gentle encouragement wasn't enough to nudge me out of my creative funk.

I hadn't painted since graduation. I'd been thrown into work with my dad and pushed into dating someone I had zero interest in. The turmoil should have driven me toward an outlet, but I'd been too busy starting over in the city to tap that passion. I'd latched onto Cameron's life instead, ignoring the one thing that used to really make me happy.

"Hey."

Maya's concerned gaze came back into focus. "What?"

"You went someplace else for a minute. What's on your mind, Liv?"

I sighed and tossed down my pencil. "I don't know. It's been almost a year since I moved in, and I still feel...*off* somehow. Like I'm treading water and have no idea where I'm supposed to go next."

She was thoughtful a moment. "Is there anything I can do?"

"No, you and Cam have already done so much. I'm living in your house. I feel like a total leech on your life sometimes."

"Don't be crazy. You helped Cam turn this place into a home before I even got here."

"But you're a couple now, and you're about to be a family. You don't need a fourth person lurking around."

She laughed loudly. "You don't lurk. You're my friend, and now you're my sister. I like having you here. If you leave, who's going to gang up on Cam with me when I need to get my way?"

I smiled. Maya and I had gone to college together, lived in the same dorm, and a fast friendship had formed. Then she started dating my brother, and when their relationship fell apart, so did ours. I'd cut things off, resentful of how Cameron had dealt with the separation from Maya. I'd been young, too, and misguided by my mother's disapproval of her.

I hadn't always been fair, but I was more grateful than Maya probably realized that she'd come back into our lives. For Cameron's sake and for mine. After years of the silence, we were slowly rebuilding a friendship that I'd missed so much.

"I'm serious, you know. We love having you here."

I exhaled a sigh. "Thank you. I guess something's missing, is all. I'm just not sure what it is yet."

"Well, when you figure it out, I'm here for you. To talk and bitch. Whatever you need."

I nodded, pretending for her sake that whatever was missing in my life could be fixed that easily. But in a matter of weeks, Maya's life would dramatically transform. As grateful as I was for our rekindled friendship, she'd have bigger priorities than tending to the emptiness that had taken up residence around my heart.

CHAPTER THREE

IAN

I flipped through the morning news channels, landing on a story that covered the three-alarm fire I had worked the night before. The electrical fire had sparked in the basement and spread quickly, consuming most of the building. Thankfully, we were able to get everyone out and contain it. I was exhausted, but my adrenaline was still kicking hours after my shift had ended.

The news segment played out, and I caught a glimpse of my face as I worked the hose.

"Fuck," I muttered.

Will shuffled out in a pair of mesh shorts. His hair was sticking up. He glanced at the television. "Fuck what?"

"I have to pay for dinner at the station tonight. Standing rule when one of our faces hits the papers or the news."

He chuckled and went to the kitchen, emerging a couple of minutes later with a steaming cup of coffee from the fresh pot I'd brewed.

He sat at the end of the couch, took a sip, and rested his head back with a tired sigh.

"What's with you?"

He rubbed his eyes. "Ah, I didn't get a lot of sleep."

I smirked. "Sounds promising. Who kept you up?"

"No one. Got shot down, and I could have really used the company."

"Not often that you let one slip through your fingers. She must have been a piece of work. Either that or you were on your worst behavior."

"Little bit of both. But Olivia Bridge is definitely a piece of work. I'm determined though." He glanced at the clock on the wall. "Hoping to hear from her today, actually."

I stared at him, frozen as I replayed his words in my head. Had I heard him right? "Wait. Olivia Bridge? As in Darren and Cameron's sister?"

"That's the one. I take it you've met her?"

"A couple times at the gym. Darren nearly broke my face for looking too long."

He grinned and blew a puff of steam off his mug. "Can't blame you for looking. I took her out last night and couldn't take my eyes off of her. Would be a lot easier to get her under me if her brothers stayed out of the way, though. Either way, she's an adult. She sure as hell has her own mind."

Guilt swirled in my gut. I loved women, and I'd taken my fair share to bed. Will and I were cut from the same cloth that way. My friend's baby sister getting mixed up with either one of us definitely wasn't good news, especially if Darren got wind of it.

"So what's the plan?" If she'd already shot him down, maybe there wasn't one.

"Just waiting on her to make the next move. I'll let you know if it goes anywhere."

He winked, and more guilt took root.

I was between apartments and had accepted a room at Will's place a few months ago in return for some side work that he needed for his renovation. In that time, we'd gotten to know each other well. An easy friendship had formed, and women were a regular part of our interactions. We pursued them, enjoyed them, and sometimes we even shared them.

Putting Olivia anywhere near that category challenged my already taxed nerves. Darren was one of my best friends. I'd saved his life, and I knew he'd do the same for me in a heartbeat. His sister was a ten, but fuck.

I tried to focus on the television, which was now broadcasting a political story that made me want to throw the remote. Same shit, different day.

I stood and tossed the remote to Will. "I'm going to clean up and get some sleep. I'll catch you later."

"All right. Hey, I need you to help me pick out some of the materials for the condos above the Bridge site. You want to swing by there later? You owe me rent, and my bathrooms need tile."

I laughed. "Yeah, sure. I'll come by before my shift tonight."

Once in my room, I hastily undressed and fell into bed. Behind my eyelids, a vision of Olivia formed. Those icy blue eyes that I couldn't forget. Every time we met, I had to fight every primal instinct not to make a move on her. I could hardly fault Will.

Not voicing some reservation felt like a betrayal to Darren, but I couldn't keep Will from pursuing a beautiful woman.

But if he managed to get her into bed...

I groaned and rubbed my eyes. Damn. We weren't going to share her. No matter how much I might want to.

WILL

The scent of wood and dust tinged the air. I stood still with my arms crossed. The sounds of progress filled my ears, but my thoughts were far away from the work that was being done before me.

Three days had passed. I'd had Tom rip out the studs of the entryway wall and add reinforcements to support Olivia's dream glass wall. Wishful thinking, perhaps. I hadn't texted or called, and I hadn't heard a word from her either. The gauntlet had been thrown, and I'd be damned if I was going to beg.

Cameron had come by to discuss progress. Neither of us had mentioned Olivia, but I sensed an undercurrent of tension between us that hadn't existed before. Perhaps he'd learned of my dinner with her, but for the sake of our working relationship for the remainder of this project, I sincerely hoped that Olivia had omitted the finer details of our conversation.

A vision of her pressed against my car flashed across my mind. Her brown hair blowing in wisps. Her soft pink lips, parted and full. Her body communicating in a thousand subtle ways that she wanted me to kiss her. I should have, and then she would have given me an answer right then.

Instead, I'd let her go.

I hadn't wanted to give her time to think. But the less impulsive part of me knew her surrender would be all the sweeter if she could talk herself into it and save me the guilt. No room for regret. Still, I wasn't quite sure how to handle seeing her again if the answer was no. I wasn't used to getting shot down.

Only time would tell. But how much time?

I cursed quietly as the rest of my crew went to work nailing up drywall, the next phase of turning the first floor into a fully outfitted fitness center in a few short weeks. On an average day, I'd be preoccupied with the transformation. Today I was preoccupied with something else entirely, and it was driving me fucking crazy.

Fuck it.

Kevin, my drywall guy, was carrying sheets in a few at a time. I went to help him and spent the next four hours making a total mess of myself. The work was labor intensive, but I relished it. My back hurt, I was covered in drywall dust, and I'd almost forgotten all about Olivia Bridge.

Until she walked in the front door.

"Boss!" Tom hollered through the hum of drills and motioned toward her.

She stood a few feet away, looking like the goddess that she was. Tight dark jeans and heeled black boots. A simple white tee under the same little blazer that didn't cover an inch of her tits. My palms tingled and my cock throbbed. Why did I want this woman so damn bad? If I were smart, I'd have started looking elsewhere as soon as she'd driven out of sight the other night. Now I'd been dreaming of her for days and wanted to fuck her more than I wanted air.

I brushed myself off and stalked toward her. "You come to check on progress, princess?"

She lifted her chin. "I came to talk."

I hesitated, trying to read her, but she wasn't giving me anything.

"It's loud in here. Let's go upstairs."

I led the way to the yet unfinished condos, which were completely quiet, thanks to the expensive soundproofing we'd installed between each floor. The sound of her heels on the unfinished floor marked her entrance behind me.

I slowed at the center of the large room and turned to face her. "What did you want to talk about, Miss Bridge?"

"You know me well enough by now. You can call me Olivia."

"We're hardly intimate." I raked her in again from head to toe, taking my time. Why'd she have to show up looking so fucking edible?

Her lips tightened, and she looked past me quickly. "About that."

"You're referring to my proposal? Do you have an answer for me?" On the inside, I prayed for progress. If she showed any weakness on the matter, I swore then and there I'd show no mercy.

"I do."

I held her stare. "You made me wait. Not sure if we still have a deal," I lied.

She cocked her head. "Really? I didn't see a wall when I walked in."

I shrugged. "Yeah, I had a little chat with Cameron. I reconsidered your suggestion, and I think you're right. Aesthetically, it was worth the extra pennies." Lies. I'd made the call well before her big brother had come poking around for updates. I'd done it for her and no one else.

"I guess there's no reason for me to be here, then." She didn't move an inch.

"No more suggestions? You're good with me taking the reins from here?"

She exhaled a breath through her nose. "What is this about, Will? I don't want to play games."

I went to her until our bodies were inches apart, until I

could smell her expensive perfume and see the pebbles under her shirt. The ache to haul her against me raged. But I was dirty, and she was too perfect right now.

"It's really simple. I want you to say yes to me," I said quietly, fisting my hands to keep from touching her. "I won't be happy until you're under me, Olivia, and once you're there, I plan to make you come a thousand different ways. You don't want games? Making me wait when you know we both want the same thing—that's you playing games. That's you trying to win. Say yes, and we both win."

She stared up at me with those eyes that cut right through me. Her lips were parted again, like she wanted to say yes. To give as much as I wanted to take.

"Fine." Her voice was barely a whisper.

I lifted an eyebrow. "Fine?"

She exhaled a shaky breath and broke eye contact. "I'm saying yes." She swallowed and met my gaze again. "But I have terms."

"Name them."

"Good. Not sure if you noticed, but I don't like being told what to do."

I pursed my lips to suppress a smile. "There's only one ruler in my bedroom, princess. You have a voice, but I call the shots."

She crossed her arms, bringing my attention away from her beautiful face for only a second.

"That's fine. I'm talking about outside of it. I'm not going to be at your beck and call. If you want me, you can tell me. But I'm under no obligation to come running every time you have a pressing need."

Fair enough. "I want what you want."

She swallowed. "You have to use protection, always."

I smirked. "That's a no-brainer."

Relief flooded me, settling in my shoulders and feeding a fresh rush of desire through my veins. "You'll have to excuse my forwardness, but since you've made me wait longer than I expected to, and since I've been hard for you for days, when might I have the pleasure of your company...Olivia?"

She stepped away, glancing around the room like she was suddenly interested in it. "I'm free tonight."

"Perfect. I'll have a car pick you up after work."

"I can make my own way. Cameron's going to get suspicious if you keep picking me up in private cars."

I nodded. So Cameron didn't know. Thank fuck. She completed her circle of the room and came toward me, leaving more space between us than I had.

"And we should think of tonight as a trial run. If this doesn't feel right for whatever reason, I reserve the right to change my mind and forget you exist."

If she only knew how much that challenged me... "Harsh, but I'm confident you'll leave happy and wanting more."

"Your confidence is reassuring, but you need to know I'm not cheap and I don't want to be treated that way."

I frowned. "You're anything but cheap, Olivia. I would never call you that or treat you that way."

"I'm glad to hear that."

"Have you negotiated this arrangement to your satisfaction, then?" I had a feeling the terms meant less than the power she was trying to hold onto in changing them. I'd never hold her to anything. I just wanted to get inside her, if only for a night.

"I'm satisfied. For now." She lifted her chin again.

God, she was adorable when she was trying to hold her ground. She didn't like the games, but watching her play them was a huge fucking turn on.

"I'll meet you at your place tonight. Text me the address. I'll be there at nine."

"Dinner?"

She shook her head, seriousness shadowing her eyes. "You don't need to wine and dine me, Will. I know what this is about."

OLIVIA

This is crazy. You're crazy.

The voice in my head had been harassing me the whole way to Will's. I'd taken the train and walked from the station to his building. Once inside the lobby, I changed into heels. I tossed my flats into my oversized purse and leaned back against the wall. I closed my eyes and drew in a deep, steeling breath. My nerves couldn't get the best of me now.

I'd entertained this. I'd said yes to this.

"Liv?"

My eyes opened to a familiar face. Ian Savo was walking my way. He looked like he was going out, dressed in dark jeans and a black collared shirt with the sleeves rolled up, showcasing his muscular forearms.

A flurry of words lodged in my throat before I finally found my voice. "H-Hi."

Something about the man had always left me a little tongue-tied whenever we'd run into each other before. Whatever their heritage, his parents had produced a straight-up beautiful man. He paused in front of me, all six-foot-plus of muscle and taut tawny skin, affording me a closer view. His combined features were lethal—dark-brown hair trimmed short to his scalp and light gray eyes.

"You here to see Will?"

My stomach dropped out, and the growing list of Ian's best features came to a screeching halt.

Shit. How did he know?

"I didn't know you and Will were friends," I said.

"Friends and roommates, for now. Let me walk you up."

"Sure." I pushed off the wall and wobbled on my heels.

Ian caught my hand, steadying me. His grasp was easy and warm, and my heart did a funny extra beat.

He didn't release me until we were in the elevator.

I watched the numbers illuminate with our climb. My anxiety seemed to climb right with it. Darren was going to kill me if he found out about this...and I didn't even want to think about Cameron's wrath.

I only had seconds left when I finally broke the silence. "I don't know how to say this delicately, Ian. But I'd rather my brothers not know about me visiting Will like this."

I chanced a look up. His expression was steady, like he knew exactly why I was here. But there was something else, something dark and hungry in the stormy gray of his eyes.

"Understood."

The doors opened, and I followed Ian out, feeling no more steady on my feet than I had been. I should have stuck with flats.

"Here we are." He unlocked the door to the apartment and let me cross the threshold first.

I took a few steps in, not seeing Will but catching his voice and snippets of conversation from another room.

The space was clean and new. A soft gray that reminded me of Ian's eyes colored the walls against ornate white trim. The kitchen was state of the art and led into an open floor plan living room. An enormous picture window offered an expansive view of Manhattan across the river. Leather and dark-wood furniture filled the space, for function over style. Everything had modern finishes but lacked the warmth that made a house feel like a home.

"So this is home?"

"For now. He's probably going to grab one of the luxury condos above the new gym when they're finished and move in there eventually."

I turned and caught him watching me again. "And what about you?"

His full lips curved into a crooked grin. "I'll land on my feet. Probably won't be anyplace half this nice, but I don't sleep much anyway."

For years, Ian had worked beside my brother through countless long nights at the station, life-threatening emergencies on the streets, and dangerous fires like the one that had nearly killed them both. But I wondered if those were the sleepless nights he was referring to now.

Before Darren had decided to settle down with Vanessa, Ian had been my brother's wingman. I imagined they made a lethal pair against the women they sought. Something about the sex-on-a-stick way he stood before me made me wonder if he was on the hunt tonight.

Of course, I wasn't one to judge.

CHAPTER FOUR

WILL

"Did you see the news tonight?"

Jia's smoky voice carried through the phone, muffled by the sounds of traffic around her. She was young, but she was married to Wall Street. When she wasn't hustling in the world of the almighty dollar, she was a stellar fuck and a friendly ally to have on my arm when Bill dragged me out to one of his business functions.

"No, why?" I walked around the room, collecting things that had been strewn about. My day had run long, and I hadn't had much time to get the place presentable for Olivia. God knew she'd find every flaw.

"They're starting to cover the Youth Arts investigation. The SEC is involved now and looking into more deals at the firm that might have run through Reilly and Dermott. As Reilly's business partner, Bill's name is right there with all of it."

I chucked my work boots into the closet with a loud thud. "Fuck."

"What are you going to do, Will? You need to get a handle on this before the investors bail. He'll lose everything."

"It's his business, not mine. Let him clean up his own messes."

"I know you're angry, but you need to be logical. Millions of dollars are at stake, not to mention the life he comes back to if all this goes sideways. You can't stick your head in the sand and pretend like this isn't happening."

"Like hell I can't," I muttered, biting down on a slew of curses because I could hear my father's voice in her words.

She sighed after a moment. "I'm just trying to help, Will. It's hard for me to watch this too."

The front door closed, and I heard Ian's and Olivia's voices. "I have to go, Jia. I'll talk to you later."

I ended the call and muttered a string of curses to myself. I scanned the room, deeming it all satisfactory until I saw myself in the mirror. I ran a nervous hand through my hair. One minute I ruled my world—the one I'd built on my own dreams and ambition. The next I was the son of a fraud who'd helped con millions out of an unsuspecting few. It was like a second skin, and I couldn't fucking get away from it.

But I had to. At least for tonight. I shoved Jia's news and my father's failures from my mind and found Olivia in the kitchen. Ian was leaning against the counter staring at her like he wanted to eat her alive. Fucker.

"You staying?" I shot him a look only he'd understand.

He frowned. "No, I'm going to the pub down the street with some guys from work."

"All right. I'll see you later."

"See you later, Liv." He held Olivia's gaze a second longer than he needed to before leaving.

When she shifted her focus back to me, concern filled her gaze. "Are you okay?"

"I'm fine," I said tightly. I moved to the built-in bar and knelt down to the wine fridge. "Wine?"

I pulled bottles out and returned them, searching for something to fit this mood. Except there wasn't a bouquet that would take me out of this haze of hatred fast enough.

Her heels clicked beside me. Her tight-fitted black dress revealed the toned expanse of her leg just below her thigh. She reached high on the shelf and brought down a single malt scotch. "How about something stronger?"

I stood and leaned my hip on the counter. "You like that stuff?"

She smiled, uncorked the bottle, and poured two fingers of Lagavulin into two cut-glass lowballs. "Reminds me of my dad. I used to hate it, honestly, but over the years, I've taught myself to like it."

I took a glass, threw back a healthy gulp, and swallowed with a wince. "Seems very unlike you."

She refilled my glass and smirked. "Okay, I admit it. My roommates would always drink up the vodka and tequila. They wouldn't touch this stuff, so I acquired the taste."

I laughed, and for the first time in the history of me fucking women, I actually wished we had some time to kill over dinner. A little friendly conversation to quiet some of this noise in my head. Didn't ease the physical ache that had been plaguing me for the past few days, but I was beginning to legitimately *like* Olivia Bridge.

She leaned on the counter, facing me, and held the glass between her delicate palms. I resented how I felt in this moment. She'd agreed to being with me, something I didn't imagine was an easy decision for her. Now I was too wrapped up in Jia's news about my father to fully embrace it.

I sighed and rubbed my forehead. "I'm sorry. I just got some shitty news, and it's making me a little edgy."

She sipped from her glass and licked her lips. "It's okay. Do you want to talk about it?"

I shook my head and stared to the floor. "Would you want to talk about your father going to prison?"

When she answered with silence, I lifted my gaze to hers. Her cool blue eyes were soft and kind, offering solace without words. Without another word, I took her hand and led her to the living room. We settled beside each other on the couch, and her eyes took on that apologetic look again. I pinched the bridge of my nose and exhaled slowly. I didn't want to talk about Bill's troubles, but I couldn't get the shit out of my head either.

She reached out and touched my hand. "I can promise you my life isn't any more perfect than yours. The way we were raised, you know as well as I do, it comes at a price."

She could say that again.

"I sure as hell know it," I muttered. "I can't say cleaning up his mess is worth any price, though."

She laced our fingers, like silk and heat coming together. The simple contact warmed my chest faster than the liquor. I wanted to drag her against me then and kiss the lips I'd imagined for days. I wanted to strip her down and bury myself so deep in her I couldn't remember my own anguish. Slowly, desire replaced my ebbing anger.

She spoke softly. "I love my dad, but when he wants things for me that I don't want for myself—it's a hard pill to swallow from a man who's been a shadow half my life. It took my brothers a long time to break away from the expectations. Sometimes I wonder if I ever will."

"I have a lot of respect for your brothers. Doing what they've done isn't easy."

"Thanks to people like you."

"It's not just the money, you know. I'm trying to carve out my own dream here. Last thing I want to do is end up like my dad, wrapped up in dollars and cents. But that's what he wants, of course. Doesn't give a damn about what gets me up in the morning."

"You're passionate about what you do."

I tightened my grasp, enjoying our contact a little more with each passing second. "After my parents split, I lived with my mom for a few years in Paris. When I came back here for private school and stayed with my dad, I was always looking for details that would remind me of home. I got preoccupied with it."

"So you were a thirteen-year-old with an eye for architectural detail?"

I grinned. "Pretty much. And now I walk into a property, the building could be totally gutted, and all I can see is possibility. I'm compulsive until it's realized its potential."

She dragged her fingertips over my wrist, like she was painting along the vein lines. "I get it. Sometimes I feel that way with an empty room. It's like a blank canvas. Probably doesn't hurt that I watched my mom redecorate about a thousand times. Every time she was upset at my dad or something, she'd go on a mission, changing everything around."

I chuckled. "I'm afraid to ask what you think about what I've done with the place."

She looked around, her eyes seeming to light and pause on little details. "I haven't gotten the full tour, but the interior architecture is impressive. I think I'm recognizing your style. But it's definitely a bachelor pad on the surface right now."

I stared at her in silence a moment, draining the liquid

from my glass. I savored the smoky peat on my tongue, but I longed to taste her. Why was I being so careful with her? Why the hell hadn't I just fucked her against the wall the second Ian left? I should tug her under me right now and take her without another word. But I wanted her words...

"Why did you say yes? With all the shit going on with my dad, I can't imagine why you'd risk being associated with me." I held my stare, silently imploring her to give me more.

"I said yes. Does it really matter why?"

"We're going to be intimate. What's the harm in being honest, too?"

She glanced up at me with thoughtful eyes. "I'm attracted to you."

I fought the smile tugging at my lips. "I'm flattered, but I hope there's more."

She leaned her head against the couch with a soft sigh. "A lot of what you said about me the other night was true. The way you said it made it sound ugly and shallow, but I'm still trying to figure it all out, what matters and what doesn't. I can let my parents or my brothers or the society that raised me determine what matters, or I can go with my instincts. Maybe I'm being reckless and impulsive, but..."

"But what?"

"I feel things differently when I'm with you," she said softly. "You piss me off, Will. The other night, my God. You're lucky you weren't wearing your dinner."

I laughed, and she smiled.

"When you painted my life that way, you insulted me, but you also made me question my world. I've been doing more of that since I moved here, but nothing has ever been quite that jarring. And you...want me. You're not the first person who has, but somehow, the way you express it makes me feel desirable on a primal level that I've never experienced before."

"So in other words, I'm a crude bastard, but you kind of love it."

She shrugged. "Like I said, I reserve the right to change my mind."

"I won't let you."

She traced the rim of her glass and bit her lip gently. "I've said too much."

"Yes, but that's okay. I'm glad you did. I asked for your honesty, and you gave it to me."

Her dark eyelashes fluttered up, framing her hooded gaze. "Except now I feel vulnerable, like I need a piece of you, too."

"Come here." I gently tugged her toward me.

The second her glass hit the table, I circled my arm around her torso and brought her up against me. Her hand fell lightly on my chest, and I could see the rapid flicker of her pulse at her neck.

I trailed my fingertip along her jaw, slowing over the silky ridges of her lips. Where she'd seemed sharp before, she was soft, melting against me, leaning infinitesimally closer. Her breathing was uneven, and her legs shifted.

This was it. I couldn't wait anymore. I had to have her.

OLIVIA

I'd forgotten all the harsh words that had left Will's lips the second they touched mine. Because his kisses were magic. Unexpectedly soft and slow. Full of restraint and a tenderness I'd never expected he was capable of. I sighed into them, letting myself fall into the pleasure of his touch. He tangled his fingers in my hair and then roamed over my body, touching and teasing.

The drugging sweeps of his lips made me dizzy. When I opened and sought his tongue, he evaded me, dragging his lips instead over my cheek and along my jaw. He returned to nip gently at my lips, kissing and sucking them until they felt swollen and hot.

When he caressed down my thigh and his hand disappeared under the hem of my dress, my legs seemed to part on their own. So far everything Will did was magic, and I welcomed more of that heavenly, warm buzz between my legs. My breath rushed out when he stroked me through my panties, putting pressure where my clit was already aching for contact. I shifted my hips, and he answered by pushing the thin fabric aside. He traced a finger up my wet slit.

He lifted the corner of his mouth. "You're bare, princess. I love it when I'm right," he whispered.

I smiled because I couldn't help it. "Shut up."

"You'll forgive me in a minute, I promise."

He glided easily through my folds. "So smooth and so fucking wet for me. Can't wait to watch you come, Olivia."

I fisted my fingers into his shirt and gasped as he slid back and forth from my clit to my opening.

When he put his mouth on me again, the kiss was hungry... demanding. Then, for the first time, I tasted the smoky liquor on his tongue as he simultaneously slid two fingers deep into my pussy. I clenched around him, unprepared for the invasion but badly wanting it.

I closed my eyes with a moan.

He held me tight against him and entered me again gently, sending another ripple of pleasure through me.

"This is just the beginning, Olivia," he whispered against my lips. "I'm not stopping until you shatter around me, until you're hoarse from screaming my name. You have no idea how badly I want you right now."

Heaven knew I wanted him too. Against all reason and better judgment, I threw it all out the window and fell into the lust ripping through me. I arched and lifted, seeking his touch everywhere—where our mouths hungrily met, where his fingers twisted and fucked me, against his broad chest that both warmed me and trapped me to him.

Where his touch was tender before, he devoured me now, claiming me, pumping into me to the time of this erotic rhythm he'd created.

I released a desperate moan, but he silenced the sound with the ferocity of another kiss. My body climbed with sensation. My nipples ached under my clothes, and my skin burned where our bodies touched. I wanted more of his skin against me. I hungered for his cock inside me. More than anything, I craved release from the intense need he was creating. But inside each moment, I reveled in the wonder of it all, the pressure, the friction, the anchor points where he ruled my body.

After a few more perfectly placed flicks against my clit and glides inside my sensitive flesh, I began to unravel, no longer able to hold back and savor the magic in his touch.

"Oh, God!" I seized around his fingers, coming with a broken cry against his lips. The orgasm crashed over me hard and fast, a wash of relief and bliss.

I clung to his hard body like I was drowning, trying to catch my breath. I hadn't come under a man's hand since... I couldn't even remember the last time someone had stolen my breath that way.

Eager to return the pleasure, I reached for him, molding my palm around the outline of his cock in his pants. He exhaled a breath as I marveled at the size of him. I couldn't want him any more than I did right now. I hadn't had someone touch me with such selfless dedication for as long as I could remember. And right now, I wanted to forget everything outside of this moment and drown the judging voices that had plagued me since I'd met Will.

I reached for his zipper, but before I could release him, he'd tugged me up against him and kissed me hard. Without another word, he lifted us off the couch. I circled his waist with my legs, and he carried me to the other side of the apartment. His bedroom was dark, save for the city lights twinkling through a large picture window and a soft light from a small bedside lamp.

He lowered me to my feet beside the bed. Its puffy white bedspread was almost as inviting as the man standing before me with more heat and hunger in his gaze than I'd ever seen.

I lifted to my toes and pulled us close, sealing our mouths. Our tongues tangled, our bodies brushed together as we tugged at each other's clothes. Pulling down the sleeve of my dress, he attacked the flesh he revealed. The fabric tore as he tugged the garment down, letting it fall to my feet. My head fell back with a sigh. He dragged his tongue up the column of my neck and nipped at my ear.

"There are a few things you need to know, Olivia."

"What's that?" I wondered breathlessly.

He unclasped my bra and slid his palms over my sensitive nipples. "I'm in charge. I told you before. I call the shots."

I nodded, because right now I had complete faith in his

ability to give me more pleasure than I ever imagined.

"That means you only come when I say, no matter how badly you want it."

I widened my eyes. "But...it just came over me."

"I understand that. But as long as I'm the one pulling them from you, your orgasms are mine. Mine to control, mine to take. Are we clear?"

I felt the dominance in his tone all the way down to my toes, and in other places that now pulsed for his attention.

"What if I can't help it?" I'd never held an orgasm for a man, and I had no idea how I'd be able to control it when Will seemed to inspire them with such ease.

He clamped his finger and thumb down on my taut bud and pinched.

"Ow." I jolted at the pain but didn't pull away.

He smirked. "Then I'll punish you, princess."

He nudged me back so I fell onto the bed. Pulling off his shirt, he revealed his impressively toned torso. Tight pectorals that led to a V of defined abdominals. Rapt and on fire for the man, I watched with more interest than patience.

He whipped out his belt and pushed his pants and boxers to the floor. His erection sprang forward, thick and virile. He took a condom from the bedside drawer and rolled it on slowly.

"What else?" My voice was breathy, a mix of lust and anticipation. I bit down hard on my bottom lip because I couldn't wait to feel more of him.

"I'm rough. But you'll like it."

He grabbed the lace tops of my panties and ripped them down without ceremony.

I held my breath. My brain was still piecing itself back together. What the hell did that mean? Climbing over me, he leaned down for another full-mouthed kiss. Then, before I could reply, he flipped me to my belly and slapped me hard on the ass.

WILL

The lithe line of her body froze. I drifted south, inhaling her scent and trailing my lips and tongue over the skin where my hand had made contact. She made a small sound of pleasure, but she was still tense, taut like a bow. I could smell her arousal. The heat radiating off her skin brought her heady scent into my lungs. I was quickly losing my mind. My willpower was like a rubber band that had been pulled too tight for too long. Now I was ready to fucking snap.

But as willing as Olivia had been moments ago, an air of tension lingered between us...

I rolled her back to face me.

Her eyes were wide and bright. Her cheeks were flushed pink. "What exactly do you mean by rough?"

Her words were strained, and in that moment, I regretted the little swat as much as I enjoyed watching the red handprint form on her ass. How could I explain what I wanted without scaring her out of my bed? Olivia Bridge wasn't a virgin, but she had a lot to learn about the way I played. There was only one way to teach her...

When I pushed her legs apart, she opened for me, giving me a glorious view of her bare pussy. Her chest moved under rapid uneven breaths.

"I'm going to give you a taste of how I like it, princess. If you like it too, I'll give you more than you can handle. If you don't, you tell me, and I'll fuck you slow and sweet like Prince

Charming. How does that sound?"

I dropped down on my elbows, hovering above her. I gazed into her hooded blue eyes. Every inch of my flesh buzzed with need.

She licked her lips absently.

"I like you vulnerable, Olivia. Never be afraid to show me that side of you."

I slid my palm over the curve of her cheek and drew massaging circles around the knot of her jaw. Our lips brushed together, and I inhaled her next breath. "I'm going to take care of you, princess."

"I know," she whispered, softening as she wove her fingers through my hair.

I lined myself up to take her fast and hard, inching into her tight heat. I was barely inside her. Her flesh hugged the tip of my aching cock. "God, you feel good," I murmured. Then, feeling no resistance from her wet pussy, I slammed home.

Her jaw fell with a silent cry. I didn't wait. I couldn't wait. I drove hard, again and again, melding our bodies together, sinking her into the bed as I sank into her.

She was tight, primed for everything I wanted to give her. Her body wrapped around me in every way, arms and legs and her beautiful wet cunt hugging my cock.

Fuck, she was so ready and willing, open and vulnerable, trusting in what I hadn't yet been able to show her. And the way she'd given in to me was perfection next to the dozen or so scenarios I'd played out in my sordid fantasies.

She dug her heels into my thighs, urging me faster and harder.

God, she was ready...and waiting.

"You want to come for me already, don't you, sweetheart?"

"Yes," she whimpered. She clenched down around me, and her lip trembled.

As much as I wanted to make this last and draw out her pleasure, nothing about being inside Olivia was making me want to slow down. I closed my eyes, savoring the delicious grip of her body on me. "Come for me."

She moaned softly and pressed her nails into my flesh. I pumped harder, slamming my hips to hers. I tensed my jaw, trying like hell to exercise restraint, but she'd given me no reason to. Her eyes closed and her chin went heavenward as a throaty moan escaped her lips.

Heaven help me. Desire rushed down my spine. Heat raced like fire through my veins. And I had a clear premonition that the look on her face would be indelible on my mind for a very long time.

The orgasm seemed to swallow the air from my lungs, sweeping down into my throbbing cock. I banded my arm around her hips and drove until I felt the end of her. She screamed, and a violent tremor shook her body.

After a few deep thrusts, I came hard, shouting her name into the tornado of sex and mindless delirium that filled the air around us. Somewhere in the haze, I wished I could have come inside her and marked that place that made her shake...as mine and only mine.

CHAPTER FIVE

IAN

The vodka had just about worn off, but the Red Bulls hadn't. The sun had been up for an hour when I stopped staring at the ceiling and finally went to the kitchen. I'd spent the night throwing back some drinks and talking shit with pals from work. I'd even talked to a few women that I could have pursued, but I couldn't stop thinking about Liv in Will's bed. The potent visual flooded my thoughts every time I contemplated bringing someone home.

Thousands of pretty girls in New York, but the irrefutable truth was that no one could hold a candle to Olivia Bridge. She wasn't a diamond in the rough. She was just a fucking diamond—beautiful, refined, smart. A prize for any man.

Except she was Darren's sister...and Will's new fucktoy.

It had been a late night at the bar, extended further by a few more hours of listening to Liv's primal screams. I'd been hard half the night, and now my body refused to succumb to sleep.

I scowled and pushed scrambled eggs around a frying pan, eager to satisfy at least one of my basic instincts.

I'd never had anything but an easy camaraderie with Will, but right now I fucking hated the man. I hated him for being the one to have her last night. If I hadn't been so honorable for once in my life, I'd have been the one making her scream *my* name.

"Oh, I'm sorry."

I turned, and Liv was standing in the middle of the kitchen, wearing nothing but a white T-shirt that she was tugging down at the hem. Her makeup had worn off. Her hair was tousled, her lips were full, and her skin glowed. She was impossibly beautiful.

I took a deep breath and reminded myself to be good—whatever the hell that meant. For the moment, I'd try to pretend like I hadn't heard her in the throes of ecstasy for hours. I wouldn't let on that I'd spent those hours fantasizing about all the ways I could take her over the edge, with or without Will.

I cleared my throat. "You hungry?"

She chewed her lip and eyed the food cooking on the stove. "A little, actually."

"Sit." I motioned toward the stools that lined the kitchen island. "I'll make you a plate."

She took a seat and tucked her hair behind her ear shyly. I turned away and tried to focus on the task at hand. But having her in the same room was distracting as fuck. Either that or I was still half drunk.

I finished cooking the eggs and the sausages that sizzled on the burner and made us each a plate. We ate in silence, and as the minutes passed, the tension saturated the air between us. She was close enough to touch, and that's all I could think about—tangling my fingers in her hair and kissing her breathless.

When she finished, she set down her fork and pushed her plate away. "I wanted to thank you for your...discretion," she said quietly, breaking me from my single-minded thoughts.

"Thank you for yours."

Her brow wrinkled.

"Darren pretty much forbade me from even looking at you. It's been nice to cheat a little. Even if he'll skin me alive if he ever knew what I know."

She blushed with a small smile. "You saved his life. Hopefully he'd forgive you. I doubt he'd forgive me."

"Big brothers are overprotective. I get it. I've got four little sisters."

"Yeah..." She picked up one of the little green fruits that were piled into a bowl on the counter. She rolled it between her fingers, studying it, but her thoughts seemed far away.

"Try one," I said, grabbing one for myself.

"What are they?"

"*Quenepa.* I get them at the Caribbean market down the street. Reminds me of the Dominican. They call them *limoncillo* there. Little kids would sell them on the beach, and I ate them like crazy." I cracked the green skin of one with my teeth before popping the sweet fruit into my mouth.

"Did you grow up there?"

I worked the flesh off the fruit and removed the seed, reaching for another.

"No, my mom did, though. I used to spend summers there with my sisters to see family. You know, until we grew up and had to find real jobs." I smirked, but something told me she didn't know that much about summer jobs. Darren was as down to earth as they came, but he and his siblings were born into money. The kind of money I knew nothing about.

She shrugged with a smile. "Nothing like the summers of youth."

"No kidding. Now it's running into burning buildings and laying tile. Not nearly as fun."

"Seems like you've all got side gigs. Like risking your lives every day isn't enough." She folded her arms and leaned in.

I shrugged. "Yeah, but I've had this one since high school. I learned the trade from my dad. He put me to work as soon as I could be trusted with power tools."

She laughed. "Do you still work together?"

"Nah." I shook my head and avoided her penetrating gaze.

I was mixed up enough. Last thing I wanted to talk about was my father...or that gaping hole in my chest that his death had left behind. I tensed my jaw. Nope. Wasn't going there.

"I guess I should get cleaned up." She stood, came beside me, and reached for my plate.

"I can get this. Don't worry about it." I rose, stopping her. But as I did, I sensed her heat. My breath caught being this close. Close enough that I could inhale her lavender scent and see the small reactions of her body. Her short breathing, her nipples getting hard under Will's T-shirt. Her back was to the counter. Another few inches in her direction, and I'd have her pinned.

Her gaze flickered up to mine and then lowered down my bare chest. She reached out and softly traced the mosaic of ink that stretched across half my torso.

My heart raced. All my senses went on high alert, reacting to her proximity. I tensed, silently praying that this would be her last night here. I'd never known Will to let a girl stay overnight. I had no idea what his plan was. I didn't want Will to hurt her, but I couldn't do this. She was temptation personified, and I was so fucked right now.

"What does it mean?" Her voice was as soft and sensual

as her touch.

I shook my head, my jaw tight. "Doesn't matter."

A hundred women might have asked me the same question, but for the first time since the needle had hit my skin, I wanted to say it out loud. I wanted to tell her. But I couldn't... wouldn't.

When she pulled her hand away, I caught it and pressed it back against my ribs. My hand covered the delicate planes of hers. I took the last step that had us nearly touching, and she sucked in a breath. I caressed up her arm, slowly, reveling in her softness. I sifted my fingers through the silky strands of her hair and angled her face up to me. Her eyes were hazy. Those beautiful rose-colored lips parted like they were begging without words. And she didn't move, even as my skin burned under her touch. I bent toward her, craving those luscious lips, inhaling her scent into my lungs. Even as my mind screamed...

Don't do this.

Don't fucking do this.

OLIVIA

"Good morning."

Will's husky voice filled the room. My heart ricocheted off the walls of my chest a few dozen times before settling into a panicked rhythm. Oh, God.

I pulled my hand away from Ian, but I couldn't move any farther. He had me all but pinned against the counter. Then his touch fell away, and he stepped back. That small relief took the edge off my panic, but nothing about his stolid expression implied that he was rattled by Will's presence.

If Will cared, he didn't show it either. He was dressed

already, in jeans and a blue collared shirt that set off his eyes. He opened the cabinet and pulled out a mug.

Ian walked past him. "Help yourself to breakfast. I'm going to get some sleep."

Will didn't look up as he poured his coffee. "Long night?"

"You know it."

The corner of Will's mouth lifted. That small sign of levity lifted away a little more of my anxiety about what he'd walked in on.

But what the hell was I thinking? There was something really wrong with me. Apparently lust was a contagious disease that had taken over my mind and my body since I'd met Will. He'd kept me up late, and just as I'd slip off to sleep, he'd come at me again. I'd welcomed it. I'd opened for him, accepted him, let him bring me to the brink again and again and then push me over until I barely knew my own name. I seemed to only know his, crying it out like a prayer every time he'd let me come.

The man fucked like a god, and now, after months of no action, I couldn't get sex off my brain. One look at Ian's shirtless tattooed body had me clenching in places that were already very well used. And even if I'd only spent a night with Will, somehow those places already seemed to belong to him. But did they?

I brought my hand to my mouth, trying to ignore the tingle in my lips that Ian's closeness had inspired. Like the truly wanton creature I'd become, I had wanted him to kiss me. There was no doubt.

Ian disappeared down the hallway into his room, and Will was watching me now. My heart thundered in my ears. I wanted to say something, but his careful gaze seemed to say it all. He walked over to me casually, taking Ian's place in my bubble and caging me with his arms on either side.

Shaking his head with a soft sigh, he said, "Oh, Olivia. Beautiful, sexy girl. What are we going to do with you? I leave you alone for a few minutes, and Ian has you in his clutches."

I expected an edge in his tone. Bitterness or a hint of anger. But I sensed nothing like that. Still, I was riddled with unexpected guilt.

"It was nothing," I said, trying to convince myself of my own words.

"A kiss?"

"He didn't kiss me."

He cocked his head, his gaze fixed on my lips. "An almost kiss? You wanted his lips on you though." He traced the bow of my mouth. "I'll bet you wanted even more than that."

Was he teasing me? Taunting me because less than twenty-four hours into our purely sexual relationship, I'd nearly betrayed him? Was exclusivity implied? We hadn't negotiated those terms.

"Will...I'm sorry."

He hushed me, pressing his finger to my lips. His thoughtful gaze seemed to search mine. I was exhausted, aroused, and completely mixed up. I hadn't even been with Will long enough to comprehend what it would be like to lose his presence from my life. Inherently I knew I didn't want that. But I had no idea how far I'd let things go with Ian. That alone frightened me.

"I don't know what came over me. He just..."

"He wants you. The way I want you."

A silent moment passed between us, those few words lingering and echoing through me. He bent and kissed me softly. He lowered his hand to the tender place between my legs, where I was shamefully wet.

His eyes went dark, and all signs of humor left his expression. "I don't care if Ian started this. I'm going to finish it. Because I can't get enough of you right now."

In one swift movement, he lifted me onto the island. My heart couldn't slow down.

"Are you sore?" He shoved the hem of the shirt up.

"A little, but—"

"Lie back."

I froze. I was naked under his shirt. And we were far from alone in the apartment.

He lifted an eyebrow and spoke with more force. "Lie. Back."

I lay back on the granite as he spread me. "What are you— Ah!"

His mouth landed between my legs. He centered his tongue on my pool of arousal, spreading moisture up and over my clit. I tensed, but he held my thighs apart, continuing his assault on my pussy.

He moaned against me. "Christ, you taste good."

I sighed. The counter was cool and hard against my back, a stark contrast to the heat and softness of his mouth as he ate me like a starving man.

I was barreling into the orgasm before I could think better of our position and my vulnerability... But he probably liked that. Maybe that was what this thing with Ian was about— capitalizing on a weak moment. But hell, if this was my punishment, I could handle it.

I threaded my fingers through Will's hair, holding him to me as I shifted my hips against his mouth. I swore nothing in my life had ever felt this purely...erotic.

I had no idea what made me open my eyes.

I sensed Ian before I saw him. His energy drew my gaze toward his. As Will moved between my legs, Ian's muscular frame filled the threshold to the hallway that led to his room. His hands pressed against the walls on either side. His dark lips were parted and wet.

He was watching, like a goddamn voyeur. And because I was drunk on lust, I didn't care. And I didn't think. My hands left Will's dirty-blond locks. I skimmed up my thighs and hips, lifting my shirt up over my breasts. Cupping each breast, I gently twisted my nipples. They were sore and sensitive from the night before, and the pain shot right to my core. I was so close...so aroused and climbing higher with every passing second.

With one hand on the wall, Ian brought his other to the place where his erection visibly grew beneath his sweatpants. He bit down on his lip and squeezed, giving me the briefest view of its impressive girth. His abs tightened with the motion, and in that moment, he was all muscle and feral lust. It was too much. Two beautiful men and their attentions fixed on me... open...vulnerable...

I moaned when Will began rotating between the pressure of his fingers and the exquisite texture of his tongue on my clit. *Good God...*

Something inside me detonated. I couldn't take it. I was falling and then flying high and crashing hard into another incredible orgasm.

My eyes closed. I cried out loudly, bowing off the counter. The orgasm seemed to ride out in waves, marked by my breathless cries and Will's dedicated lapping against my oversensitive clit.

As the pleasure tapered off, little aftershocks rippled through me. When I opened my eyes again, Ian was gone and Will stood before me. He wiped his mouth with the back of his hand and lifted me upright.

"I have to go," he said breathlessly.

"But..."

I reached for him, but he caught my wrist.

"If I let you anywhere near my cock right now, I'm going to be even later than I already am."

I pouted my lip a little. "Okay."

"See me tonight."

The hint of desperation in his voice made me want to give him everything. All of it, all the time.

A vague memory of me telling him he couldn't beckon me whenever he wanted floated across my mind. I didn't really care about that, not in my current mind-set, anyway. But through the fog, I remembered that I did have plans.

"I would, but I'm having dinner with my brothers." Being gone last night most likely would have already raised suspicions. I couldn't bail on our weekend dinner, even if Maya was probably going to grill me about Will again.

"Are you going to make me wait again?"

I smirked. "Not too long. I promise."

"Call me after. If I can't feel you, I want to hear you." He brought his mouth over mine, kissing me tenderly. "How can I want you this badly already?"

I kissed him back, the same question echoing in my mind...

WILL

"So what do you say?"

"Huh?" I lifted my gaze from my picked-over lunch and focused on the man seated across from me.

I'd agreed to this meeting with my father, but as soon as the conversation turned to the fund he wanted me to take over, my thoughts had drifted.

To Olivia. I shouldn't have let her stay over. I'd planned to break her down, shatter her until she was screaming my name. I wasn't expecting to ravage her all goddamn night. I couldn't leave her alone. And this morning, seeing her with Ian... Jealousy wasn't a word in our shared dictionary when it came to feelings associated with the women we fucked. But something had tightened in my gut when I saw her in his arms.

All the more reason to let him seduce her. Once he'd had her, that feeling would surely go away. Getting possessive over Olivia wouldn't serve anyone. I'd promised her nothing but pleasure. Either of us could deliver on that. And the arrangement between Ian and me had been set months ago. Why renege and screw up a good thing?

He could have a taste, but I wasn't letting her go. In fact, not knowing when I'd see her again was proving a constant distraction. In my youth of privilege, I'd managed to stay away from the hard drugs that I could easily afford, but I imagined this might be what it was like to come off a really good hit of heroin. I was tired and restless, and I wanted to crawl inside of this woman next chance I had. Lose myself there and hide away from the problem that was currently looking me in the face.

Bill Donovan was aging before my eyes. The investigation had been underway for months and clearly had taken a physical toll on my father. More of his hair had turned from brown to white, and his eyes seemed tired. The stress was eating at him.

I almost felt sorry for him.

"You look terrible," I finally said.

He exhaled and rubbed along the deep grooves on his forehead. "I guess that'll happen when you're facing jail time."

"You sound so certain."

His expression didn't change, but his shoulders hunched slightly.

"Was it worth it?"

He shook his head. "I ask myself every day. It's easy to cut corners when you're flying high. Christ, people do it every day."

"So you don't regret it."

"Obviously," he snapped. "I fucking regret it now."

I clenched my teeth. Bastard. His only remorse was getting caught. "I'm afraid I can't help you, Dad."

He dropped his fist on the table loudly enough for the silverware to rattle. "Goddamnit, Will. I need you to step up. I let you fuck around long enough. Didn't I? I gave you fun money, whatever you needed to get the girls, get your little ventures going. Playtime is over. We're talking about real money here. The kind of money that ensures the next four or five generations of our family are taken care of."

"I can't do this. I'm not like you."

"Despite being raised with a silver spoon in your fucking mouth, you are. You're money wise. You're good with people. You can wheel and deal and make people feel safe writing you checks. You were *born* for this. If I thought for one second you'd fuck it up, trust me, I wouldn't have wasted my time grooming you to take things over. I just didn't think it would have to be so soon."

"You understand that I've never wanted any part in it?" I'd wanted to tell him for so long, and somehow, now that his ruin seemed imminent, the words could finally come.

"This isn't a life sentence, Will. If Reilly or I get indicted, the investors will bail, without a doubt. We need you to come in and instill confidence. Become the figurehead for a while until the dust settles and one of us can take over again."

I laughed and shook my head. "This guy—your business partner—skimmed millions from his friends so people like you could get fat kickbacks. You really think there's anything I can say that's going to convince investors to let you continue playing with their money?"

"There's a six-month lock-up on the investments. That gives us time to repair the damage. But I can't do it alone."

"You mean you can't do it from behind bars."

The grooves between his brows deepened. "Nothing is certain right now. I told you. We need to plan for contingencies."

He was right about one thing. Nothing was certain. Nothing about his tone or demeanor was confidence inspiring, and the way the news was spreading around, Bill Donovan and the future of Reilly Donovan Capital was heading south. The suggestion that I could do anything to unfuck the situation seemed unlikely.

The instinct to help my father, even as I disagreed with it in principal, still nagged at me. Was the fund really clean? I couldn't imagine being part of the company. If the money was tainted at all, I had no choice. I wouldn't go down the way my father was going down. That much I knew.

CHAPTER SIX

OLIVIA

"Oh, good, you're here. You have to tell me everything." Maya pushed a glass of wine into my hand as I entered her kitchen.

Darren straightened from checking on the food in the stove and exchanged a look with Cameron. "What's going on?"

"Never mind. Come on, let's go sit." Maya waved him off and pulled me toward the dining room area where Vanessa was already sitting at the long table with her wine.

While Darren and Cameron stayed busy in the kitchen, I was essentially sandwiched between my brothers' wives. Two new sisters in the space of a year. Our family was growing faster than I could keep up with. A week didn't go by without one of us hosting a family dinner, a ritual that kept our close family even closer. Except none to date had included our parents, a fact that I regretted.

We were a stubborn family. My brothers had broken out on their own not long after college, defying our parents' wishes for their futures, and nothing had been the same after that. Long periods of silence, awkward dinners, tense holidays, and words that couldn't be unspoken. Sometimes I felt like I was the only one keeping that line open between the two broken halves of our family, but I wondered if I'd always be able to do that.

"So what happened last night?" Maya's voice was hushed.

I glanced back to the kitchen, worried that we were still within earshot of my brothers.

"Did you meet someone?" Vanessa's light-green eyes brightened.

"Um..." How did I respond to that? "Sort of." Technically I'd met Will. The rest fell into a very weird category that I wasn't sure I could really talk about.

Vanessa smiled broadly and leaned in. "Who is it?" She clasped her wineglass, and her diamond shone brilliantly in the light.

Maya quickly answered for me. "Will Donovan. He's the investor for the new gym."

"Oh, wow." She blinked. "Wait, that's Bill's son, right?"

I nodded, and her excitement dimmed. Her days at Reilly Donovan Capital had been short-lived, but I knew from Maya that she carried a lot of resentment toward her ex-boss, David Reilly. Thankfully, she'd landed a much better position at the Youth Arts Initiative, the very one that Will's father had defrauded. Still, I wasn't ready to hold anything against Will. From what I could tell, their business dealings were very separate, and the few words he'd shared on the matter seemed weighty with disappointment.

"So you still haven't really answered my question. What happened? Did you stay over?"

I glanced back at my brothers, who weren't saying anything but weren't making eye contact with me either. I wanted to give Maya the benefit of the doubt and assume that the pregnancy hormones were altering her better judgment. She was all but throwing me to the wolves with this line of questioning.

"We had drinks and talked. We're getting to know each other better," I said, aiming for the most diplomatic answer I could. It beat admitting that the man had spent half the night dedicated to pulling multiple orgasms from me.

"Sounds promising. When are you seeing him again?"

I shrugged. "I let him know I had plans tonight, so I'm not sure."

Maya clapped her hands. "Oh, we should have him over for dinner one night. That would be perfect."

Cameron approached the table, serving dishes in hand. "Probably not the best idea to mix business with...family."

Maya frowned. "Ironic, don't you think? Since we're all family and half of us work for the family business."

"That's different," he answered tightly before sitting down beside her.

"How?"

The way Maya was glaring in his direction told me Cameron wasn't going to win this argument tonight. His lips formed a thin line, and he plated up his food. The rest of us followed suit, and I was grateful for the moment to have something to do with my mouth other than discuss Will.

Darren dropped down into the seat beside Vanessa. He leaned toward her and kissed her square on the mouth. She smiled under the kiss.

When she returned to her food, he whispered in her ear, "Beautiful."

Her cheeks colored a lovely shade of pink, and she nudged him back with her elbow. We ate in silence for a few minutes before Vanessa spoke up.

"Liv, are we all set for the shower next weekend? Do you

need me to do anything?"

"No, I think I have it covered," I said.

We both glanced to Maya, who shot us a smile. She knew we'd been arranging a baby shower for her, but other than the date, everything else would be a surprise.

"Boys invited?" Darren asked between bites.

Vanessa nudged him again, harder this time. "No. Girls only."

"Ah, that's too bad." He shot her a wicked grin, like he was pretending to be disappointed.

I'd almost welcome the comic relief he'd bring. He had a way of softening my mother. She loved her sons, and even though I knew she got under Darren's skin too, he seemed to absorb the blows better than the rest of us did.

"Speaking of celebrating," Maya said playfully. "Now that you two skipped out on the usual wedding drama, we can expect some baby news soon, right?"

I widened my eyes, anticipating Darren's discomfort on the subject, but he seemed unaffected. Maya was on a roll tonight, but I was glad the focus had shifted away from me for the time being.

Darren pointed his fork in Vanessa's direction. "Talk to her. I keep trying to knock her up, but she wants to wait until she has a year in at Youth Arts."

"It's a nonprofit. If I'm out for any length of time, it's going to take a toll on the organization. I took on a lot of responsibility when I accepted the job, and obviously there's been a lot to manage in recent months."

He shook his head. "Never met a woman so damn committed to work."

Vanessa rolled her eyes. "We had a four-month

engagement. I think you can be a little patient."

My mother had vetoed just about every wedding plan they'd suggested and subsequently sucked the romance out of the entire planning process. Deciding that one Bridge wedding in a year was enough, they'd opted for something quick and simple. Darren had whisked Vanessa off to Spain for a romantic, albeit unexpected, elopement followed by an incredible reception in New York that even my mother couldn't complain about.

Maya rubbed her hand over her belly. "Well, hurry up. Baby Bridge is going to need a cousin."

"Noted," Darren said.

The conversation moved to less touchy topics, from the rapidly progressing renovation to fresh stories from Darren's calls on the fire department. After an hour, I was full, slightly buzzed from the wine, and ready for my bed.

Maya stood up with her dish, but Cameron rose quickly, taking it from her. "I've got it. You go sit and relax."

She smiled, and he bent to give her a peck on the lips.

"Love you," she whispered.

One by one, everyone started moving to clean up, but Cameron exiled everyone to the living room. I cleared my plate and went to join them, when he called my name.

I circled back. Cam was leaning against the counter, arms crossed, with a dishtowel slung over his shoulder. We shared many of the same features, the dark hair and blue eyes, but he was nearly twice my size. Tall and padded with muscle from years of dedicated hours at the gym. If I didn't know him so well, I'd be frightened of him, from his size alone. Especially now when greeted with his stony expression.

"Is everything okay?" I asked.

"You tell me. What's really going on with Will Donovan? Should I be concerned?"

I hesitated a second. "Concerned about what?"

His nostrils flared slightly. "I don't know, Olivia. Maybe you sleeping with our investor?"

Blood rushed to my cheeks. I wasn't in the habit of talking relationships or sharing any of the dirty details of my personal life with my brothers. I'd be content if they just assumed I was a virgin for the rest of my life, and I guessed they probably would be content with that lie too.

"Do you think you might be jumping to conclusions a little bit?"

He whipped the towel off his shoulders and began wiping down the counter. "I wasn't born yesterday. And the way Maya keeps prying, seems like she's got the right idea too."

"Why is this anyone's business?"

He paused to level another hard stare my way. "Because it *is* business, Liv. You shouldn't be complicating it with personal shit like this. Whatever you've got going on with him, I don't like it."

My embarrassment quickly morphed into indignation. "I hate to burst your bubble, Cam, but whatever I have 'going on' with Will is really none of your concern. Kindly butt out."

He leaned in a fraction. "As long as we have a working relationship with him, I think it *is* my concern. I don't want you getting involved with him."

I brought my hands to my hips and worked my jaw. He could be so pigheaded sometimes. I silently prayed that my nephew showed up soon so both he and Maya would get off my case. I was having a hard enough time figuring out what the hell was going on with Will without the added complications.

"You don't want me getting involved because he's an investor. Is that your only reason?"

"He's mixed up in things that you don't need to be dealing with."

"Is this about his dad? Will has nothing to do with that."

He scowled. "How do you know? You believe everything people tell you now?"

I was the one to lean in this time. "Oh, so his money's green enough to fund our project, but because his dad's in trouble, I can't have anything to do with him? I mean seriously, Cam, do you just make these rules up as you go?"

"He's not good for you."

"Who is?" My voice had dropped to a whisper. "Was Maya good enough for you? Was Vanessa good enough for Darren? What do you think Mom would say? No one's ever going to be good enough, and you know it."

"We're not going down that road again, I swear to Christ, Liv."

I held up a hand, silencing him. "I love Maya, okay? I pushed her away and I judged her when I should have given her a chance. I was stupid because I didn't understand that your happiness was at stake."

He was silent for the first time.

"I don't know if this thing with Will is going anywhere, but I can't deal with you guys hovering. I need to be my own person. I need to make mistakes and figure things out as I go. I don't want to be led around by the nose anymore. That's why I came here, remember? For a chance to start over and be *me*, not the person everyone else wants me to be."

He drew his hand over his face and sighed. "I'm never going to stop being your big brother, Liv. All my instincts tell me this is wrong."

I wilted, drained from the whole exchange. "Save your instincts for your baby, Cam. I'm a big girl. I can cross the street on my own now."

"This can't affect the build-out or the business."

"It won't." I hoped I could absolutely keep that promise.

"And he better not hurt you..." His hand turned into a fist.

"I'm going to be fine," I said, wanting to believe that, too.

Cam turned away after a long moment. We finished cleaning the kitchen in silence. His concerns tumbled through my head. I wanted to be indignant, but I knew his words, even if gruffly and pigheadedly delivered, came from his heart.

Cam had always been there for me when I was little. When Darren would pick on me endlessly, Cameron was always the compassionate one who would play with me and keep me entertained when no one else would. He was the ultimate big brother, always making me feel safe and protected. When he was deployed and I was in college, he wrote me letters, brief but heartfelt. The smallest gesture was enough to remind me that he cared, that our bond was still as strong as ever, even if he was battling his own demons overseas.

I was grateful for Cam, and I always would be. But if I was going to carve out my own path here in the city and in this new life, I had to do it on my own. I had to make my own decisions and own my mistakes. Otherwise, the risk was worth nothing.

★ ★ ★

The night ended early. Maya was tired, understandably so, and Darren had a look in his eyes like he wanted to hurry home and talk Vanessa into making a baby. After a nearly sleepless night in Will's bed, I was ready to put the day behind me too.

I walked around my apartment, tidying up as I went, tired but unable to really rest. I had too much on my mind, and even as midnight approached, I couldn't slow down enough to sleep. I reached for my phone and contemplated calling Will. He'd asked me to, but I also didn't want to come across as needy, even though I missed his presence already.

I put my reservations aside and pulled up his number. He answered after the first ring.

"Olivia."

"Hi," I said softly. "Can you talk?"

"Of course. I've been watching bad TV for two hours, waiting for you to call."

I smiled. "Sorry."

"Don't be. How was dinner?"

I blew out a breath. "Awkward, to be completely honest."

"I rely on your honesty."

I didn't reply, because I worried he was talking about what happened between Ian and me that morning. A wave of heat rushed over me, embarrassment mixing with the lust-fueled memory.

"I can't stop thinking about this morning," I said finally, because something felt unresolved about all of it. I wanted to get past it and move on, one way or the other.

He hummed quietly on the other end. "Me neither. I'd love a repeat performance tomorrow."

I smiled again, warming further at the memory of his mouth on me, licking me straight into one of the most incredible orgasms of my life. "I meant...before that."

He was silent a moment. "Ian?"

I nodded, even knowing he couldn't see me. "What would

you have done if he'd kissed me? Tell me the truth."

"I would have laid you out on the island and eaten you like my last meal, same as I did this morning."

"I know we're not exclusive—"

"We are." The abrupt way he said it left no doubt. "I'd planned to tell you once we passed the trial run. But I swear to God, if you let someone else into that luscious body while we're together, I won't be held responsible for my actions."

"Okay, but if that's what you want, why don't you care that Ian..." What could I say? *Came on to me, put his hands on me...*

"Because things are different with him." His voice was low, like he was confessing a dark secret.

"Explain that."

"This is really something we should talk about in person. If you come over, I can explain."

I hesitated, gauging my energy for a late-night ride to his place.

"Right after I take advantage of you, of course," he continued. "Savagely and repeatedly."

His was a tempting offer. Not only was I burning with curiosity, I was already craving his company. But that could be another scenario that didn't leave me time to think. His lack of concern when it came to the attraction between Ian and me was troubling, and I was compelled to get to the bottom of it.

"Just tell me, Will. I can handle it."

"I'd hoped to spend a little more time with you before this came up." He sighed, and more seconds passed. "I told you I don't do relationships, Olivia."

My heart sank a little, even though he'd been perfectly clear on those terms. Was I already starting to care more than I should? I waited, hopeful and anxious at once about what he wanted to tell me.

"Ian and I have similar tastes when it comes to women."

"And..."

"And sometimes we share them."

My heart fell, landing like a cold stone in my stomach. Any latent hope I'd had about getting to know Will better, about exploring our chemistry and wondering if it could possibly go anywhere, shattered. If my thoughts had been a jumble before, they were a whirlwind now.

"Talk to me, Olivia."

I searched for words, but it seemed like he'd said them all. "I don't know what to say. I don't think I'm what you want—"

"You're what I want, okay? It sounds complicated, but it doesn't have to be. This is why I wanted to talk about this in person. I can already hear you freaking out, and that's not what I want."

I rose to my feet and started pacing around my room. "How am I supposed to respond to this? What do you want from me?"

"I want *you*, Olivia. No one else exists for me right now."

"Right *now*." I couldn't hide the uneasy tone in my voice. Who knew what tomorrow would bring...

"I haven't been exclusive with anyone for a very long time."

"And sharing me with your roommate counts as exclusivity?"

"I want you for myself, and I trust Ian to be with you if that's what you both want. But he's the only exception."

"This is completely insane. Do you realize that?"

"If three consenting adults choose to spend time together—intimately or otherwise—I don't see that as insane or deviant or whatever else you want to label it. You want to spend your life playing by someone else's rules, go ahead, but I call that a waste of time."

He'd cut me off at the knees with that last comment, and I struggled for a reply.

"I'll be honest with you, Olivia. I don't usually see women more than once or twice. Most of the time, the person I'm with accepts that for what it is and enjoys it. That's not what I'm asking for, because I think I want something different with you. I haven't been able to get you out of my head since you walked onto the work site and started bitching at me about that fucking wall. And after spending most of last night inside of you, I can't think straight right now."

"Me neither," I admitted, feeling the smallest measure of relief that I wasn't the only one who was totally mixed up at the moment. I sighed and dropped back down onto my bed. "Did you two like *plan* this already? Did you know this is what you wanted from me when you asked me to have dinner with you?"

"Not really, no. I met you, I was attracted to you, and I acted on it. But Ian and I don't observe boundaries like other people do. His attraction to you is obvious. And from the looks of it, you're attracted to him, too."

I couldn't deny that I was. My body reacted to his before my brain could talk me out of it, and it had been that way every time we'd interacted. Still, I couldn't imagine myself seeing two people at once. Breaking away from expectation was an attractive notion, but how far was I willing to go?

"What if I say no?"

He was silent a moment. "Then we'll figure it out."

"What does that mean?"

He sighed again. "Come over and let's talk about this. I

can explain it better."

"I can't tonight."

If I hadn't just spent one of the best nights of my life in his bed, I could have easily dismissed all of it away. Never in a million years was I going to have two lovers. Sure, I was attracted to them both. The idea of them knowing about each other seemed unbelievable until I thought about how unfair it was when someone was left in the dark. Will wasn't painting a picture of betrayal and heartbreak, though. This was open and honest, even if it was unconventional.

"Then I'll come to you," he insisted.

"No," I said firmly. Never mind the rattling confession about sharing women with Ian. I couldn't have Cameron run into him here and deal with the inevitable drama.

I heard him curse quietly on the other end, and then the sound of ice hitting a tumbler. "Tomorrow."

The edge in his voice told me he wasn't asking anymore. He was demanding, and even though I'd told him he couldn't make those kinds of demands on me, I knew better. He had more control over me already than I cared to admit.

But what the hell was I walking into? Even talking to him and entertaining this conversation was probably a step in the wrong direction.

Maybe Cameron's instincts were right and mine were all wrong. Didn't change the fact that I wanted to see Will tomorrow, and I knew I would. I couldn't deny the way he made me feel, and I couldn't ignore my growing attraction to Ian either. I wanted to talk about this insanity until it made some sort of sense.

Tomorrow, maybe it would.

"Tomorrow."

CHAPTER SEVEN

WILL

I climbed the steps of Olivia's Brooklyn brownstone, fueled by coffee, another restless night, and a burning desire to see her again. The call box showed three buttons. The second one was scratched out. Above, *M. & C. Bridge*, and below, *O. Bridge*, was scrawled in messy lettering. Before I could buzz her, the door opened. Cameron walked through, a satchel slung over his arm. He was dressed as I normally saw him, in jeans and an athletic shirt donning the Bridge Fitness logo.

"Cameron, hey." I smiled, like there was nothing at all uncomfortable about me showing up at his sister's apartment at eight in the morning.

He leveled a hard stare at me. "Can I help you with something?"

I hesitated. I wasn't afraid of being upfront with him about seeing Olivia, because I planned to see more of her. But after last night's conversation, I had no idea what the future had in store for us. Things were tenuous, and instead of adding to the potential shit storm and admit I was here to see his sister, I could come up with a bullshit excuse about wanting to talk about the renovation. Except my hands were full with coffee and pastries from the bakery down the street. Not sure I could sell Cameron on that gesture being for him. Had to go with the truth.

"I actually came to see Olivia."

His expression didn't change. Without moving from the doorway, he created a wall between me and the woman who'd completely taken over my brain.

I lifted an eyebrow. "Is there a problem?"

"I hope not." Cameron's voice was low and unwavering.

I knew in that moment that he cared a hell of a lot more about his sister than any potential repercussions his actions might have on his business. Even though he was an impediment to me getting what I wanted, I respected him more for it.

He didn't move, as if he were waiting for an answer.

Did he want some kind of guarantee that I was going to do the right thing by Olivia? Did I even know what that meant? I'd never had to think about it too hard before. But the way he was protecting her now made me want to do the same thing for her, because deep down, I knew she was worth it.

"There's not going to be a problem," I finally said, believing the words as I uttered them.

Whatever happened between Olivia and me, I wouldn't hurt her. I wasn't going to fuck her and leave her, discard her and her feelings. I wasn't going to take her heart and break it. Anything we did we'd go into with full disclosure.

After another tense moment, he moved down the stairs and began his walk down the tree-lined street. I held the door, shifting my gaze from Cameron through the doorway that would take me deeper into this situation with Olivia.

The scent of the coffees in my hand spurred my next steps. I needed more coffee, and I needed this woman.

I stepped into the hallway that led to her first-floor apartment. I knocked on her door. She didn't answer, so I knocked again, longer and louder. A few seconds later, she opened it and stood before me. I tensed my jaw to keep it from landing on the floor. Her hair was a tangle, and her eyes were soft and tired, like I'd woken her. She wore only a ribbed navy-blue tank top and matching blue panties.

"What are you doing here?"

I collected myself and shot her a grin. "I slept like shit. Figured you might have too. I brought coffee." I extended the cup to her. "Cappuccino, your favorite."

Her brow wrinkled as she accepted it. "How do you do that?"

I masked a smile, enjoying the thrill that always came with being right.

She moved to the side so I could enter and closed the door behind me. "You shouldn't have come here. If Cameron saw you, he'd lose his mind."

I laughed a little and watched her perfect ass sway ahead of me into her living room. "Too late for that."

She turned abruptly, her eyes wide and alert. "What happened?"

"Nothing. We just passed each other on my way in."

"Did he say something?"

I shrugged. "It's fine. Nothing you need to worry about."

She sighed heavily and took a seat on the edge of her couch, covering herself with a velvety gray throw. I sat at the other end, taking in the details of the place she called home.

The apartment wasn't enormous, but it was well appointed. The cherry hardwood floors were new and covered with a couple of expensive rugs. The furniture was designer I guessed from the quality of the material covering it. Everything was cool, from the white linen curtains to the series of square-cropped ocean photographs that adorned the walls through the room. And Olivia was the centerpiece, warm and beautiful. Though I guessed she'd rolled right out of bed, I didn't want her any less than I had hours before. Why the hell did I crave her the way I did?

She blew the steam off the top of the cup and sipped carefully. She met my imploring gaze after a moment. "Thanks for the cappuccino. You were right. I didn't sleep very well. I couldn't stop thinking about what you said."

"And what are you thinking now?"

She circled her fingertip over the rim of the cup. "I'm thinking I'm crazy for even talking to you about any of this. Deciding to be with you was already outside of my comfort zone. This thing with Ian..."

The hesitation in her eyes warned me and heartened me. She was bound to me, enough to question her attraction to Ian and accept what he was going to do to her. That bond wasn't a figment of her imagination either, a pathetic one-sided longing. It existed. A real thing—taut and tense, strengthening between us. I trusted Ian with her body, but no matter how many hours he spent inside her, I knew she was becoming mine.

"You have doubts. That's normal," I said.

"Will, I don't even know where to start. I am attracted to Ian, but I'm not like you. I don't rove the world sampling all of life's earthly pleasures, throwing every rule and convention out the window as I go."

I laughed at the picture she painted, but maybe she wasn't completely wrong. I wanted what I wanted. I enjoyed sex, and all the money and privilege in the world couldn't measure up to losing myself for a few minutes inside a beautiful woman. And right now, all the beautiful women in the world couldn't measure up to the one beside me at this very moment.

"Come here." I reached out to her, palm upturned.

She hesitated.

"Please," I uttered quietly.

Some tension melted off her shoulders. Her mouth relaxed as she shifted to the middle cushion beside me. I took her coffee with one hand, setting it safely away. Then I caught her thigh and pulled her over so she straddled me. Her hands rested on my shoulders and crept softly around the nape of my neck.

I stifled a groan, immediately on edge. Through her panties, her pussy was warm against the bulge in my jeans. Her tits were right at eye level too. I ached to uncover them, mold my palms around their perfect softness, and suck each sweet rosy nipple into my mouth until she cried out.

Instead, I gazed into her eyes, skimming my palms up the sides of her torso until I reached her face. I cupped her cheeks and brought her lips to mine, kissing her tenderly.

"Don't give up on me just yet," I whispered against her lips.

"I don't know what I want, Will."

Longing and surrender came through with her words, and I knew then what I had to do.

"Let me show you what you want, Olivia. Trust me with your body and your pleasure. You don't need to think before you act. Not with me. Give in, and let me take control of a situation you already know I can master."

"I want to, but—"

I pulled her to me again, silencing her doubts. She

moaned, kissing me deeper, shifting her hips against mine. Maybe we were done with words. Maybe I needed to show her another way...

I stood, lifted her with me, and brought her to the bedroom. I dropped her down on the bedspread, enjoying how the morning light cast a warm glow on her body. Her knees were bent and slightly parted. Her arms were high, her fingertips tangled in the mass of dark-brown locks that lay across the blue paisley bedspread.

I pulled my shirt over my head and threw it to the floor. She bit her lip as her gaze traveled the length of me. I went for my belt, pulling it swiftly from its loops.

"Sit up."

When she moved upright, I lifted her tank top over her head. I caught her hands and looped my belt around them, securing them tightly. She didn't flinch or question me, which I took as a promising sign.

"I'm giving you a chance to trust me," I murmured.

I finished and tested her bonds. She was secure.

"Does that feel okay?"

Her gaze flickered up to mine. "Feels fine. Should I be worried?"

"The opposite. You should be relieved. I'm in control now, so you don't have to be. Lie back, and let me blow your mind."

A ghost of a smile passed over her lips, and she lay back, resting her hands above her head. I undressed and fished out a condom from my wallet. I rolled it on, noting how the ritual was already starting to piss me off. Something about Olivia made me feel uniquely possessive.

I fed the fantasy I'd had more than once about coming inside her. I didn't seem to have much control over my primal instincts when it came to her. As she writhed on the bed in front of me, I fought the urge to spread her and take her hard and rough. Not this time. This time I had to make a point. I had to earn her trust.

I caught her foot and rested it against my chest. Her toenails were perfectly manicured and painted a pale pink. I pressed a soft kiss to the pad of each toe. Then I went to her ankle and worked my way up to her toned calf, kissing and sucking. The inside of her thigh was like satin. I licked the crease between her thigh and the hem of her panties, shifting the fabric just enough to catch the lip of her pussy with my tongue.

"Do you like this? The way I touch you and tease you?"

She sucked in a sharp breath and arched against me. "Yeah."

I pressured her hips down to the mattress and nuzzled against the cotton panties that separated me from the object of so many indecent thoughts as of late. Olivia's delicious pussy.

I inhaled her, smelling her arousal, catching the hint of moisture through the fabric. My cock was painfully hard, straining to be inside her.

I was losing control. I'd come here to make a point, and the only one I was making was that my cock was hardwired to respond to her scent, her touch, her everything.

"Do you trust me to do things to you that no one's ever done before?"

She nodded, her breaths coming rapidly now.

I yanked her panties down, tearing the fabric. I moved up her body, trailing my lips over her silky skin. I hovered there, barely touching her.

"And when I'm so deep inside you that you shake and

scream. Do you like that too?"

"Yes," she whispered breathlessly.

"I want to give you that. I want to take you over the edge, over and over again. So does Ian. He wants to be the name on your lips right next to mine. Imagine feeling what you feel now, but with both of us. Two people who want to give you more pleasure than you can handle."

The heat radiating off her body seemed to multiply. She balled her fingers into tight fists and arched her back off the bed. I closed my eyes and breathed her in, a deep intoxicating breath that was meant to calm me down but only made the beast inside me hungrier.

"Give in to me, Olivia. Give me what I want. Tell me you will."

Neither of us could afford love. But we could have this. We could share this. Once Ian had her, heaven help me, maybe I could disconnect from some of these dangerous feelings. I'd never wanted anything or anyone so damn bad. And even as I questioned if I could truly share her with Ian, I'd deliver on the pleasure I'd promised. I ached to see her come apart under the passion that we'd bring to her in the same bed.

Give in to me...

I demanded without words, without an inch of our flesh touching and tempting her. I wanted her surrender, but the next step was hers to take.

Her bottom lip trembled as she searched my gaze. Her own was hooded with lust and glimmered with trust. It was the trust that gutted me.

"Yes." Her voice was a whisper.

OLIVIA

I was up against years of careful upbringing, a lifetime of meticulous plans and decisions made to ensure a future as close to perfection as one could attain.

And in the space of minutes, Will had stripped me down, physically and in every other way. I was naked and raw, as bare as my desire. Bound yet somehow freer than I'd ever felt before.

Despite being plagued with doubts most of the night, when I was in his arms, I was ready to let go. I was tired of overthinking and worrying about every potential misstep. Being with Will had been nothing but liberating, stimulating in more ways than one.

I felt safe, and deep down, I did trust him. The good girl inside me warned me to be careful, screamed "no" when my body screamed "yes." But the woman he had uncovered wasn't good anymore. She was a shell of need, and she wanted to be filled—with life and experience and the kind of toe-curling pleasure that only Will had given me.

He was pushing inside me in seconds, making me his all over again.

"Fuck," I gasped at the searing pleasure of our bodies coming together. My thirst for more curled around the incredible sensation of him filling me—completely and so perfectly. I expected him to come at me like he had before, fast and hard, but the way he moved felt deliberate and meaningful. He brought our hips together slowly, joining us inch by inch and pulling back again.

His lips hovered over mine. "Olivia...say it again. Say yes. I need to hear it. I need to know it's what you want."

I'd already given in, but I'd give in a thousand times for a minute of this kind of bliss.

I whimpered as he thrust again.

"Yes...I'm yours."

He stilled. I could feel his heart racing against my chest. His eyes were dark with need, shadowed by the messy locks that fell off his forehead. His expression was tight and vulnerable at once.

He didn't say a word, only pressed his lips against mine. Soft at first, and then firmer, until I could taste his tongue. I kissed him with everything I had until he broke away.

"You're goddamn right you're mine."

In the haze of desire, something in my heart twisted. The last of my resistance melted into pure surrender. His hands were everywhere then, pushing my hands down as he drove hard, rocking into my body. Pulling my hips up to meet his fierce drives, he fucked me straight into oblivion.

I moaned his name between my cries of ecstasy. Nothing had ever felt so amazing, so complete.

He wrapped his muscular arms around me, holding me tight and bracing me against his rough movements. "I'm not letting you go. Can't...won't..."

I felt his strength and his passion in every touch, every undulation pulling me deeper into feelings I didn't want to think about. Our flesh was slick with sweat. I twisted my wrists in the bonds of the belt, and the pinpricks of discomfort only added to the intensity of the moment. Something about giving him this much control had me spiraling out of my mind and into my body, owned so completely by his.

"Don't let me go. Oh, God, don't stop... Will!"

I shattered. The orgasm seemed to swallow me whole,

taking me under, suspending space and time.

My broken cry echoed off the walls and fed his passion. He sped up and hit a place inside that had me quaking in his arms, crashing into another powerful release before the other had even waned. He shoved into me so hard I didn't know where he ended and I began. We were one, and I was coming longer and harder than I ever had in my life.

His abs and every other muscle bunched and tensed. With a curse, he buried himself inside me one last time with a low moan.

My head buzzed. Only our breathing and the faint sounds of the city outside filled the air. After several minutes, he lifted on his elbow and stared down at me. His skin was flushed and his grin wicked.

"You came without me, princess."

Whoops.

"Does that mean you're going to...punish me?" My tone was teasing but held a glimmer of the fear I felt. He'd threatened punishment before, but I wasn't quite sure what that meant.

He laughed out a breath. "Sure does. As soon as I catch my breath."

His erection hadn't flagged, so I silently hoped my punishment involved more pleasure than pain.

A second later, he rose and disappeared into my little adjoining bathroom. He returned, reached for his jeans, and tossed another condom on the sheets. His weight dipped the bed as he came for me.

"Let's see what we else can do with that belt."

IAN

I had a few days off, which meant my time belonged to the side work that Will needed. The renovation was moving at a steady clip, and I had to catch up when I could between shifts at the station.

I was working on the master bath in the penthouse condo above the new home of Bridge Fitness. The floor was nearly done—a simple design that came around a custom centerpiece that I hadn't figured out quite yet. Will had given me creative license to come up with something that hopefully he'd like. For being the bossy type, he didn't seem to have a lot of specific preferences regarding this particular aesthetic, which was fine by me.

As I laid out materials to start my work for the day, Will came into the room, his boots scuffing along the subfloor. "We need to talk."

I halted what I was doing and glanced up. I hadn't seen much of him for the past few days. I figured he was working extra hours at the site, but whatever it was, he looked more intense than usual.

"Everything okay?"

"It's about Olivia."

We hadn't discussed my rendezvous with Liv in the kitchen after their all-night fuck fest several nights ago, and I hadn't seen Olivia since. I didn't figure any of it needed an explanation, but the look in Will's eyes hinted that something else was at stake.

"Is there a problem?"

He glanced away, gnawing at his lip for a second before returning his focus to me. "I want to be careful with her. This isn't going to be a once-and-done thing for me."

I stood and faced him, man to man. We were the same height and of similar build. He was leaner where I was a little stockier, but we were evenly matched. I'd never felt threatened by Will, but something about this conversation was putting me on the defensive.

"What are you saying? You want me to back off?" I sure as hell didn't want to. If that's what he wanted, I had to start looking for a new place to stay as soon as possible. I couldn't have her that close to me. I couldn't listen to her cries of pleasure night after night and keep my hands off of her. There was just no way.

"No, I like the arrangement we have. I just don't want to scare her off because of it. We talked about it, and I think she'll be fine. But I don't want to take anything for granted."

I lifted my eyebrows and rubbed my chin. I couldn't imagine how that conversation might have gone. That she might be open to being with us both was as shocking as it was arousing. I was that much closer to having her for myself, and the prospect had taken over my thoughts in an instant.

"What did she say?"

"She panicked at first, of course. Getting her into my bed to begin with wasn't exactly easy. She's not like the others, Ian. You know I can talk anyone into having us both for one night after a couple martinis. It's a fantasy, not a commitment. I want her to know what she's getting into."

I thought about his words. We'd never hooked up with the same girl more than once or twice. Negotiations were easy. They started with an indecent proposal and ended with a yes or a no. At the end of the day, we were a hard combination to resist. I hadn't known anyone to leave unsatisfied, but Will and

I weren't the kind of guys to get tied down. Had I heard him right?

"You want a commitment?"

"No." He bit out a curse under his breath. "Just be careful with her, all right?"

I winced and took a step toward him. "Have I ever been anything but careful with the women we've been with?"

His expression softened. He ran a hand through his already messy hair. "Sorry, you're right. She's got me twisted up. I don't know what the fuck I'm saying half the time."

"You haven't been around the apartment much. What's up?"

He shrugged. "I've been here trying to push the pace. If we can wrap up and get the gym open early, all the better."

"Why the rush?"

"To be honest, I'm sick of getting death glares from her brother. I'm biting my tongue for now because I respect him, but I'm not going to back down. I'm pretty sure the only reason we haven't come to blows is because of the business relationship we're both trying to maintain. Working on this project together is an uncomfortable complication. I want to get past it as quickly as possible."

I nodded. "Understandable." On both sides.

I wasn't sure what the future held for him and Olivia, but if I was going to be involved in any way, I only prayed that Darren never found out.

CHAPTER EIGHT

WILL

"Thanks for making the time," Jia murmured into my ear as she hugged me. When we separated, she took a seat across from me at the barroom table and glanced at the cocktail menu. "What's good here?"

"Everything," I said.

We'd agreed to meet at Superhero, a new bar that had opened up in the neighborhood. The drinks were strong and the atmosphere was relaxed.

Jia's dark-brown hair was held up in a twist. I imagine she'd changed out of her requisite pencil skirt and designer blouse in favor of the dark jeans she wore with a silky top that rippled every time a breeze came through the open-air bar.

When the waitress came by, she ordered a cocktail. Leaning back in her chair, she eyed me. "So how's it going?"

"It's been busy. Trying to renovate multiple spaces at once is no small trick."

"I can't wait to see the new condos when they're finished."

"It's going quick. I think I'm going to snag the penthouse for myself though."

"What about Ian?"

A smirk curved my lips. "What about Ian?"

She played with the square diamond stud that sparkled

in her ear. "You two make quite the team. I'd hate to see that change."

"I haven't thought much about it, to be honest. The roommate situation was supposed to be temporary, but if he wants to crash at the new place, I have no issues with that."

"That's reassuring," she purred. "We should catch up. Maybe tonight?"

"I can't," I answered automatically.

"Come on. I could use some downtime." She reached over and brushed her fingers over the back of my hand. "I might even miss you, Will." Suggestion glimmered in her deep dark eyes.

Jia was a beautiful woman. Dangerously so. She pined after no one, took what she wanted, and left shame at the door. Those qualities made her a perfect bed companion on nights when I wanted a hard, uncomplicated fuck.

Tonight wouldn't be one of those nights.

"I met someone."

The dark wing of her eyebrow lifted. "You're in a relationship?"

"No, but she's someone I plan to spend a lot more time with." As soon as possible, in fact. We'd barely seen each other the past few days outside of work, and the withdrawals were harrowing.

Jia didn't speak for a second, her smile tight. "Sounds serious."

"It's not serious at all. Nothing against you. She's just who I'm focused on right now."

She sat back in her chair, withdrawing her touch. "Focused on or preoccupied with? I've never heard you talk about someone this way."

I resented the unimpressed tone in her voice. I drank from my glass of scotch, refusing to give her an answer. Olivia had caught me completely off guard. I had pursued her, thinking I was taking another rich girl to bed. I didn't expect her wit or her fire. And I didn't expect her submission to be so goddamn captivating. I didn't expect her to respond to me the way she did, like she wanted to give as much as I wanted to take, even as it betrayed everything she'd been taught.

"Can I ask who she is? She must be striking to give you pause."

I worked my jaw. As far as I knew, outside of Ian and her brother, no one knew about our little affair.

Jia laughed quietly. "God, Will. I'm not going to tell anyone. I'm just curious."

"Her name is Olivia Bridge. Our families know each other. Under the current circumstances, I'm sure she'd appreciate if they didn't know we were fucking."

She nodded. "Understood. Reputation is everything these days."

Glancing out to the street where a couple was walking hand in hand, she looked almost wistful. When she returned her attention to me, her expression was harder.

"I spoke with Bill recently. He thinks I can talk some sense into you. According to him, pissing away a billion-dollar opportunity isn't a matter of choice."

I shrugged, pretending not to care even as fresh guilt took root. "He's the one pissing it away, not me."

"You have the power to turn this around, you know," she pressed.

My jaw was tight. Frustration coiled in my muscles. "Is this why you wanted to meet?"

"It's not the only reason, but since you're not up for company, I suppose it is now."

She crossed her arms. The defensive position told me she wasn't fond of being rejected. But something else was at play. The way she jumped from sharing a bed with Ian and me to something she knew was a hot topic was unsettling. Jia worked from an agenda, always.

I laughed quietly when it struck me. "He wants to bring you on, doesn't he?"

She hesitated a moment, her dark eyes steady with calculation. "Yes, he's mentioned it. They were scouting for a COO before all this happened. We've been in loose discussions since then. He doesn't trust a lot of people right now, but he trusts me. Would that bother you?"

"You can do what you want, but why would you want to be associated with this shit?"

"It's a mess, Will. No doubt about it. It's risky getting anywhere near it. You know this as well as I do. But it's an opportunity to make a jump. I'm sick of climbing the ladder at the firm. If I can help you turn things around with Reilly Donovan Capital, it's a game changer for me."

"If he has you, why the hell does he need me?"

She stared out to the street and back to me again. "I'm not going to jump without you. I need you just as much as he does."

OLIVIA

I'd spent the past few days between the two gyms. The renovation was moving ahead of schedule, and Cameron and I were suddenly busy with the finer details of getting the gym functional and ready for members. I also had a ribbon-cutting to coordinate so we could announce to the neighborhood that we had officially arrived and were ready for business.

Through it all, I'd seen Will regularly enough. As promised, he heard my opinion from time to time. As promised, he bent to my wishes. When he pushed back, I never hesitated to make my case, which seemed to intrigue him as much as it irritated him. By the end, I could tell he wanted to resolve the matter once and for all back at his apartment, and most of the time so did I. But the tension that strained his interactions with Cameron made me want to focus on the task at hand—getting this done so we could all move on with our lives.

In the meantime, being with Will had created a different kind of tension in me. An unsettled edgy feeling had gnawed at me ever since I'd originally agreed to be his no-strings-attached fuck buddy. Except new strings were popping up all the time. Exclusivity, except when it came to his head-to-toe gorgeous roommate. And his fiercely passionate style of fucking that pushed me past all my boundaries and resulted in a seemingly never-ending stream of sheet-tearing orgasms.

I needed to burn off some of that tension, so after a long day filled with details and a level of multitasking that challenged even me, I found myself on the treadmill, eager for the burn in my muscles. I set an aggressive program on the machine, put my headphones in, and began.

Only a few minutes in, my phone rang, and my mother's name appeared on the screen.

I turned off the treadmill and slowed my pace as the machine did. "Hi, Mom."

"Olivia." Her tone was tight, which wasn't unusual for her, but most of the time she called me after a couple of lunchtime cocktails, a regular indulgence that she and her socialite friends shared on any given day of the week.

"What's going on?"

"I'd like to ask you the same thing. What do you think you're doing, seeing Will Donovan, and why am I only now hearing of this?"

I collected my water bottle, stepped off my machine, and walked away from the noise of the gym as quickly as my feet would carry me. Cameron was in the back office and all the rooms were occupied with classes, so I went outside.

"Who told you that?"

"Everyone knows everyone, and there's certainly nothing more interesting to talk about up here. You will end this at once. I'll not have you married off to the son of a convict."

I rolled my eyes so hard it hurt. "You're getting a little ahead of yourself, Mother. I'm not marrying anyone, and as far as I know, no one's been convicted of anything. Even if charges come down on Will's father, it has nothing to do with him."

"Rumor says he's going to take over his father's hedge fund. If that's the case, he is involved enough. We invested a million dollars with Reilly and Donovan."

My jaw fell. "What? When did this happen?"

She sighed. "Back in the spring. You know Vanessa used to work there. Darren lost his temper and got into some trouble with Reilly. Frank did what he felt was best to de-escalate the situation. At the time, it seemed like a sound investment."

"How come no one ever told me?"

"Why on earth would your father keep you informed of his investments? You left here with hardly any notice. You still haven't explained why. We thought things were going well with Rob, and suddenly you're packing your bags and running off to the city with your brothers."

I clenched my teeth. Everything about this exchange was upsetting and hurtful. I loved my mother, but her claws were constantly out. She rarely cared about how her words fell or how her cold demeanor affected those around her. I'd adopted her coldness because it protected me from people I needed to keep at a distance. But I'd never been able to lash out with words quite the way she could. Watching from the sidelines as she shredded my family and those close to us was one thing. Being the target of her discontent was another.

"I told you I was done talking about Rob."

My father's rising star had been a distant memory well before Will had entered my life, and I had no desire to relive my time with him. The one night I'd let him get too close still made my skin crawl when I thought of it.

"He's handsome, comes from a great family, and your father is bringing him up through the company, mentoring him. He could be a partner at this rate. It would have been a good match."

"You pushed me at him! You both did. Do you want to know the truth? I slept with him, and I hated every minute of it. I woke up in the morning, and I didn't recognize myself. I had to leave."

She made a sound of disgust. "I don't want to hear about those things. You know that, Olivia."

"Then you don't want to hear about what's going on with Will, either. Stay out of my love life, and I'll spare you the details."

"Olivia," she snapped, her tone loud and sharp. "You don't speak to me that way. What has gotten into you?"

Panic tightened around me, a familiar sensation when I was at risk of upsetting my parents, the rulers of the purse strings that kept me in the life I'd grown accustomed to. Unlike Maya and Vanessa, who'd had to work and struggle to stay afloat through every year of school, I'd wanted for nothing. Clothes, trips, beauty appointments. Long after graduation, I still relied on my parents to bridge the gap between my income with helping Cameron and affording a life of privilege.

Being "cut off" was a real and present danger. Then Will's words from the day we'd met echoed in my mind. The way he described my life had angered me, no doubt. But it had made me a little sick too. It made me wish I could crawl out of my skin and be someone else, anyone but that girl...

"I can't talk right now, Mom." I couldn't stomach telling her any more. This conversation had to end.

"You're ending it with Will, correct?"

"No, I'm not."

"Olivia, do I need to come down there and talk some sense into you? This isn't like you. You're worrying me, and when your father learns of this, I can guarantee he's not going to be happy."

"I have to go." My voice was hollow.

I ended the call and leaned back against the building. She called again, and I sent it to voice mail, something I never did.

But something had to change. Even as I questioned the choices I'd made since meeting Will, I knew deep down that I was changing, and not just on the outside. This wasn't a new style or a dramatic haircut. This wasn't a move or an expensive soul-searching vacation. I wasn't trying on something just to feel different for a little while. The foundation of who I thought I was for so many years was crumbling. And as much as I may have wanted to please and appease my parents, I wasn't sure I could help it.

I had to break away, and my parents had to know it, once and for all. Even if it cost me financial stability. Even if it cost our family this last tie that kept my parents and my brothers connected. I had to risk it all if I was going to find the person I wanted to be.

The thought was liberating, but devastating. If my foundation was crumbling, a new me had to be built. I didn't know how I would be able to do that. Warm tears cooled as they streamed down my cheeks.

"Liv, are you all right?"

My eyes flew open at the sound of a male voice, smooth as velvet. I swallowed when Ian approached me. He was dressed in workout clothes. I rushed to wipe away my tears, but he'd surely seen them. Concern filled his gaze. In my experience, most guys didn't know what to do with a crying woman, but Ian didn't shy away.

He came closer, brushing his thumb across my cheek. That simple touch made my heart beat faster.

"What's wrong?"

"Nothing," I lied.

"Do you want to talk about it?"

I shrugged. "Not really. Family stuff."

He glanced through the glass windows of the gym and back to me. I thought I caught a flash of hesitation, even guilt, in his eyes.

"Want to get out of here for a little while?"

"Where?"

"Why don't we go for a run?"

I contemplated his offer. I wanted to curl into a ball and cry out the rest of these toxic emotions, but burning them off along with the rest of the tension that had built up over the week didn't sound awful either.

"I'm not sure I'll be able to keep up with you."

His smile was warm. "I'm not worried about that. Come on. Just a jog around the neighborhood."

I inhaled a deep breath and nodded. "Sure. Let's do it."

IAN

I stashed my bag in the locker room and joined Liv outside again. Being seen with her like this, so close to Darren's domain, was probably a mistake, but I hated to see her upset. That and I couldn't deny wanting to spend some time with her. According to Will, she could become a regular fixture in our lives. He talked about her like she was precious and worth protecting. That inspired mixed feelings in me. As a friend, I worried that I was moving in on something that could mean more than the casual flings he was used to. But Will wasn't asking me to back down, and I'd desired her from afar for too long to walk away on my own.

I silenced my doubts and shot her a smile that she quickly returned. "Ready?"

She nodded. "Ready when you are."

We took off, and I let her set the pace. I wasn't so much interested in pushing myself physically as getting her mind off of whatever was bothering her. Family stuff I certainly could relate to. I could also relate to not wanting to talk about it. I hadn't talked about my dad's death to many people. The guys from the station had come to the funeral and paid their respects. My mom broke down almost every time I came by. I'd watched my sisters cry and held them through the sobs, pushing down my own.

But I wouldn't talk about it. I couldn't. I'd hardened against the waves of grief that seemed to crash over all of us. They came less frequently as time passed, but the pain hadn't lessened and neither had my anger. We'd all thought his slow decline had come from age and a lifetime of backbreaking work. We didn't find out until the end that cancer had been eating away at his body for years. He'd worked through it. Took new jobs, carried on with life, a little slower, thinner, weaker. We never knew until the end. He'd been robbed, and so had we.

At an intersection, Liv looked up to me. "Which way?"

"This way." I pointed to the right. Without a second thought, I took her in the direction of a place I'd avoided for nearly a year.

We jogged another few blocks before the old studio came into view. My heart raced, not from exertion but from a rush of emotion I wasn't sure I was ready for yet. I considered passing by and circling back to the place where we'd started. Instead, I slowed in front of the run-down stretch of storefronts, not unlike a few others we'd passed. Not all of this part of Brooklyn had been revitalized and not every venture had made it. That's what made this place cheap enough to rent, and I'd refused to let it go.

I stared at the old metal door marked with a dozen worn stickers and no other indication that it led to my father's old workshop. A padlock and chain protected its contents.

"What's this?"

Beside me, Liv was catching her breath and looking between me and the door that represented a Pandora's box of unwanted emotion for me. I opened my mouth to speak, but I struggled for the words. Instead, I went to the lock and spun the dial through the combination until it clicked open. I unhooked the chain. Each movement resonated inside of me. I felt like I was moving forward mechanically, forcing myself through each step. Even though I'd contemplated this door a dozen times before, having Liv with me seemed to push me through.

I opened the door that led up a narrow staircase. The air was stale, but tinged with the smells of the studio ahead—wood, chemicals, and even the faintest scent of the homemade wine he'd made here too. I pushed on until we stepped into the large studio. There were no dividing walls, only places designated for one function or another. This was his sanctuary, his place away from everything, to create and simply be.

Liv touched my arm, and I caught her thoughtful gaze.

"This was my dad's studio. I haven't been up here since he died." I swallowed over a grimace. "Sorry, Liv. We can go."

"You don't have to be sorry." She scanned the untouched shadowy room. "Can I look around?"

"Sure."

I imagined it all through her eyes. It must look like a real dump. Immediately I hated myself for letting it sit this way for so long. I opened the shades. Billows of dust floated through the air. Dozens of boxes of materials sat against one wall. Another wall was distinguished by an extended work surface where an unfinished project lay scattered. Vats, a short wine rack, and the rest of his winemaking operation filled one corner. Then, where the light hit the strongest, an entire wall of glittering color. His art, a lifetime of work that hadn't made its way into the hands of friends or strangers. The pieces he'd kept for himself.

Liv went to them, walking along with wonder in her eyes. That wonder reminded me of the admiration I'd had for my dad's art since I was a boy. That same wonder had brought me into the trade. Now I didn't do it for the money but as a way to keep him close. She paused in front of one piece—a sun and a moon, joined. Shimmering gold and bright yellows blended into a night as cool and vibrant as Liv's unforgettable eyes.

"You can touch them," I said. I joined her and marveled at the piece that always seemed to be the centerpiece of his collection. "This one was always my favorite. Dad used to tell me it meant rebirth and strength. I didn't get the rebirth thing for a long time. Had to grow up enough to appreciate what that really meant. But I liked the strength part. I remember always wanting to be strong like him."

She turned toward me, her eyes soft. "You are strong."

"On the outside, Liv. Not in all the ways that matter, though."

She didn't speak, and I cursed myself for getting too close to a topic I didn't want to talk about. But for some reason, she made me want to talk, even if it hurt. Even if it was awkward like it was now.

"I'm glad you brought me here. Seeing this reminds me that some people don't give up."

I searched her eyes for meaning until she looked down and toyed with the small charm that hung from her bracelet.

"I used to paint in college. Majored in it, actually. But I haven't picked up a brush since I left campus. It's been years now."

"Why did you stop?"

She shrugged. "I'm terrified, to be honest. I sketch sometimes, or I work on little crafty projects. I can decorate rooms all day long. But I look at my box of paints, and I'm petrified."

"What are you scared of?"

"I'm not sure. Nothing ever feels right. I've spent a lifetime trying to be perfect, Ian. Art has nothing to do with perfection."

"If you can understand that, you can get past it. You can rise above whatever is holding you back."

"I'd like to think that, but it's not so easy."

I traced the wave of a sun ray, a path I must have traveled a hundred times while my dad worked here, a short train ride away from the home I'd grown up in. Liv was worried about perfection. I was already too broken to reach for those heights.

"Mosaics are born from imperfection. Broken pieces come together to make something beautiful, almost like they were fated to fit together and become what they are," I said.

Knowing that Olivia had abandoned her art hit me in the same place where I felt my father's death—the place where memories reminded me of all the days the cancer had robbed him of.

I let my hand fall back to my side. "After my dad died, I couldn't work for a while. I decided I needed a break. I couldn't stick white subway tile to a wall without thinking about him, let alone try to do him justice on something like this."

"But you got past it."

"Yeah. I missed him so damn much. I finally broke down and took a job, and when I did, I realized it was the only way I could keep him close enough. Nothing else gave me relief. Doesn't take away the pain, but it keeps him close."

"And your tattoo...that keeps him close too."

I remembered her touch that morning in the kitchen, painful but oddly welcome. And without having to tell her, she'd known. The mosaic stretching across my skin was homage to him, to the pain I couldn't quite let go of.

"It does."

"It's really beautiful. I'm sure you've made him really proud."

Her words wrapped around me, seeming to crawl inside and make me want to have her even closer. I caught her cheek, reveling in her soft skin. I'd had her this way before, so close but just out of reach.

"You're beautiful too, Liv. Inside and out. Perfection doesn't exist, but if it did, it already exists inside you. All your doubts, your flaws, your fear. Use all of it. Don't waste it because you think the world won't love every stroke."

She swallowed, and her eyes glistened with emotion. "I'll try," she whispered.

Whatever hurt was there, I wanted to take away, swiftly and completely. I pulled her into my arms and pressed my lips to hers. I flicked my tongue along the seam of her lips until she opened for me with a sigh. Then her tongue and her taste were all mine. I drank from her like she was cool water on a summer day...like she was the one thing I never knew I needed.

Leaning into me, she curved her soft body along the hard planes of mine. I guided her arms around my neck, and the kiss deepened. When she moaned, everything went out of focus but her. Heat ricocheted through me, hardening my cock. I wandered my touch over her curves, where her clothes molded tightly over her perfect body. Cupping her ass, I pressed her against my erection, adding more tension than relief to my current situation. She gasped, tightened her hold on me, and answered with the smallest movement of her hips, adding more friction between us.

I kissed her breathless, trying and failing to control my raging desire. I could have her here, somehow. But she deserved better, and I wanted to take my time with her. I longed to unwrap her, taste every inch of her incredible body, and fuck her slowly until she begged for more. I couldn't do that here, even as my cock ached to find a place inside her.

"Liv...goddamn, I want you, but we can't do this here."

"I know. I'm sorry." Her soft words puffed against my lips.

"See me tonight." My voice was need and desperation. I had to have her. I couldn't wait much longer...

Her questioning gaze flickered up to mine. "What about Will?"

Goddamn Will. I didn't especially want to share her, but if she hadn't already been his, she wouldn't ever be mine. Plus, he'd already warned her about us. The truth was I would have her any way I could...

"See *us*."

CHAPTER NINE

OLIVIA

My hand shook as I hit the button that would take the elevator car to Will and Ian's apartment. We'd talked about this, but that didn't change the fact that I was scared to death of what I was walking into. A sexual situation with not just one dominating man that I couldn't bear to resist, but two.

My mother's slanted opinions and unfair demands echoed in my ears. They were quickly silenced by the bell announcing my arrival. I didn't have room for her in my thoughts. Not tonight.

Will opened the door before I had a chance to knock. He looked freshly showered, shirtless, his hair falling in dark wet strands every which way. He smiled and pulled me close for a kiss that instantly took my breath away.

He stepped back enough to look me over. "Wow. I feel underdressed. You look...damn."

His ravenous gaze worked me over from head to toe.

I had a closet full of cocktail dresses, and more times than not, no place to wear them. So tonight I'd chosen a satiny cream dress with thin straps and an almost indecent slit up the thigh. Late summer was quickly becoming early fall, but the days were still hot and I could pull it off. His gaze fell to my feet, where I wore matching cream-colored heels that laced up the ankles.

"Good God," he murmured. "I think tonight's going to be a real exercise in restraint, princess. I'm ready to fuck you through the door, but our friend has been waiting oh so patiently, and I can't deny him now."

My breathing became ragged, and my confidence wavered. Will pulled me close again. "Shh, don't be scared."

I exhaled an unsteady breath. "But I am."

His gaze softened with concern. "We're not trying to take anything from you, Olivia. This isn't about us. You're the center of it all. You and your pleasure. If it's not making you happy, it's not what we want. Okay?"

I nodded, heartened by his words but still wary of the unknown. How could I please two men with appetites like theirs? I was one woman, perpetually frightened of falling short, historically out of my depth when it came to enjoying sex for the sake of sex.

"I don't want to do something wrong."

"It's just us, here and now. Open yourself to it. Give in to it. If you do that, you're doing everything right." He stilled. "Do you want this?"

Was he asking my brain or my heart? Because they were of two opinions on the matter. "I don't know what I want until I'm in the moment. I'm trying to feel my way through all of this, and even though it always feels right with you, sometimes it's scary too."

"Tell me what you're afraid of."

I reached for that honesty I'd promised him our first night together. "I'm afraid of getting hurt. Of feeling used. I don't want to be someone you...fuck and dispose of."

He winced, and his hold on me tightened a fraction. "I

won't hurt you."

"And Ian?" His name left my lips in a whisper.

Will licked his lips, his gaze serious. "Olivia, I have a feeling this is new territory for all of us."

"Not for you two."

He shook his head. "You might be surprised. We're all taking risks here. You have to trust me."

"I do trust you," I murmured.

He released a breath, relief smoothing his gorgeous features. "Ian's in the living room. Do you want a drink?"

I shook my head. "I'm fine." Three fingers of scotch would certainly have eased my nerves, but I wanted my wits about me. I had to know what I was going into.

"Go get comfortable. I'll be out in a little while. You don't have to wait for me."

I nodded, but those last words had me shaky on my feet again. I inhaled a steeling breath and left Will's embrace to find Ian sitting on the long leather couch in the living room.

I paused a few paces away. The heat in his gray-eyed gaze threatened to turn me into a puddle on the floor. That and he was sexy as hell—chiseled features carved by the gods and an enviable body. I bit my lip, suddenly scared and anxious by the prospect of seeing the man totally uncovered. All the way down to the substantial erection that he was already sporting through his jeans.

"You're trying to kill me in that dress, right?"

I laughed and smoothed my hands down the slick material. I bit my lip, imagining his hands on me instead, the way they had been earlier. He'd barely left an inch of my sparsely clothed body untouched at his father's studio. I hadn't wanted him to stop, but he seemed to possess more willpower than I had.

"You look nervous." His voice was low, as dangerous as his lascivious gaze.

I stared down at the floor, gathering my courage. "Guilty as charged."

"You have nothing to be nervous about. You've got both of us by the balls, Liv. Enjoy it."

He motioned me to come closer, and that small vote of confidence spurred me forward until I stood between his thighs. He gazed up at me, his jaw set tight. His tongue traveled along his lower lip as he drank me in.

"That first night, I heard you coming all night. I couldn't sleep, couldn't think straight. I'd wanted you before, but that's when I knew I had to have you."

My heart hammered, and my nipples beaded under the dress. I hadn't been able to stop thinking about the way he touched me at the studio hours before. I was on fire for the man, and nothing could soothe me except having his hands on me again.

"Touch me...please." I was desperate for it.

He bent forward, bringing his palms to my knees and moving them slowly up my thighs and under my dress. He circled around to my ass, teasing the skin under the hem of my panties. Heat arrowed to my pussy, where I wanted contact more than anything.

He brought his lips along my thigh where the slit didn't cover and teased a little circle around that small bit of flesh with his tongue. I grabbed his shoulder for leverage, sensing my knees might not hold out.

He stood abruptly, tugged off his shirt, and reached for me. Pushing the straps of my dress down, he devastated my mouth with a ravaging kiss. The lust and longing I'd felt before seemed so small compared to the sensations racking my body now.

My dress fell to the floor, and our flesh came together. Finally, skin against skin. He was scorching, his beautiful dark skin taut over slabs of hard muscle.

"I've wanted you for too long. More than you know," he rasped.

He dropped back onto the couch, bringing me with him so I straddled his thighs. The friction of denim against my skin heightened my need.

"What about Will? How does this work?" I whispered, suddenly aware of Will's extended absence from the room.

"Will calls the shots. And I do whatever the fuck I want in the meantime. Right now, I want your mouth on me, Liv."

On cue, I separated from his mouth and trailed my lips down his neck. He smelled spicy, like smoke and musk. I sucked at his skin, marveling at his taste, and worked my way down.

I curved my palm over his broad shoulder and then down his rib cage to his narrows hips. I brought my knees to the floor between his muscular thighs and trailed my lips and tongue along his tattoo, half expecting it to taste different than the rest of him. The pattern of geometric shapes created an ornate mosaic that stretched over his pectoral and around his torso. It was deep reds, oranges, and purples—colors that reminded me of pain, but set together, created a breathtaking design.

I rubbed his erection through his jeans. He hissed between his teeth, and his gaze turned molten. Grabbing my hair, he angled me up. He leaned in like he was going to kiss me again, but instead hovered there, a breath away. He worked the button and zipper on his jeans and freed his thick cock.

"Is this what you want?"

I whimpered in reply. Of course I had to pick two enormously endowed men to take to bed at once. I tried not to think about how I could possibly please them both. Ian's scent, the silky head of his cock teasing my lips, and his possessive hold on me had my head spinning with desire. Arousal pooled between my legs as I shifted my thighs against each other. Every sensation was on high alert.

"I want to know what you taste like," I whispered.

He loosened his hold on me, allowing me to take him into my mouth as far as I could. His deep moan filled me with satisfaction. I twirled my tongue around the head of his cock and then lowered down his impressive length, each time trying to take more of him than I had before. I inhaled through my nose, taking in the scent of him. His breathing was uneven, and his fist tightened and released around my hair when I sucked him harder. I reveled in the little signs of his undoing, reminding me that even though I was on my knees, I had power too.

The sound of bare feet shuffled behind me. Then out of the corner of my eye, I saw Will drop into the leather chair adjacent to the couch. I closed my eyes, wanting to stay focused on Ian's pleasure and not think too much about having an audience. Except when I did, the ache in my core became painfully acute. I sped up my strokes.

Finally, Will's voice cut through the room. "Olivia." That single word demanded all of my attention.

I let Ian's cock slip from my mouth and looked to Will. He flicked a finger, motioning me toward him. I looked up to Ian's flushed face, his full lips parted through ragged breaths.

"Go," he said.

"On your knees, princess," Will ordered gently, before I could rise to my feet.

Slowly, I traversed the space between the two men. I knelt between Will's thighs. Where nervous energy had pulsed through me before, I only trembled with lust now.

In Ian's arms, I felt frantic, a mirror of fierce desire that threatened to overwhelm all my senses. On my knees, waiting breathlessly for Will's next command, somehow I was free. When he challenged, I didn't rile. I found an unexpected peace in his dominance. And I trusted that wherever he led me, unimaginable pleasure followed.

"Did you enjoy that?" His voice was gravel and lust.

I bit my lip with a smile. I did. Giving Ian pleasure was intoxicating, empowering. I couldn't wait to do the same to Will.

"Let's take your panties off."

I stood and slid my lacy nude panties down my legs. I flicked them off my ankle and canted my head with a flirty grin. "Happy now?"

He shook his head with a smirk. "Why do I have the distinct feeling you're going to put me in my grave with that smart mouth of yours?"

"I promise not to suck you to death," I teased.

"I'm not sure I'd mind. Get back on your knees, princess."

I dropped down and stared up at him. He brushed his thumb back and forth over my lips. They felt swollen and tingly. They ached for something between them. As if he sensed that, he pushed two fingers past my lips.

"You can suck on these while you take my cock out."

I sucked the salt off his fingertips and worked to unfasten

his belt. He gasped as I tongued him the way I planned to tongue his cock as soon as I got my hands on it. I tugged his boxers down, freeing his cock. Then I took him in my mouth as I had Ian.

He released a heavy sigh, and his head fell back. "Fuck, that feels good."

I lost myself in the act, so focused on his pleasure that I nearly forgot my own until I heard more clothes drop to the floor behind me. Then I felt Ian's heat. His presence hummed through me without actual physical contact. He pressed a hot kiss between my shoulder blades and then trailed his tongue down my spine, eliciting a shiver over my whole body.

"How is she?" Will murmured over my head.

I jolted when Ian dragged his finger up my wet slit, from my clit to my anus.

"She's beautiful. And she's drenched."

"Perfect."

I heard the condom wrapper rip. Then Ian's broad hand came to my hip. The head of his cock nudged into the opening of my pussy. I shifted restlessly. I tightened and released my internal muscles, as if I could somehow draw him into me. Feeling painfully empty, I whimpered in desperation around Will's cock.

He grazed his thumb along my cheek. "Olivia's waited long enough. Give her what she wants."

I pressed my nails into Will's thighs and moaned as Ian filled me slowly. Inch by delicious inch, he rooted deeply. Unimaginable pleasure coursed through my veins. Ian's hands were everywhere, caressing down my back, up my sides, and around to my front to tease my nipples and clit. He was a master of gentle strength, seeming to know intuitively how much I could take.

Will sifted his fingers through my hair and caressed my cheeks as they hollowed around his cock. "How does it feel to be so filled up, princess?"

I was grateful to have my mouth occupied because I couldn't possibly answer that question with words. I was on fire, burning up from the inside out. Giving and receiving more pleasure than I could handle.

I took him as far as I could and then lifted to tongue and suck his head. I circled the base of his cock with my hand and began stroking quickly. He gasped out a curse. I didn't know whose orgasm I was racing toward—his or mine. Hopefully both, because Ian's thick penetration and rugged thrusts were already bringing me to the brink.

Then Will pulled me off of him abruptly, his hand tight in my hair. "Are you in a hurry?"

I was breathless and oddly missing that second invasion. "I want to come. Please, let me. Please." I barely recognized my own voice, so raw it was with need.

Ian dug his fingertips into the flesh of my ass and shoved deep into me, harder than he had before. A cry tore from my throat. I clenched around his penetration, harnessing all of my willpower not to fall apart. I was trembling, taking every inch of him over and over again.

"She's so fucking tight." Ian's words were strangled. "She's right there."

Will bent toward me and lowered his voice. "I'm going to let you come all over Ian's cock, Olivia. Then you're going to let me fuck your mouth and come down that beautiful throat."

Sounded like an incredible plan, as long as he let me come. Right. Fucking. Now.

I hated his rules. But I loved this feeling.

Hated it. Needed all of it.

I was turning inside out, and it was all Will's fault.

"Please." I wanted to cry for how on edge I was. I was ready to come without his word, even if it meant facing his punishment. Because the slap of his belt against my ass was nothing next to the torture of holding an orgasm while they both were taking me this way.

"Come for us," Will whispered against my lips. "Loud and hard. We want to hear you. Does Ian's cock feel good in you? Tell me."

"Yes, yes... Oh, God!"

Ian's rhythm sped up. "I'm there, baby. Come for me."

I felt him in a deeper place, and then I shattered into a million little pieces. I screamed Ian's name. Unintelligible sounds fell from my lips and flew across the room like shards of glass. Reflections of light and desire cut through me like a sharp blade.

Light-headed and wilted with my release, I wanted to melt into the ground when Ian slipped out of me. Will stood, lifting me on my knees. I held my palms to his thighs to keep my weak balance.

"Now you're mine."

The certainty in his tone raced along my sensitive nerves.

He fisted his cock, and I opened for him. Still recovering from my orgasm but dedicated to his, I welcomed him back into me—his hard heat, his firm hand moving me how he liked. Fast penetrating strokes. Until only he moved and I received the brunt of his movements.

"Now," he groaned. "Take all of me."

I relaxed my mouth and let the next few strokes push to

the back of my throat.

"Fuck. Fuck!" His curses hit the air as his salty release spilled into my mouth.

I swallowed, stroking my tongue over his pulsing erection until he pulled me off again. His knees buckled, and he fell back into the chair. His cock rested against his belly, still glistening from his come and my mouth. Satisfaction hummed through me from the inside out. He caught his breath a moment and held my stare through his half-lidded eyes.

"Don't you look like the cat who ate the canary?"

A smile curved my mouth. "I ate two. Do I get extra credit for that?"

He laughed roughly and let his head fall back again. "Olivia...you get extra everything for that. I'm not nearly finished with you."

WILL

Faceless men surrounded me. Suits and bare feet, hands clasped politely at their front. And ahead of me an open wall. A busy street lined with trees and people passing by. Except this place was dark and cold. Small and crowded, but somehow it felt abandoned, forgotten.

I needed to get out. I didn't feel entirely in control of my body, but my legs moved me toward the opening in the wall. Olivia was there suddenly, standing still as strangers passed by her in groups and pairs. She had a look in her eyes like something had gone wrong. I moved more quickly because I needed to fix it. I needed to take that look away. But I hit an invisible barrier before I could reach her. Glass, so perfect and clear I couldn't have seen it before.

I pounded my fists against it. I shouted her name, but the sound only echoed off the dark-gray walls. The faceless men began to shift, moving closer. But I had nowhere to go.

I couldn't breathe, like the oxygen suddenly had been sucked out of the room.

"Olivia!"

I screamed her name. I didn't think she could hear me, but she came closer. The bodies on the street pushed her back and forth. The faceless men were close, too close. I felt a hand on my shoulder, pulling me back into the darkness. I scrambled out of the man's grasp, desperate for Olivia to reach me.

There was no escape, but something told me she was the answer, my only hope.

I flattened my palms against the glass, and then she was there. She reached up, mirroring my position, tears brimming her eyes.

I could feel her warmth through the glass. Then her skin.

Our fingers intertwined as the barrier miraculously disappeared.

Air rushed into my aching lungs, and I hauled her against me. I could feel her, smell her sweet scent. Relief flooded me, and when I opened my eyes again, only we were on the street. No men in suits, no gray room.

Her cool blue eyes held me, her dark-brown hair flew in the wind, and her arms came around my waist as we held each other.

She was home in a sea of strangers. Safety in the wake of a nightmare that had disappeared with her touch.

I opened my eyes to the darkness. The impossible threats in the nightmare had my heart beating wildly in my chest. Olivia was curled up beside me, her head nuzzled against my shoulder. Her hand rested on my stomach. I repositioned her palm to my heart, willing the damn thing to slow down.

What the fuck was that all about anyway? I had no clue. All I knew was that I was damn glad the beautiful woman in my dream had somehow saved me. I drew in another deep breath and closed my eyes. I tried to relax and slip back to sleep, but I couldn't yet. The dream still felt too real.

So did the feel of Olivia against me, holding me, saving me...

I was too tired to question why she'd been able to. All I knew was I wanted her again. My need to have her never seemed to wane, and now... Now something other than primal desire drove my actions. I was unsettled, and somewhere inside my tired brain, I knew being inside her would make the world right again.

I turned, rolling her gingerly to her back. She moaned sleepily and fell against my pillow. God help me, she was beautiful. Every inch of perfection...a dream. Except real, in my bed, in my arms.

Ian had taken off after our earlier rendezvous, as he usually did in the evenings. Didn't stop me from making love to her half the night. I still wanted her, yearned for her like the air I'd been deprived of in the dream.

I lowered and captured her lips. I tasted her, breathed her in. Sex and rain. And goddamn, she was mine.

I moved down her body, taking position between her thighs. I licked her roughly, too impatient to let her body catch up with my desire. Her small cry filled the room, and she lifted her pussy against my mouth.

My head was buzzing. My need bled into hers until I was blind with it. I couldn't wait another second to have her.

I rushed back to her mouth, kissing her deeply. She wrapped around me, her silky arms and legs warm from sleep, holding me close. My cock slid through her wet folds, and my breath left me in a rush. I had to have her, now.

"Is this okay?"

She nodded, her eyelids heavy with desire.

Not wasting another second, I guided my cock into her, exhaling a shaky breath as I did. I was ready to come at the first sensation of her scorching heat gloving me. Heaven help me, I wanted her this way every time.

I was ready to spring into loving her hard. Instead, I held her there, enraptured with everything about her, the way our bodies melded and entwined like we were designed to always be this way.

Her eyes glimmered in the night, bewitching me as the air seemed to press out of my lungs. Except it wasn't fear robbing me of air this time. It was something else entirely.

"What is it?" she murmured into the quiet night.

My heart slammed against the walls of my chest, forcing the words out. "Olivia...I think I'm falling in love with you."

She blinked, her lips parted.

I wasn't expecting her to say it back. I wasn't expecting her to say it at all. Maybe I'd lost my goddamn mind in that nightmare, but I'd meant it when I said it.

She sifted her hand through my hair and traced my lips softly. "Then make love to me, Will."

Without another word, I melded our mouths together, sealing the words with a tender kiss. When I breathed, I breathed her. When I thrust, I was making us one, fueled by an irrational need to make her believe it.

When she came, I couldn't hold back. Her cries, the

desperate way she clung to me... I followed her down into the incredible feeling, a slave to the way she came apart around me.

"I love you." I breathed the words against her, filling her, making her mine...

CHAPTER TEN

OLIVIA

I still couldn't entirely wrap my head around what had gone down last night. I'd been with two men, and one of them had professed his love to me in the wee hours of the night. Granted, Will had been inside me when he'd uttered the words, which I worried could have skewed his true feelings. The tender way he made love to me afterward made me want to believe it, though. He'd never been that way before. And while I'd grown to love the rough side of him, I couldn't help the way my heart swelled to know his gentler side.

His confession added another string to a no-strings arrangement that he'd promised would remain uncomplicated. If he was falling for me... Where did that leave Ian in this tangle of rule-breaking desire?

I cared about Will. I couldn't deny that, but something existed between Ian and me that I couldn't deny either. If it was just physical, our chemistry was off the charts. If it was more... How could I let myself fall in love with Will when I was being pulled in Ian's direction too?

My vagina had become a traitorous bitch. She wasn't good, and she wasn't patient. As soon as these two men had come into my life, she became constantly hungry, desperate to be filled, and she didn't seem to care if it was Will or Ian who met the need. Maybe this was who I'd become—impulsive and unrecognizable, thoughts hazy with lust.

I was so tired of honoring the rules. Now, suddenly, nothing was out of bounds.

I contemplated all of this on a hamster wheel of sleep-deprived thoughts as I set out favors for Maya's baby shower luncheon. Guests were due in less than a half hour, and like an idiot, I'd agreed to plan the entire event myself.

My mother had never approved of my brother's choice, but since Maya was now his wife and about to make her a grandmother, she'd agreed to sponsor the event while never lifting a finger for it.

When she appeared in the private room I'd reserved, I knew it wasn't to lend a helping hand.

"Olivia. I thought I might find you here early."

She offered a wry smile that sent a wave of dread through me. The day of reckoning had arrived, and I couldn't feel any less prepared for it. All I could hope for was mercy that she'd go easy and not want to ruin Maya's day. I had a sinking feeling she truly didn't care, though.

I straightened and smiled like nothing was wrong. I went to her for a hug and two air kisses like I was one of her friends in the Hamptons. When I pulled back, her tight expression morphed into a grimace.

"You look awful, Olivia. Have you been sleeping?"

I winced at the insult. "I was up late getting things ready for the shower." I certainly wasn't getting anywhere close to the truth.

"Well, we need to talk. I don't appreciate you cutting me off and not returning my calls. What's gotten into you?"

I sighed. If she only knew...

"Mom, I can't talk about this right now. Guests are going to be showing up any minute."

"No, we are talking about this now. I want to know what you're going to do about Will Donovan." She put a hand on her hip.

"Why do you care so much?" I knew why, but I wanted to hear her say it.

"He's not good for you, and you know it."

Regret and anger swirled in my gut. She had said the same thing about Maya when she'd come back into Cameron's life. Vanessa hadn't been a suitable match for Darren in my mother's eyes, either. No one would be good enough for her children, but somehow I knew the fight for my future would be a harder one.

"I'm sorry he's not the right brand of white collar for you, Mother. But I care about him, and I'm seeing him. I don't know if it's going to go anywhere long-term, but you can't freak out on me every time I date a guy."

"Your father is concerned. Having invested in Donovan's shoddy fund is damaging enough, but having his daughter tied to this debacle is a slap in the face. Don't you see that? This isn't about you, Olivia. Stop being so selfish."

I swallowed over a wave of tears. "Can we talk about this later?"

Past her rigid frame, I saw guests entering the restaurant through the front door.

"Tell me you're not going to see him anymore." Her voice was strained and threateningly quiet.

The crumbling foundation of who I was seemed to crack, breaking wide open. I couldn't be who she wanted me to be. Not anymore.

"I'm sorry, Mom. I can't do that."

WILL

"Thanks for coming by." Bill's eyes were slightly glossy as he ushered me inside.

My father was a fifty-year-old bachelor, and nothing about his luxury high-rise apartment felt like home. Everything inside was modern and cold. Black and whites and grays. The decor was sparse and high contrast. Olivia would probably hate it.

"What's going on? You said it was urgent."

"Frank Bridge is on his way here."

Inside I cursed, but I didn't let on in any other way that I was concerned. If I'd been struggling to keep my cool with her brothers, I didn't know what the hell I was going to do with her father in front of me. But how would he know that I was with Olivia?

"What does that have to do with me?"

He walked to the wet bar and refilled his glass halfway with an expensive scotch, the kind he saved for the best days and the worst days.

"Rumors are going around that you might be taking over the fund. I'm guessing whatever he wants to say to me he wants to say to you too."

I frowned. "He's an investor?"

Bill nodded and sucked back a gulp. "His son was fucking around with Reilly's assistant, Vanessa. Socked him in the nose, so Frank invested to make the problem go away. I'm pretty sure the girl could have filed harassment charges against Reilly anyway. Idiot had a hard-on for her that just wouldn't go away, but who knows how far that would have gone? Now that we're in a whole different world of shit, I'm sure Frank's rethinking his decision."

"Is that why you're drinking at ten a.m.?"

"No. I just got a call from my lawyer." He set the glass down and his shoulders hunched. "I'm being indicted. We all are."

"Fuck," I said through gritted teeth. No matter how I despised his actions, I couldn't celebrate the news.

We'd expected this, but somehow the reality that he was going to face legal action devastated me more than I could have imagined.

"Who's being charged?"

"Reilly, Dermott, me, and a handful of others who took the kickbacks. The charges against Reilly and Dermott are more serious. Regardless, Reilly Donovan Capital is going to crumble as soon as this hits the press. We'll be finished."

He filled his glass a little more, moved to the couch, and dropped down. He stared out to the terrace. "Life can change in an instant. Things start moving too fast and you forget to think everything through. People get cocky, greedy. Before you know it, you're knee-deep in shit, praying you did at least one thing right that'll save you from sinking all the way down." He drew his hand down his face and sighed. "I'm sorry, Will. For all of this. You don't deserve it."

I stood before him. My father. My flesh and blood. I battled between my anger and my compassion. I was his only lifeline.

I had to decide, now or never.

"Dad."

He made a small sound of acknowledgement but didn't

look up.

"Dad, look at me."

He lifted his gaze.

"What's the most important thing in your life?"

He blinked, his eyes sadder than I'd ever seen them. "You, Will. After things fell apart with your mother, all I had was you. Nothing's changed."

"Swear to me that the fund is clean."

He nodded, his jaw tight. "I checked everything myself. I took the kickbacks, Will. I don't deny it. But Reilly was making a career out of it. I knew what he was doing, and I warned him to slow it down. He was getting too greedy. Then he brought the nonprofit on as an accredited investor, and I got worried. I made Adriana check every exchange, every source. It's clean."

I wanted to believe him, but I had to be certain.

"You know I don't care about the money. Nothing you can say will change that. I know it's important to you, but something has to mean more to you than the fucking money. If it's me, you have to swear on *me* that the fund is without a doubt clean. Because if I do this for you and I find out that it's not, we're finished. I mean it."

His expression was blank, like he was facing the ultimate truth. "It's clean, son."

The door buzzed and broke the moment. He rose slowly, and a few seconds later, he was walking into the room with a tall, dark-haired man with light-brown eyes, dressed in an expensive suit.

"Frank, I'd like to introduce you to my son, Will Donovan. Will, this is Frank Bridge."

"It's a pleasure to meet you."

"Bill, we definitely need to talk, but I'd like a word with

your son."

My father looked between us, confusion written on his features.

I cleared my throat. "Why don't we get some fresh air on the terrace? Can I get you anything to drink? Coffee? Scotch?"

"I'm good," he said.

I nodded and gestured toward the outdoor space that would give us privacy. I glanced back at my father and shook my head imperceptibly, communicating without words. He held his place inside. This was on me now.

Outside, New York City sprawled.

Frank scanned the cityscape on the horizon before looking back at me. "My wife tells me you're involved with Olivia now."

"To be fair, I've been involved with Cameron and Darren for months."

"You'll have to excuse me, Will, but your investment in their small business doesn't concern me as much as your personal interest in my only daughter."

"I understand."

His smile was tight. "Then you'll also understand why I don't want her anywhere near you or the trouble surrounding your father and his associates."

"Let's talk about that for a minute. Dad just informed me that you were an investor."

"I am. It was a delicate situation, and it seemed worth it at the time. Obviously circumstances have changed for Reilly since his pitch. But being involved with him after what he pulled with the charity looks bad for me. I have my own investors and reputation to consider."

Our business reeked of trouble, and it would get worse before it got better. I could pretend it wouldn't and hope for better results, or I could be up front with him. Frank Bridge wasn't the only investor I had to convince of giving us a second chance.

"My father is being indicted along with the others."

He stilled. "You're certain."

"The lawyer just called this morning. It'll be public by the five o'clock news."

"Why are you telling me this?"

"I'm telling you because I want you to know that I think what my father and his associates did was deplorable. I've managed to stay pretty far away from his affairs, but I never imagined any one of his ventures would come to this. That said, I believe the fund is clean. You know as well as I do that it's been successful, even in this short time. I'd like to see it have a fighting chance."

He laughed and turned to face the city. "Let me guess. You're going to try to talk me into keeping my money with Reilly Donovan Capital *and* convince me that you're worthy of my daughter."

"I'm going to take over the fund." The words slammed down on me as I said them aloud. Was I really going through with this? God, my father owed me everything for doing this...

He glanced at me sidelong. "That's risky business."

"Obviously we need fresh leadership. Let me prove that we can be a fund you trust before you make a decision."

"How about you keep my million, and you walk away from Olivia. If you care for her, you'll understand why that's the best thing."

The prospect of leaving Olivia was gut-wrenching. I wouldn't walk away, not unless she wanted me to. Even then, I'm not sure I could bring myself to let her go.

I was falling in love with the woman, and no amount of money was worth giving her up. Maybe I was too cocky for my own good, but I wasn't going to let someone push me out of the way, either. She was worth fighting for, and I had every intention of doing that. It wouldn't save the reputation of this venture, but businesses could be rebuilt. I'd never find someone like her again.

"You're her father. She loves you, and I know she respects you. But she's a grown woman, and she's going to do whatever she wants to do. I can't stop her any more than you can."

"When you're one half of the equation, you can. Just walk away. People do it every day."

"I'm not going to walk away from her. Not for a million dollars, not for ten."

He narrowed his eyes and moved his lips to speak, but I cut him off.

"Before you threaten me, think about this for a minute. I'm in love with her, and even the promise of certain ruin wouldn't get me to back down right now. So let's say, for argument's sake, that there's nothing you can do about Olivia and me. If you're really worried about her being associated with me, help me spin this the right way. I don't want this job, but I'm taking it because I believe the fund has a future. I don't want to see this fail, and if you stand with me, it won't."

"You want me to vouch for you so you don't lose investors."

"Yes."

Bridge had been a major player back in the day. He'd gone into private investing over a decade ago, but his connections ran deep. Having him on my side wouldn't fix everything, but it would be a step in the right direction of repairing this goddamn mess.

He shook his head. "It's not a bad plan, but it's not enough. When this hits the news, your investors are going to walk. No doubt about it."

"We have a lock-up period. I have six months to prove myself."

"That's not as long as you might think."

I paced the terrace. The sounds of traffic floated up. This city was chaos sometimes. Thrilling and intoxicating. Crushing and sobering. All I ever knew was that life could turn on a dime.

"Reilly is your problem," he said.

I turned and met Frank's stare.

"You can't just step in front of them and expect people to forget what they did," he continued. "If you want to instill confidence and keep this together, you need to do something drastic."

"Like what?"

"Reorganize. Buy your dad's shares. Cut Reilly out." The words came quickly, but his advice was anything but simple.

"They're the only shareholders."

He shrugged. "If you can't figure it out, you shouldn't be running the fund. If you have no stake, why should I trust you with my money?"

I clenched my jaw tight. He made a point, even if it stung. Taking over full ownership was never in the plans, though. My brain was scrambling to come up with a scenario that would work. Even if I was able to oust the owners, my father included, Frank hadn't exactly given his blessing when it came to my relationship with his daughter.

"What about Olivia?"

He walked toward me, his expression impassive.

"You've got thirty days to impress me, Will. And if she suffers from *any* of this, trust that there will be consequences."

I wasn't in the habit of tolerating threats, but threatening someone to protect Olivia wasn't beneath me either. I didn't reply as Frank left the terrace. I watched through the sliding doors as he shook my father's hand and swiftly disappeared. A few minutes later, my father joined me.

"What happened?"

"We need to talk," I said.

IAN

Darren was checking the engine when I joined him. The stalls were open, and fresh air blew in from the street. Early fall was in the air, cool and dry, promising an imminent change in the seasons. We worked over the truck, checking that everything was stocked and in place for the inevitable emergencies that would call us out over the course of the day.

"Vanessa's doing an open mic tonight. You want to come? I'll buy you a beer."

I shook my head. "Thanks, man. I've got plans though."

"Hot date?" He winked.

I laughed nervously as Darren waited for an answer. "Something like that."

I hadn't seen Liv in a few days, and that wasn't sitting well with me. I'd never cared this much before. The chase and the satisfaction of getting a girl into bed—all of that usually went away as soon as I got what I wanted. Not with Olivia. Every day that went by without seeing her felt a little more perilous, like I could lose her. And I wasn't ready to lose her.

After our last night together, I figured Will would keep

her close, but he'd been scarce too. When he wasn't putting hours in at the renovation, he was commuting to his father's office downtown. He'd agreed to take over where his father left off, but he didn't seem any happier for it. I had no idea where that left things between him and Liv, but I was done waiting. She'd agreed to meet me at the studio after my shift. I'd been counting down the hours until then.

Darren closed down a side compartment and moved to the next one. "You ever going to get serious about someone?"

I shrugged. "Maybe one day."

I'd fucked around for so long, though, I had a hard time imagining it. Dad used to ask me when I was going to bring a girl home to meet the family. I'd brushed him off, figuring I had time. Then he died, and something inside me broke. I was angry, and all I wanted to do was bury that anger. I didn't take women home for the pure fun of it anymore. I took women home to forget, to feel something intense just long enough without needing to open up to anyone. Then I could walk away and try to work the rest of it out on my own.

Will was my insurance policy that made sure nothing serious ever took root. Because once someone shared a bed with the two of us, any potential for a real relationship dissolved. I tried to remember that when the need to see Liv gnawed at me, but being with her wasn't fitting into any of those neat little boxes.

"Who've you got plans with?"

I hesitated, running my palm over my scalp. What the hell could I say to that?

"What's going on, Savo? You seeing someone?"

"Sort of." I frowned, because I had no idea how to describe the situation with Liv, even in the vaguest terms. This felt like the most dangerous conversation I'd ever had in my life.

He let out a short laugh. "No shit? Tell me about her."

"I don't know. She's...amazing. Basically fucking perfect. But I don't know where it's going. I'm not really in the right place to be the guy she needs." Jesus, I was rambling, but Darren's smile just got wider.

"Sounds pretty familiar, actually."

I shook my head. "Nah, it's complicated."

He had no idea.

Darren had done a complete one-eighty when he met Vanessa. For years he'd been my wingman, my go-to guy long before I'd run into Will. One week on an island with Vanessa, and Darren was a goner. I didn't recognize him. I'd hated to watch him torture himself through the ups and downs, but he seemed happier now than he ever had doing the bar scene with me.

I refused to believe anything like that could be possible for me.

I tried to get back to work, but Darren wouldn't let up.

"Do you care about her?"

My stomach seemed to drop out when I considered that. Never mind I was talking about my "feelings" for Olivia with her fucking brother. I'd taken feelings out of every hookup I'd had for years. But when I thought about Olivia, about how she responded under my touch, the way she seemed to seep under my skin, body and soul—that was a feeling I couldn't deny.

"I do care about her. But even saying that sounds idiotic."

Darren stopped what he was doing and leaned against the truck. "What do you have to lose, man?"

What did I have to lose? An uncomplicated lifestyle that I could rely on while I worked out the rest of my shit.

"I like to keep things simple. Straightforward. I don't really have time for anything else."

"You don't have time because you're too busy wasting it with a bunch of people you're never going to settle down with. If this girl is different, you should be focusing on her and seeing where it can go."

I widened my eyes. "Who said anything about settling down? For fuck's sake, Bridge. We're not all waiting to be you, Mr. Domestic Bliss."

He laughed and slapped my arm. "Don't knock it till you try it. Happier than ever."

I shook my head and shoved him off with a laugh. We wrapped up and returned to the kitchen, where the other guys on our crew still lingered with their coffees. I could almost guarantee Darren wouldn't be grilling me on relationships in the present company, so for now I was safe.

Because if Darren ever found out I was sleeping with his sister, our friendship would be anything but safe.

CHAPTER ELEVEN

OLIVIA

The studio was almost unrecognizable from the last time I'd seen it. The space had been aired out. All the surfaces had been dusted and cleaned. The mountains of boxes that had lined the walls were stacked in the hallway before I entered. The concrete floor was smooth and had been painted white.

"I like what you've done with the place." My tone was teasing, but I had a feeling this fresh start was an important milestone for Ian.

He hadn't opened up to me about the details, but the pain Ian carried from his father's death radiated off him at times. So did his passion, his hunger for me. Whatever was at the source of it, a potent energy drew me to him, to soothe, to feel, to feed...

My heart sped up when he was near, and I couldn't blame it all on the physical chemistry that pulsed between us. I ached for his presence, his tenderness. On the outside, he was perfection—tall, gorgeous, and strapped with muscle. On the inside, he was gentle and more thoughtful than I had ever imagined. Those stormy gray eyes could see right into me at times, as if he knew parts of me that I barely knew myself.

"I think you're going to like it even more soon." He moved across the room, systematically relocating several gallon-sized cans from the perimeter of the room to the center, two in each hand, his biceps flexing with the effort. He straightened and walked toward me, a secretive glimmer in his eyes. "I've been paying the rent on this place for months, but I hadn't decided whether I should keep it or not. When you walked in here the other day, I knew I had to."

I scanned the room again, admiring the vibrant work that decorated the wall, imagining the countless hours that had gone into their conception inside these walls. "It's a great place to create."

"It will be. But it's been little more than a shrine, and that's why I couldn't set foot in here for so long. It's time to change a few things."

I lifted my chin toward the center of the room. "You painting?"

He grinned slowly. "No, you are. This place needs some color."

I glanced around at the walls.

"The floor," he said.

I frowned and met his gaze. "The floor?"

"I've got all the colors. Trays for mixing. A dozen brushes. I want you to make it yours. Do whatever you want. Picasso, Pollack. Do your thing."

My pulse raced, not because of the intoxicating effect he usually had on me, but because I hadn't picked up a brush in... *years*. I swallowed over the knot in my throat and tucked my hands into my jeans.

"But I don't have a plan or anything. I'd need time to come up with something."

He shook his head, undeterred. "You don't need one. Just do whatever you feel like. Right now."

I let out a nervous laugh. "I'm sure I don't need to point

out that this is a huge canvas."

He circled his arm behind me and ushered me to the center of the room. I walked stiffly, keeping my hands stuffed safely in my pockets. I stared at the clean white floor, trying to catch up with what he was asking of me.

"You can do this. Want me to help get you started?"

I nodded without making eye contact. I needed all the help I could get right now.

"All right. Pick a color."

I stared down at the gallons of paint. Could I really not even pick out a color? I glanced up at Ian, who was waiting for my answer.

"What's your favorite color?" I asked.

He laughed softly. "Blue." Without asking, he knelt down, popped the top of the can open, and handed me a brush.

I took it, though it felt foreign in my hands. I stood frozen in place while he opened the rest. Every color in the rainbow was set before me. Still, I couldn't move. Seconds passed in awkward silence while I contemplated my next move.

"What's wrong?"

I gnawed on the inside of my cheek because I couldn't put it into words. Maybe I wasn't ready. Maybe I never would be.

This place meant so much to Ian, and here I was, challenged to put my imprint on it. I felt beyond unworthy for the task.

"I'm not sure I can do this. This place means so much to you..."

"Liv." He brought his hands to my face and forced my gaze to meet his. "Listen to me. It's a floor. It will see wear and tear. It'll get dirty. The paint will chip. And one day, a long time from now, maybe it will be painted fresh. Today, I want you to make it yours. Give yourself permission to do this...for *me*."

I wanted to say yes, even as I doubted my ability to do what he was asking. I wanted to thank him for caring enough to see the empty place where creating used to fill me up and make me whole. But my throat was tight with emotion and I couldn't speak, so I nodded and swallowed hard.

"Blue." He pointed to the brush and then to the waiting blue paint.

Brush in hand, I knelt on the concrete. The floor was cool on my knees where my ripped jeans didn't cover. He'd told me dress in clothes that I could get dirty, and now I knew why.

I took a few deep breaths, trying to catch the ideas floating across my mind. Lines and colors. Shapes and feelings. I pushed the paint tins out of the way so I could focus on the center, which seemed like the best place to start.

Ian's steps moved away from me, and a second later, I jumped at the sound of music echoing off the walls. Loud rock filled the space. At the workbench, Ian stood beside a stereo.

"Okay?" he shouted over the music.

I smiled broadly, happiness bubbling up inside me. "It's good."

Returning my focus to the center, I dipped the brush into the paint, all the way to the metal, and pulled it back. A solid cyan coated it. The music was loud enough to silence the little voice in my head that tried to tell me I couldn't possibly do this. Not after so long.

Instead, I thought in visuals. This place had meant pain for Ian for so long, so I searched for happiness and found a sliver of memory.

The ocean and long summer days at the beach with my brothers. Those few days every year as a child when everything felt perfectly right. Salt on my skin, laughing and exploring the shore. My mom's smile was warmer than the sun, and my dad's time was only ours. Everything around the memory blurred, growing darker when I started to think about how we'd grown apart in the years since. I returned to the happy memory. It was decidedly blue.

The first stroke was emotion—raw and unafraid. That thick wash of blue invited more. More colors, uneven lines, mistakes, and feelings that only had one outlet. I took the rest of the brushes out of their packages to see what I had to work with. I pulled my hair into a messy knot on top of my head and returned to mix up a soft gray—early morning clouds that hovered above the water.

The music played, and the world disappeared. The once daunting canvas beneath my feet disappeared bit by bit, under an ocean of memory. I felt Ian's gaze on me at times, but when my focus broke, I found him sifting through boxes of broken glass at his father's workbench, seemingly adrift in his own creative magic.

I lost time. I had no idea how many minutes or hours had passed, but eventually my back and hand began to ache. I sat back on my heels and rolled my shoulders. I couldn't finish tonight, but I had definitely left my mark. The design had worked out from the center, layers of color, uneven rings, and diversions. Seagulls cut through the waves of blue. Sand melted into the waves and clouds. Next time I'd bring out the sun.

I cocked my head, strumming with energy and unexpectedly pleased with the results. The painting was abstract but bright and vivid. Folding my happy memory into the piece for Ian to gaze upon felt right. I hoped I'd given him a measure of what he wanted to add to the space.

"That's awesome." Ian stood behind me a few paces, his focus fixed on my design.

I smiled broadly, pride beaming out of every pore. "You really like it?"

He nodded with a sweet grin. "I love it, Liv. Why the hell did you stop painting?"

I drew in a deep breath. Then I let it go the same way I'd let go of the fear that had held me back for so long. "I guess whatever made me stop is in the past now. If I weren't so sore right now, I'd keep going. I feel like I could go all night."

When I glanced back at Ian, a familiar heat darkened his eyes. His lips curved up into a wicked grin. "I can go all night if you can."

A rush of desire surged between my thighs and made my breasts tight and heavy. "Ian..."

He held out his hand and I took it, rising as he lifted me against him.

"I'm a mess," I murmured.

But he didn't seem to care as he crashed his lips against mine. I moaned and melted into him. That familiar frenzy worked its way through me. It tingled along my limbs and exploded at my core, making me want him with a fierceness that made me question my own sanity.

"Let's go home," I said, desperate to get a bed under us.

"No. Here. I can't wait."

My gaze flickered up to his. "Are you sure?"

He nodded. "Dad always wanted me to bring a girl home to meet the family. Here you are. Close enough."

I smiled, and he tugged my shirt and bra off, giving my nipples a teasing pinch. He knelt down, undid my jeans and pulled them to my feet. He kissed my thighs and belly on his way back up. When he stood before me, he sifted his fingers through my hair, angling me to meet his molten gaze.

"And every time I walk in here, I want to remember this moment. The war you won inside yourself. How perfect you feel in my arms...all around me."

Tying me even further to this place that held such importance in his world felt dangerous, but I was too high on Ian and this perfect night to say no. He stepped away to unzip a duffle bag in the corner of the room. He pulled out a thick blanket and laid it on the floor. I went to him, my body flushed with heat, my heart skipping every other beat in his presence.

As he stripped, I lay down on the blanket and waited for him, enjoying the view a little more with each passing second. The man's body would make sculptors weep. When he came to me, he wasted no time divesting me of my panties and burying his gorgeous face between my legs. I gasped, unprepared for his savage hunger. He nudged my thighs wider.

"Open up for me. I want to see every inch of you, baby."

I obeyed, and in seconds, his velvet tongue against my sensitive tissues had me riding the edge of an orgasm. The hint of teeth against my clit pushed me over. I arched higher, and my cries echoed off the studio walls. As I came down, he lifted away and rolled on a condom. Sated as I might have been, I was counting down the seconds until he was inside me.

He moved up my body and took my mouth in a fevered kiss. My taste lingered on his lips, mingling with his as we devoured each other. Our tongues dueled, chasing and tasting. I held him to me, touching and tugging. Suddenly he couldn't be close enough. When he pulled away enough to look into my eyes, his were hooded with lust and soft with emotion.

"I don't know how to say it. It sounds crazy...but I want to love you, Liv," he whispered roughly, like the words hurt to say. He closed his eyes and swallowed. "I'm not sure I know how."

My heart twisted painfully in my chest, like a tornado of emotion powering through me. I wanted to love him too. Every cell in my body wanted that. My mind shouted yes.

I couldn't deny him something I wanted so badly too. I cradled his face in my palms, accepting the fall where a different me would have fought it. I gazed into those captivating gray eyes and let myself feel it all.

I brushed my fingertips over his full parted lips. "You're loving me right now."

A wordless moment passed between us. I grazed my touch down his chest, floating over the hard ridges of his abdomen, until I reached his cock. I positioned him against my slit and moved my hips to urge him to me.

Taking my lead, he began moving into me slowly. His heated gaze held mine. I stretched around his thick penetration. He tunneled deeper and claimed more of me as I savored the sensual glide of our bodies becoming one. With every inch gained, he retreated fully before sliding into me again. The maddening rhythm ensured I was ready for everything he gave me.

With one hand, he held his weight above me. He slid the other under my lower back, protecting me from the hard floor. I lifted my hips into his careful thrusts, desperate for the pinnacle moment when we joined completely.

"This is more than sex, Liv. Tell me you know that."

I gripped his shoulder tightly. "I know."

The sex was unmatched, but he was right. We'd crossed over into something that meant so much more. Because it did,

I was quickly losing my mind to the intensity of the moment.

"You feel so good..." I closed my eyes, the buzz of our closeness lighting up under my skin everywhere we touched.

When I opened them, he brushed his lips over mine tenderly, filling my lungs with his smoky scent.

"I could stay inside you for hours, baby." His muscles bunched and flexed as he buried himself inside me completely with a shaky sigh. "Fucking you... Christ, it's better than anything I've ever experienced. Can't wait to feel you come apart around me. I want to take you there, over and over again."

I gasped at the feel of him reaching the deepest part of me.

His rhythm picked up. My walls clamped down around him, adding an intense friction to every invasion. I clawed at his tight skin, wild with the sensations rocketing through me. A frenetic heat skittered over my skin and pulsed heavy at my core. I craved more the way I craved the release that would bring it all to an end.

"Ian!" I trembled beneath him, anchored by his powerful drives.

Banding an arm around my hips, he fucked me harder and at an angle that sent me into orbit. Colors flashed behind my eyes. Seizing around his cock, I screamed the air from my lungs and clung to him through the powerful release.

He slowed his undulations as I came down, but he was still thick and hard inside me.

"Did you come?" I asked breathlessly.

His lips curved up into a wicked smile. "Not yet, baby. I want to see if I can make you scream my name a few more times. Can you take it?"

He flexed inside me, putting pressure on the place inside that threatened to make me come on the spot. I bit my lip, aching for the stroke of his cock against that spot, again and again.

I nodded with a breathy sigh. "Yeah. Definitely."

★ ★ ★

The lights buzzed and flickered above us. I rolled to my side, molding myself against Ian's warm body. His eyes were closed, and one muscled arm rested over his forehead.

I was still reeling—from the multiple orgasms, and even more from the way I was falling hard for him. My heart hurt when I thought that maybe the affection I felt for him could be totally one-sided. Then I thought about his words...that he wanted to love me. He was too smart, too seasoned with women and protecting his heart to say something like that without meaning it.

I was falling for Ian too, but how could I love him with half my heart?

Will knew I was meeting Ian tonight, but that didn't allay the sliver of guilt that took root. Still, Will had pushed for this. We'd all walked into it with our eyes open.

Didn't change the fact that every time we were together felt like a free fall into feelings I wasn't completely ready for.

I drew circles on Ian's chest, marveling at how far we'd come in such a short time.

He moved his arm and looked over to me. "What are you thinking about, baby?"

I exhaled deeply and followed my thoughts to the last time we'd been together. The night had ended in Will's bed, only because Ian had left. I hadn't mentioned it, but his absence had bothered me more than I wanted to admit.

I released the frown I was holding and sighed. The rules were changing at every turn, and Ian's absence right now, after what we'd just shared, would gut me.

"The last time we were together...you left. I wasn't sure what to think about that."

"I figured Will wanted his time with you. That's all. My schedule is a mess with work. Most nights I don't sleep really well, so I usually go out. I go for a walk or grab a drink before I turn in."

I was silent a moment. His reasons were sound, but that didn't change that I wanted to be close to him.

"Did it bother you?"

I shrugged. "I guess I felt a little vulnerable after what we did. I didn't know what to expect. Now I do."

He turned to his side, facing me with his head propped on his elbow. "I'll stay next time. I like this—being close to you, touching you." He captured my nipple between his fingertips, teasing the hard tip before cupping my breast gently.

His tender touch threatened to rev me up all over again. The few guys I'd been with in the past were always once and done. Will had turned that expectation on its head, challenging my stamina while more than proving his own. I had a feeling Ian wasn't much different, and a part of me wanted to find out.

"I care about you, Liv. Never doubt that," he said, his eyes turning serious. "Will does too. You're important. What we have here, it's important to both of us."

"I know. I guess I'm still trying to wrap my head around everything that's happening with us."

With the return to coherent thought, I was thrust into the odd reality that I was sleeping with two men. Two very different men. The way they carried themselves, the way they smelled and fucked and talked was uniquely them. They shared an apartment, a passion for unbridled sex, and me.

Ian brought his hand to my chin and lifted my gaze to his. "I want you to be happy, Liv. You just have to tell me what you want, okay?"

My chest tightened. "You seem to already know."

Tonight had been amazing in so many ways.

"Ian, you don't know what tonight means to me." I swallowed over the emotion rising to the surface again. "I can't explain it. It's been so long since I've painted. Losing that part of my life has been kind of devastating. You're the first person who's ever noticed anything was missing."

He held my gaze for a moment. "I know what it's like to live with that kind of emptiness. I don't want that for you. You're talented, truly. It's a goddamn crime if you let anything stop you."

Tears stung my eyes. I hid them by nuzzling into his shoulder. His strong arms came around me like they belonged there. I settled against him with a shaky sigh, feeling grateful and safe and cherished all at once. He held me tight, his strength surrounding me as silence stretched between us.

We lay that way, entwined and lazily caressing each other as the seconds turned to minutes. I traced the jagged edges of his tattoo. After a moment, he caught my hand and brought my fingertips to his lips, gently kissing them.

"Tell me about your dad," I whispered.

He turned his stare to the ceiling, his expression becoming taut. "I don't really like talking about it."

I let our fingers slide together and rest on his chest, under his heartbeat, strong and steady. "Is that why you don't let yourself get close to people?"

He was silent a moment, and I worried that I was pushing too far.

"Maybe," he finally said. "I trust you, Liv. It just hurts. I want to be stronger than the grief, you know? It's not easy to show that side of myself to someone else. Especially someone I want to be strong for."

I lifted up on my elbow and stared down into his beautiful eyes. I stroked down his nose and over his full lips before kissing him.

"I know you're strong," I whispered against him. "And I think sometimes allowing yourself to feel it all makes you even stronger, even if it hurts. You don't need to prove anything to me."

His features were pinched with doubt. I didn't want to push him. Whatever was eating at him had been festering for a long time. If he wanted to tell me about it, he would. I lowered again, relaxing against his chest.

His voice was low, tight with emotion as he began to speak. "My parents were crazy about each other."

I held my breath, waiting for him to continue. He stroked his fingers through mine rhythmically.

"They had to be to have five kids together and still be as in love as they were at the end. They were inseparable. We were all close. Things weren't always easy. We struggled sometimes, but we always had each other. I grew up knowing, without a doubt, that we could get through anything together. My sisters and I grew up, and we did the usual things. Family dinners and holidays, but the past couple years my dad started getting really worn down. We noticed but didn't think much of it. Figured he was just getting older and slowing down a bit. Then he collapsed one day when we were doing a job. The ambulance rushed him to the hospital. He died a few days later. I watched him take his last breaths."

His grief seemed to permeate my skin, tugging painfully at my heart. "What happened?"

He exhaled a shaky breath. "Cancer. We found out that he'd visited the doctor a couple years earlier. They'd detected it then, but he denied any treatment. He didn't think it was worth the fight." He squeezed his eyes closed and pinched the bridge of his nose with a sigh. "Felt like someone cut something out of me."

I wrapped my arms around his torso and held him tight. I listened to the sound of his heart and his breathing. I couldn't imagine losing a parent, even as strained as our relationships were at times.

"I wasted so much time, Liv. I'm angry because he let me waste it. I'm angry because he didn't fight to keep our family together longer."

"He doesn't want you to be angry," I whispered.

He held me a little tighter. "I know. I want to let it go, but it's so fucking hard."

I kissed his chest and gazed up at him. "Think about the love he had for you, all the love he created with your family. Don't let your anger ruin that amazing gift."

He shook his head, his jaw tight. "It's so much easier to be pissed off."

"You need to let it go, Ian, if you want to make room for the good things he'd want for you."

"Like what?" His voice was barely a whisper.

I trailed my lips over his torso and along the ink that marked his pain. "Like love."

CHAPTER TWELVE

WILL

Thanks to Olivia, the event looked more like an opening at an art gallery than a ribbon-cutting. Music filled the air but didn't interfere with people having conversations. Servers buzzed around, refilling drinks and offering gourmet refreshments.

I'd been going nonstop all week, and tonight felt like the culmination of many things. After months of hard work and a pile of my money invested, Olivia and her brothers were one step closer to making their dreams a reality. After spending the past several days poring over every page of fine print I could get my hands on at Reilly Donovan Capital, I could appreciate the Bridge siblings' hard-won milestone even more.

I'd officially filled my father's shoes. Even though I stood by my choice, every day my own dreams seemed a little further away than they'd been before I'd taken on the position. The lawyers were drawing up the papers, and in a few days I'd become the official CEO of the company, my fate sealed for the foreseeable future.

I didn't have much choice though. As predicted, the news of my father's indictment had dropped like a bombshell on the company. And, as promised, I had been there to field every call. The investors were angry, and the lock-up period on their investments pissed them off more, but it was the only lifeline I had. Nothing was certain, but I made promises I hoped I could keep—significant structural changes, attractive investment opportunities, and a future of stability and growth. I schmoozed and sugarcoated every morsel of good news I could until I felt like I had a handle on all the major players.

I had six months to deliver. But Frank Bridge was right. It wasn't a lot of time to work with.

His advice had been sound. Reilly was undoubtedly a scumbag. Deep down, even my father knew it. Perhaps that had made him a shrewd and valuable business partner in their line of work, but a man whose morals were so askew had no place near the fund. I had to get him out, but I wasn't sure exactly how yet.

As I ruminated on that, Olivia's parents walked through the doors, their rigid figures clear through the flawless glass wall that separated the entrance from the rest of the building. As if immediately sensing their presence, Olivia went to them. I couldn't hear their words, but even across the room, I could sense the unease. Olivia's tense smile, her mother's stiff posture, her father's gaze shifting around the room like he'd prefer to be somewhere else.

I made quick strides toward them and held out my hand. "Frank, good to see you again."

"Will." He accepted it, shaking my hand firmly, but his expression revealed nothing.

"Oh, *Will*. I'm Diane, Olivia's mother."

Diane was Olivia's height, with short silver hair and a severe glare under her forced smile. I answered with a warm one, determined to melt the ice queen who had produced the most amazing woman I'd ever met.

"It's a pleasure, Diane. So glad you could make it."

"Of course, I wouldn't miss it," she said, her lips forming a thin line, making me doubt her sincerity.

I had a feeling she wasn't brimming with pride when it came to her sons' career choices. Even I questioned why they'd take my money over their parents' when it was so readily available, but I'd come to respect them more for it. I wouldn't want to be operating under Frank Bridge any more than I wanted to operate under my father. Even if I'd been tasked with cleaning up the mess from his epic failure, at least I was working with some autonomy now, an option that had never been open to me before.

"Let me show you around, Mom." Olivia hooked her arm with her mother's, effectively splitting us up.

Diane lifted a flute of champagne off a passing tray and watched with a bored look as her daughter showed her around the facility. Frank lingered by my side, watching as I did.

"Her mother expects perfection," he said flatly.

I lifted an eyebrow. "You don't?"

He slid his gaze to me and then back to the humming crowd. "I expect it from you, not her. I want her taken care of, but I also want to see her smiling. My sons are intent on doing things the hard way, but at the end of the day, they seem satisfied. I hate to admit it, but she's happier here with them than she was working for me."

"She deserves happiness."

He answered with a nod. "She and Diane don't always agree, but they're very close. Olivia may not need her approval, but she'll want it."

I smiled, because it masked my irritation well. "Let me guess. I haven't been approved."

"You'll have Diane's approval when you have mine."

I nodded, hating that I was in a position to prove myself to him.

"How's it going with Reilly?" His question was a sharp reminder of the absurd timeline he'd given me.

Tick tock. Apparently he was going to hold me to it.

"I'm meeting with him this week," I answered tightly.

"And your other investors?"

"They're not happy. No surprise. I managed to talk most everyone down, but you're right. Reilly did most of the fundraising, and they're ready to slit his throat. If he goes, we may have a chance."

"And your father?"

I stared down at my shoes a second, remembering the last few incoherent conversations I'd had with him.

"He doesn't love the idea of giving up his shares to me, but I'm going to talk to him about it again. As soon as he's done emptying the liquor cabinet, anyway."

Frank finally cracked a smile. "Rough week."

"You have no idea."

"Get used to it, or give it up. You'll have plenty more like this one." He squeezed my shoulder before moving into the crowd in the direction of Diane and Olivia.

The gesture both irked and comforted me. We didn't exactly have a rapport, but I had an odd feeling he was rooting for me, even if he was holding a fucking hammer over my head.

When Olivia returned, I breathed a sigh of relief. She was a slice of heaven at the end of an otherwise harrowing week. I threaded my fingers with hers and bent to kiss her. Her brothers might want to crush me for it, but I didn't give a damn. I missed the woman fiercely.

She leaned into me, accepting the unexpected display of

affection in a crowded room of family and coworkers.

"I missed you," I murmured against her sweet lips.

When she smiled, her beauty radiated. "I missed you more."

"You're beautiful, Olivia. Absolutely breathtaking. I don't think I tell you that enough."

She straightened my collar with a smirk. "When you don't tell me, you show me. Often."

"Not often enough. I want you in my bed every night, and you're not there."

Her cheeks took on a pink glow. "Neither are you, Mr. CEO."

I scowled, reminded of the long hours I had kept this week.

She sifted her fingers through my hair, seeming content for now with this stolen moment. "How are things going with work anyway?"

I shook my head. "Tonight's your night. I don't want to talk about all that."

Worry wrinkled her brow. "Is this what you really want to do, Will? I hate seeing you stressed over all this."

Of course not.

"Doesn't matter what I want. It's what I have to do. I've come to terms with that, and I've made the commitment. Now I've got to see it through."

She sighed and seemed to study me, captivating me with her cool blue gaze. "I'm proud of you. I know this isn't going to be easy for you, but if anyone can make this right, it's you. And even when it takes you away, I'll be here."

I'd taken on this challenge thinking I was doing it for my father. But in this moment, I knew I was doing it for her.

Because I couldn't lose her. I didn't need her family's approval, but having it would make her life easier, and I wanted that for her.

If I could follow through on this, after a year or two, I'd be pulling down enough money that I'd never need to do it again. I was more than comfortable, but running the fund successfully would significantly pad my already healthy income and secure future investments. If Frank Bridge was worried that Olivia wouldn't be taken care of, I'd guarantee she'd want for nothing. If I had to, I'd work day and night to make sure of it.

I twisted a strand of her hair between my fingertips, wishing we had more time, preferably alone. I regretted the crowd of people around us now and the obligations that stole away moments like these. Private moments that could lead to more pleasure than I'd expected to find in a woman.

"Can I beckon you?" I teased, but I was serious too. With my obligations mounting, I wanted her when I wanted her.

"Yes, you can beckon me. I may even come on my knees."

Her sly smile seduced me in a heartbeat. Her eyes glittered with mischief and heat.

I pulled her close and kissed her again, unable to hold back. "I love you, beyond all reason. Do you know that?"

She softened against me. "I love you too, Will. Beyond all reason."

IAN

Will's limbs twined possessively, almost indecently, with Liv's. Their bodies were close, leaving no doubt that they were together. A couple.

I watched from a distance, regretting that I didn't have

a shift at work to save me from attending the event. Instead, I was being forced to pretend like I barely knew the woman who'd effectively brought me to my knees.

No one here knew it, but I was closer to her than I'd ever been to another woman. Olivia Bridge called to me. Not just her body, soft and giving, fitting perfectly around mine. But her mind...her heart. The soul of her that reached into the soul of me.

Our night at the studio was permanently embedded in my mind. Every second. Watching her paint, entranced by the act, a feeling I knew all too well. Then baring my grief to her. It was uncomfortable and painful, but after the pain came a kind of solace that I hadn't known before. She was a welcome and unexpected salve on a year of unresolved emotions. No one had gotten that close to me before. I didn't expect anyone would again.

Will was fighting his own war. I'd known him long enough to see how the stress of his father's troubled company weighed on him, now more than ever. And I recognized that his connection with Liv was strengthening every day. He needed her the way I was beginning to need her.

I was lost in that thought when Darren arrived at my side.

"Hey." He wasn't smiling. "What's going on?"

"Nothing." I frowned, irritated that his presence was taking my focus away from the woman whose presence seemed to demand all of it.

"Want to tell me why you're eye-fucking my sister?"

I held my jaw tight, biting down on the truth and resisting the urge to call him out with the truth.

Staring at his sister? I'd been inside his sister, deep in her tight heat. I'd held her in my arms and felt her heartbeat fly after a screaming orgasm. I'd tasted her sweet mouth and the honey between her thighs. And I'd pay a dear price to be experiencing any of those sensations again right now.

The harder truth was that I could have her every way she'd let me, but I'd never be able to call her mine.

I had no words for Darren. I wasn't about to apologize, and I wasn't going to lie. One thing was certain though. I didn't belong here.

Even though it was dangerous, I left Darren and approached Liv.

She turned from Will when I said her name. Her blue eyes were bright and soft when they met my mine.

"I'm leaving. I just wanted to say good-bye and congratulate you. Everything looks amazing. You guys did a great job."

A small smile lifted her lips. "Thanks, Ian. Is everything okay?"

"Everything's fine," I lied. "Enjoy the night, Liv. You deserve it."

She frowned. Before she could say more, I turned and made quick strides toward the door. Once outside, the night air rushed into my lungs. I headed in the direction of the apartment. The weather was mild, and a walk would do me good.

"Ian. Wait."

I slowed and turned toward Liv's voice. When she caught up with me, she grabbed my hand, as if that could keep me from getting the hell out of there as quick as I could.

Her touch sent a jolt of electricity through me. That magnetic force between us couldn't be ignored.

"What's wrong? You seemed upset in there."

I closed my eyes, fighting the urge to pull her tight against me and kiss her breathless. "It's nothing, Liv. I'm just going to have to get used to being on the sidelines. It's a hard pill to swallow when I feel the way I do about you."

Her lips parted and pain washed over her expression. I began to step away, but she wouldn't let go, pulling me back by sheer will.

"Did someone say something?"

My jaw tightened when I remembered Darren's accusation. "I couldn't take my eyes off you tonight. Darren noticed. My first instinct was to tell him to fuck off, but that would have been easier to do if I could say you were mine. But you're not."

She was silent a moment, her grasp tightening around my hand. "You know that's not true, Ian."

I laughed and shook my head. "You're mine behind closed doors, Liv. I'm grateful for every minute with you, but the rest of the world will never know what you mean to me. You're with Will. That's what the world thinks."

"Who cares what the rest of the world thinks?"

"You'd care if I kissed you in there the way I want to right now. If I put my hands on you like you belonged to me. I can't even fucking look at you without your brother getting on my ass. How am I supposed to be with you like this?"

She came closer, pressing herself against my torso. Relieved, I held her to me, but my chest ached. Having her in my arms again was bittersweet. It didn't solve everything. I hadn't expected to feel so possessive when it came to having her, but things were becoming too slanted. That she could be seen with Will while I could barely glance her way wasn't ever going to sit right with me.

But she hadn't asked for this arrangement. This wasn't her fault. I buried my nose in her hair, breathing in her scent and embracing her warmth against me.

"I'm sorry. Tonight is supposed to be about you and your brothers. I just wasn't expecting it to be so hard to keep my distance."

"I'm here now," she whispered.

I shook my head, because it wasn't enough. With anyone else, it would have been too much.

"I don't know why I can't stay away from you, Liv. But if it were up to me, I'd never let you go."

I was losing my mind over her. I should have cared that being with her was turning me into someone I hardly recognized. Except I didn't. The only thing that mattered was claiming her in any way I could right now.

I tipped her chin up so I could take her mouth. Soft sweeps of my tongue met hers. My cock thickened, and desire flowed thick in my veins. She owned me, and somehow I had to accept that the rest of the world would never know it.

While I delved into her mouth, I molded my palm to her ass and pressed her against my arousal. The helpless sound she made offered no relief. It only stirred up my aching need. She curved her palms around my nape, lifting herself higher and closer, pulling me further down into my desire. I was ready to fuck her against the building, given the chance.

"What the hell is going on here?"

I broke away from her lips at the sound of Darren's approaching voice. He stalked closer, hands balled into tight fists. The look in his eyes was murderous.

OLIVIA

I jolted at the sound of Darren's voice. As he came toward us, my racing pulse thundered in my ears. Panic mixed with the rush of desire Ian's embrace had inspired.

Fuck.

I stood frozen in Ian's arms. Putting distance between us wouldn't do any good, because Darren had likely seen enough. And the wild look in his eyes made me want to keep a barrier between him and the man I was falling hard and fast for.

The door to the building swung open, and seconds later, Cameron was beside him, his thick arms crossed over his chest in a defensive pose. I cursed inwardly and stood beside Ian, our hands intertwined, creating some semblance of a united front against the wrath that I knew was coming.

"Answer me." Darren's angry gaze was fastened to Ian.

"I don't have to answer to you." Ian's low tone was laced with an undercurrent of frustration that I worried was seconds from coming to the surface.

"Like hell you don't. Get your fucking hands off my sister."

I bristled. "Darren, stop it. You're going to make a scene."

"Make a scene? You're outside the ribbon-cutting playing grab ass with this motherfucker."

The muscles in his jaw flexed. The door swung open and Will emerged, followed by Vanessa and Maya. I cursed a thousand more times to myself. I resisted the urge to escape back inside. Instead, I held my place by Ian.

Not being able to show the world that we were together had gotten us here in the first place. Even as it pained me to see him upset, I knew there wasn't an easy solution.

We'd all been honest with each other, open with our fears

and our desires. And the second we found ourselves in public, we had to start living a lie. I didn't blame Ian for being upset, and even though Darren was being a hothead, I didn't entirely blame him for being confused.

"Hey, is everything okay?" Maya touched Cameron's shoulder, but he didn't move or acknowledge her.

Darren shook his head, glanced to Will, and then back to Ian and me. "I thought you were here with Will. What the hell are you doing with Ian?"

Vanessa stood a few paces away from Darren, like she was worried about getting caught in the crossfire. "Darren, let's go back inside."

"Vanessa's right. We should let Will and Liv figure this out." Cameron spoke quietly, but his voice seemed to silence everyone else. Except Darren.

"I told you to stay away from her. You didn't hear me?" He pointed angrily at Ian, but he didn't flinch.

I made eye contact with Will. My heart beat wildly, and I fought the sudden urge to cry. Falling for two men wasn't ever what I'd had in mind, but now we were all here, facing my family. I swallowed over the knot in my throat and the uncertainty that painfully tightened my chest.

Will walked to me slowly. He touched my cheek, his eyes filled with an emotion I couldn't place. "You okay?" he murmured, like no one else was there.

I wasn't, but I was trying to be strong. I nodded. I didn't know how we were going to get through this, but I had to trust that somehow we would. I'd been careless. My family wasn't ready for the truth. I wasn't sure they'd ever be.

"I'm sorry—"

"You don't have to apologize." He turned, taking a casual

stance beside me, hands tucked into his pants. "There's nothing to figure out. I appreciate the concern, but there's nothing awry here."

We stood like that, silence stretching out between our two groups—three people who'd fallen into feelings that we'd never expected or asked for, and the rest of my family, who might never understand it.

Vanessa's jaw fell.

Darren took a threatening step forward. "Wait a minute. You're seeing both of them?"

I opened my mouth to speak, but my lip was trembling, and all the words that justified the way I felt refused to come out. They sounded right in the closed circle of my relationship with Will and Ian. Here and now, under the judging eyes of Darren and the rest of my family, they were stifled and shameful.

Tears stung my eyes, but I lifted my chin, hoping I could hold my ground without breaking down.

"Yes, I'm with both of them. What difference does it make?"

My heart seemed to buoy with relief. Speaking the truth felt infinitely better than I'd expected it to. Ian's hand tightened over mine. Will's arm came around my shoulders and I leaned infinitesimally closer, savoring his gesture of support, of togetherness.

Darren's eyes were wild and then narrowed threateningly between Ian and Will. "You've got to be kidding me. This is who you are now, Liv?"

Vanessa came to him and tugged at his arm. "Darren, stop. This is between them."

He shrugged her off. "No, I'm not going to stand here and let these two defile my sister. Not in this lifetime."

His fists got tighter, and Ian's body tensed beside me like he was ready to fight. I stepped forward, positioning myself between them, away from the security of the two men who'd worked their way into my heart.

"Darren, I don't need you to fight for me, okay? I'm fine. I know what I'm doing."

"You have no idea. I know him. I know what he does to women, and I'm not letting him do it to you. That's a fucking promise."

He'd given voice to a familiar worry that niggled at me. But deep down, I knew Ian had shown me a side that he hadn't shown the other women he'd been with. What we had meant so much more.

"Why do you get to fall in love, but I don't?"

Darren's voice was softer when he spoke next, his posture relaxed enough to make me trust he wasn't going to spring into action and take his rage out on Ian. "This isn't love, Liv. This is some fucked-up thing you don't want to get mixed up in. I don't know what they said to talk you into this, but you deserve so much better."

"How do you know this isn't what I deserve? This is a choice, not a circumstance that's been forced onto me. I know what I want, and nothing you can say is going to change how I feel."

He winced and shook his head. "This is fucked up. Can't you see it?"

My eyes were brimming with tears, and my voice wavered as I teetered on the edge of breaking down. "You're just like Mom and Dad, you know that?"

"We've always been there for you." Cameron's voice was low and clear, ringing with truth. But disappointment and discontentment marred his brow and tightened his features.

My whole life I'd watched my parents look at my brothers and me that way whenever we strayed from their firm expectations. Never had I believed my brothers would look at me that way too. I felt more alone now than I ever had before in my life.

I swallowed down a sob. I couldn't keep the tears at bay much longer.

"You're right. You've always been there for me. Until now. I need your love, not your judgment. I have a mind, and I know what I want. Who I sleep with, who I love, how I choose to spend any minute of my life is *my* choice. Not yours, not Cameron's, not Mom and Dad's."

When I thought about my parents' inevitable disapproval on top of everything else, something inside me broke. They'd find out. If I was willing to admit my feelings in front of my brothers and their wives, I'd have to find a way to stand beside them when my parents came calling for answers. Except I had no idea how I'd survive that...

Tears streamed down my face as I pushed past everyone. I hurried back inside, found my purse, and left the party without saying good-bye to anyone. My face was likely a tear-streaked mess, and the thought of facing my parents was more than I could bear.

"Liv!" Maya's voice echoed down the street, but I ignored it.

Will hurried toward me as I hailed an approaching cab. He caught my arm gently before I could duck inside. "Olivia, wait. Where are you going?"

"I'm going home." My voice was watery, and the need to cry long and hard was nearly painful.

He thumbed away the tears as they fell. "Come home with us."

Placing my hand over his, I leaned into his tender touch. I wanted to hide someplace safe, and no place was safer than with the two men who'd so unexpectedly and completely stolen my heart. But I needed time to think.

"I need to be by myself tonight, Will."

"I don't like the idea of you being alone."

I shook my head. "I need to think."

He frowned, his body suddenly tense. "I'm not losing you."

More tears fell. "You're not losing me. I just need some time, please."

His jaw bunched and his lips formed a tight line. He didn't want to let me go, but the voice that had guided me to this point told me loud and clear that I needed the comfort and security of my own apartment tonight. Quiet after the storm, time to work through everything that had happened.

"I'll be fine, I promise. It's just one night."

"One night," he said quietly but firmly.

I nodded, and he pressed a kiss to my forehead before letting me go.

CHAPTER THIRTEEN

OLIVIA

I ignored the persistent knock at the door and rolled over under my duvet with a miserable groan. If it was Cam or Darren or anyone else who wanted to throw in their two cents about my love life, they could keep knocking. I wasn't planning on emerging anytime soon.

I'd hurried home last night, desperate to escape all the prying eyes. I'd hoped to find a measure of peace in the quiet of my apartment, but my thoughts were rioting all night. I'd promptly located a bottle of wine and drank nearly all of it, rotating moods between tearful self-pity and a place of righteousness that made Darren's words undeniably shallow and foolish.

This morning my whole body ached. From the wine or the crying—or a combination of the two—I wasn't sure. All I knew was my life had become incredibly messy. And if I wanted to live out of the bounds of what society expected of me, I was going to have to come to terms with messy. I was going to have to look messy in the face and own it as my new reality.

Was I even capable of that? I'd been pushing my limits left and right, but maybe I'd finally hit a wall.

I rose slowly from bed, regretting the dull throbbing in my head. At least the knocking had stopped. I showered and made myself some coffee. I dressed for the day but had no idea what I was going to do with myself. Darren and Cameron would be at the gym, kicking off the first day at the new location. I should have been there to lend a hand, but no way could I face them today. I wasn't sure when I'd be able to. The future seemed grim, a long runway of unknowns.

Assessing the empty bottle of wine and the tissues littering my coffee table, I asked myself for the hundredth time if falling in love with two men was really worth it.

My relationship with my parents would be worth nothing once they found out. My brothers would continue believing I was either too naïve to know better or a disillusioned slut. My friends... I hadn't kept up with a lot of people since college, but my days pretending like I belonged with polite society were certainly numbered. The rumor mill and its loyal followers, many of whom would report back to my mother, would draw their own conclusions about what kind of woman I was.

I sank into the couch with a tired sigh. What was done was done. It was too late to pretend I'd made different choices. But it wasn't too late to walk away from it all.

I'd started this unexpected journey with Will. He'd led me into Ian's arms, but I was bound to Will in a way I couldn't fully explain. He was intense, determined, and unapologetic about what he wanted. His dominance affected me deeply. He'd stripped me down until I was raw and real...only me. We were the same in so many ways—raised by wealthy families who had handed us everything money could buy from the day we were born. Yet we'd missed out on so many of the things that truly mattered. Family, love, precious time that no amount of money could buy back...

For Ian, having those things and losing them with his

father's death had wrapped him in a sadness that I was determined to fight through. Ian was warm and brave, a rich texture of emotion and beauty. I was drawn to him, utterly and completely. But if my family didn't approve of Will, they'd never give Ian a second glance. My brother joining the fire service when he could have been a banker or an executive had been a crushing blow to my parents. Didn't matter that Ian was saving lives and putting his own on the line too. He'd never be good enough, even if he meant everything to me.

Will and Ian had stormed into my life, seduced my body, and captivated my heart. I'd given them all of it—my trust, my submission, my love. Choosing between them would be asking me to rip my heart in half.

It would be easier to simply walk away.

I didn't expect they'd make it easy for me, but I held the power to end it all. I could start over, try to forget what our time had meant, and one day, maybe try again with someone new. Someone who ticked all the boxes and wouldn't make things messy and complicated. Someone who didn't rock the foundation of my whole world.

I tried to picture what that might look like. Then I saw the emptiness I'd lived with for so long growing bigger and more painful. Without Ian and Will in my life, I'd become the old shell of me. Unfulfilled, lost, and searching for those missing pieces all over again. Except I'd be more brittle, hardened by fresh heartbreak.

Fresh tears burned my eyes. I set my coffee cup down. My appetite for consciousness and sobriety had effectively dissolved. My head fell into my hands, and I let the tears fall.

Even as I searched for the right answer, I knew deep down there wasn't one. I had to feel my way through this like everything else. With all the noise around me—Will, Ian, my family, and all the people in my future who'd want a say in how I lived and loved—I had to somehow stay true to myself.

Another hard knock hit the door. I drew in a deep breath and wiped away my tears. I'd loosely considered holing up at a hotel for a few nights to avoid run-ins with Cam and Maya for a while, but the last thing I wanted to do was use my parents' credit card for the extra expense. In fact, as soon as I'd weighed the possibility, I'd taken the scissors to it. I was done living under their thumb. I didn't need the finer things in life as much as I needed my freedom.

I could have stayed at Will and Ian's, but that felt oddly like running away.

"Liv, open up!" Maya's voice was muffled behind the door.

I cringed at the thought of facing her. She'd been silent in the wake of my shocking confession. She hadn't been afraid to voice her support of my relationship with Will before. I doubted she'd be an advocate for me now.

A few seconds passed before the door handle jiggled and turned. Then she and Vanessa were standing in my living room. Maya held the extra set of keys in one hand. The other rested on her hip.

"You can't just barge in here," I said.

She lifted an eyebrow. "Watch me. You're not going to shut me out, Liv."

I sank farther into the couch and covered my swollen eyes with the heels of my hands. "Maya, please go away. I really don't want to see anyone right now."

"We're taking you to breakfast, and we're going to talk through all this crap, okay?"

I groaned out a sigh. "What is this? An intervention?"

Vanessa laughed and took my hand, hauling me up to a standing position. "More like girl therapy. I had to listen to Darren go off half the night. I need a mimosa. Come on. I beg you."

The thought of orange juice and cheap champagne roiled my stomach. But nothing about their demeanor made me believe I was in for more anger and accusations.

Twenty minutes later, I was waiting for my brunch order at one of our favorite diners. Without warning, Eli dropped into the seat between Maya and Vanessa.

"Shit, what did I miss?"

Their ex-roommate and good friend had become a regular fixture since Maya had come back into my brother's life a year ago. He was a sounding board for my sisters-in-law, but I'd never quite brought my guard down around him.

Maya sat back in her seat and rubbed her belly. "Nothing. We haven't started the interrogation yet."

"Thank God. Maya said something about you having a threesome, and I couldn't haul my ass out of bed fast enough." He winked at me, brushing his jet-black hair from his forehead. "So who are the lucky guys?"

My cheeks heated as I imagined myself turning twelve shades of red at his comment.

"Our investor," Maya said in a light voice that didn't at all match the gravity of my current situation.

"And a guy who Darren works with," Vanessa added.

Eli whistled and shook his head. "I'm guessing that isn't going over so great with the Bridge brothers."

Vanessa let out a soft laugh and twisted her natural auburn hair into a messy bun. "I'm pretty sure Darren is going to have to be medicated if he doesn't calm down soon."

"Cam wouldn't talk about it. That usually means he's too pissed to speak."

Dread tightened my gut. I immediately regretted letting them drag me here when I could be safely cocooned in my apartment, away from everyone...at least everyone who didn't have a spare key to my place.

Cursing under my breath, I started looking for the nearest exit. I wasn't nearly ready for this conversation.

Then Maya reached for my hand and gave it a small squeeze. "Anyway, it doesn't matter. They'll get over it. They just need some time to wrap their heads around everything. I'm more worried about how you're dealing with all of this."

I closed my eyes, wishing I could erase the last twenty-four hours and do things differently. "I don't know."

"What happened?" she asked.

I exhaled a sigh. "Things with Will started out pretty simple, but it's gotten really complicated and really intense, for all of us. We've been living in our own little world, I guess. I won't say navigating this relationship has been without complications, but everything seemed manageable until last night. I wasn't expecting everything to be thrown into the spotlight so suddenly."

Vanessa leaned in on her elbows. "I can't imagine circumstances where Cameron and Darren would have taken the news any better. Probably better to rip the Band-Aid off and get it over with."

I shrugged. "Maybe."

"What do Will and Ian have to say?" Maya asked softly.

My thoughts drifted to the previous night. Ian had called me after I left the ribbon-cutting. He wanted to make sure I was all right but thankfully didn't press me when I asked for space. I needed to process everything that was happening. My crazy, intense relationship with Will and Ian. My brothers too, and what I was risking with this unconventional relationship.

"I told them I needed some time to deal with all of this on my own. I think they understand they can't just sweep in and try to fix everything, much as they may want to. Darren was fit to be tied last night. Obviously Cameron's brewing inside too, so having Will and Ian anywhere near my apartment is probably an extremely bad idea."

Eli rested his chin in his hand. "So this isn't just a kinky fling. This sounds serious. It must be if you were willing to come out to Darren and Cameron the way you did. I know you weren't necessarily ready for it, but I'm no stranger to coming out. It feels like you're risking everything."

I nodded silently. "I think we all fell into feelings that we weren't entirely ready for. And you're absolutely right. It feels like I'm letting everyone down, even though it's *my* life we're talking about."

"Liv, don't say that. This is your life and your choice," Vanessa said.

"Tell that to my brothers," I shot back.

Maya sighed, concern wrinkling her brow. "They'll come around."

"Cameron won't," I said.

I knew Cameron. He was the strong and silent type, committed to his emotions. He held grudges like no one I'd ever met. Getting him to reconcile with my parents was an uphill battle I had no chance of ever winning. When he loved, he loved deeply. Ultimately, no amount of time or reckless behavior could change how he felt about Maya. Whatever conclusions he'd drawn about my crazy relationship with Will and Ian last night would likely stand the test of time.

I held out more hope for Darren, whose flash of anger could potentially burn out over time. Ian had saved his life, after all. That persistent reminder might eventually break him down. At least I hoped it would.

Eli cleared his throat, drawing all eyes to him. "Can I just ask what everyone wants to know?"

I blinked, waiting for him to continue.

"Have you had them both, like at once?"

Vanessa hit him. "Eli! God, you're so rude."

He giggled and shoved his hair back off his face. "Whatever. We're all thinking it."

"What Liv does behind closed doors is none of our business," Maya said. "Even if we may fantasize a little bit about it."

"Very true." Vanessa smirked.

I wanted to be mad and embarrassed, but I found myself laughing. The levity was a welcome break from the somber note I'd left my apartment on. Suddenly I was surrounded with more support than I'd ever thought possible. I was grateful, relieved, and almost ready to face my life again.

Eli lifted his mimosa in the air. "Seriously, more power to you. You'd know better than me, but I'm pretty sure two is always better than one. You're living the dream, girlfriend."

One by one, we lifted our beverages.

"To risking everything," Eli said with a clink.

IAN

I paced outside the station, waiting for Will to pick up.

"What's up?" His voice carried through the phone.

"Have you heard from her?"

He sighed. "Nothing yet. I told her I'd give her the night to think. She knows I'm not a patient person."

"I'm worried about her, but don't think we should push her. She's under enough pressure."

"Doesn't change the fact that I want to be there for her."

"I know exactly how you feel." I rubbed my forehead. I missed her and hated to think that she was hurting and dealing with all of this alone. "Fuck Darren. I want to go over there. God knows what they're saying to her."

"I agree we can't let her sit with this for too long. But you and I need to talk before we go to her."

I halted my pacing, instantly on guard. "Why? What's going on?"

He was silent a moment. "I want a relationship with her, Ian. A real commitment."

I tightened my grip on the phone and swallowed over a rush of emotion. I knew their bond was strong, but I was ready to fight for her if I had to. The thought of letting her go filled me with a fierce possessiveness. She was his, but goddamnit, she was mine too.

"I see the way you are together, what she means to you. But you can't ask me to walk away at this point."

"I didn't say that. But I shared her with you so I could guarantee nothing got serious between us. I thought she'd be a great lay and we could all go about our lives. Business as usual. I couldn't have been more wrong about where all this would go. This isn't even about me anymore. I care about her heart more than anything. I don't want her to get hurt."

The thought of losing her gutted me, but I didn't want her to get caught between us either. "I want what you want.

Whatever the best thing is for her."

"Listen, Ian. We can share her or fight for her all day long, but it's up to her. I have no idea if she'd consider a deeper commitment between all of us. Especially after the showdown with her brothers last night."

I nodded in silent agreement. The future of our relationship rested entirely in her hands. "Then we let her decide."

"We'll give her a little time to work through everything, and then we'll talk to her. Together."

"She needs more than words, Will. She needs to know we mean it."

He was quiet a moment. "I know. I plan to show her exactly how we feel."

I hung up and returned to the station. I hadn't been on shift very long, but seeing Darren was inevitable. Any minute we could be thrust into an emergency that required us to work together. I found him in the kitchen making dinner. His expression was grim. I knew him well enough to know that he wasn't his usual jovial self.

It was probably too soon to try to make peace, but giving the standoff any energy was going to make working together a living hell.

I walked into the kitchen, stopping a few paces away from him. "Need any help?"

He didn't reply. To say the atmosphere was tense would have been an understatement.

"Fine," I muttered, turning away.

"I'm putting in a bid for a different station."

I turned back, shocked that he'd make such a rash decision. "Why would you do that? You've been here forever."

"Why the fuck do you think?" He slammed down the spatula he was using and squared his body with mine.

I tensed, preparing for the fight that he wasn't ready to give up. "You're making this worse than it needs to be. Do you realize that?"

His lips curled into a grimace. He took a step that brought his face too close to mine. "It's going to get a lot worse if you don't get the fuck away from me right now."

I held my ground, my fury rising with his. "You need to back down. Right now."

"You're the one who needs to back down. If I weren't happily married, I'd go fuck one of your sisters just to make a point."

The fury that simmered in my veins before had come to a full boil. He was so fucking out of line. I wound up to slug him, but he ducked out of the way just in time. He shoved me back hard into the counter. I was ready to go at him again when Ray, one of the guys from the engine, rushed between us.

"Boys, whoa, whoa. Calm down. Let's talk about this."

Darren squirmed away, his eyes wild with rage. "I already tried talking. He didn't understand when I said stay the fuck away from my sister."

Ray patted him on the chest, shooting a sideways glance at me. "All right. Listen, this kind of stuff happens on the department. You're not the first one to get all riled up about family ties. I mean, Greeley knocked my sister up. Twice."

Greeley hollered from a nearby recliner. "She's my wife, you dumb fuck."

Darren ignored them, fully committed to his anger. "Yeah, well, I'm not you, and Ian's not looking for a wife. How many women have you fucked?"

"If I had to make a guess, I'd say about as many as you have. You think because you're married now that you're on some moral high ground? I'm pretty sure you weren't husband material when you started seeing Vanessa. I hate to break it to you, but Liv's a grown woman. She can make decisions for herself."

"Yeah, and I have to see your face every day and think about the two of you..." He shoved his hand through his hair violently.

Ray glanced back at me, his expression betraying his concern. I'd never seen Darren this way. Except when he almost lost Vanessa. He'd gotten reckless and violent, but that rage was focused on himself. Not me.

I drew in a series of steeling breaths, willing my adrenaline down. He wasn't capable of being the bigger person, and Liv didn't want to hear about us coming to blows over this situation.

"Darren, I know you're angry, but we need to figure this out. Can we talk about this...privately? Without you trying to bust my face?"

Ray nodded and gave Darren a little more space. "Good idea. Let's take this down a notch. You guys are friends."

Darren straightened his posture and returned to the stove, ignoring me. He wasn't ready now, but hopefully he would be soon.

"I'm ready to talk when you are," I said, before leaving him and Ray alone.

I sat in a folding chair outside the station, watching the sunset melt into the horizon of buildings. Oranges and pinks and purples cascaded into each other on the canvas of the sky.

I wondered where Liv was and what she was thinking, if she was sharing the view. Not knowing was killing me. I pulled out my phone and snapped a picture before the sky lost its bright colors.

It had grown dark by the time Darren walked out. He stood several paces away, hands deep in his pockets, eyes avoiding mine. I'd already attempted to make peace. He had to be the one to talk first now.

After several moments of pacing back and forth, he stopped and turned toward me. "Help me understand, because I can't fathom how you could do this to me."

I sighed and rubbed my forehead. "Believe me when I say I tried everything I could to avoid this."

"Except fuck her. You couldn't seem to avoid that. Oh, and then you let someone else fuck her too. Sounds like this all just happened. I'm sure you didn't coax any of it along at all."

I cursed under my breath. He wasn't going to make this easy for me. "I don't expect you to understand."

"Good, because I'm pretty sure I'm never going to understand how you can disrespect my sister this way and still have the balls to face me. After everything we've been through. I mean *fuck!*"

I met his glare with resignation, because all I had was the truth. "Darren, I'm in love with her."

His lips thinned as he worked his jaw. "You can't love her. I know you."

"People change. You stood here not that long ago and told me to stop wasting time and focus on her, to see where it could go."

He shook his head. "That's before I knew the woman in question was my sister. I would have given you different advice had I known."

I stood and faced him. "You changed. For the right person,

you changed. She's that person for me. I can't help that she's your sister any more than I can help the way I feel about her."

"And Will? You expect me to believe he feels the same way and he's not just taking everything he can get from her?"

"It's not my place to speak for Will, but I'd never let him hurt her."

"Is he touting this love shit too?"

"He cares about her. We both do."

He leaned his head back and pressed the heels of his hands to his eyes. "This is so fucked."

"If you step back and look at what's happening right now, the only people who are upset are you and Cameron. Will, and Liv, and I...we're fine, outside of dealing with your goddamn death threats and judgment. But before all this blew up at the ribbon-cutting, we were fine. So stop and ask yourself if it's worth jeopardizing her happiness."

"You're not going to talk me into thinking this is good for her."

"Putting her through hell over this isn't good for her. You're one of my best friends. I don't want to lose that, but right now, her happiness comes first."

"If you're making a campaign to get my blessing, give it up. I'm never going to support this." He sliced his hand sideways through the air.

I sighed, feeling more defeated with each passing minute. "Whatever. But don't make her miserable over it. Hate me. Hate that I'm with her. But think about what all the anger is doing to her. She doesn't deserve to bear the brunt of your judgments. She's a good person, and she's got a good heart. She's figuring shit out, same way all of us are. If you care so damn much, cut her some slack. Let her live her own goddamn life."

Those last words seemed to render him silent. He simply shook his head and left me alone. At least we hadn't come to blows again, which I counted as a small victory.

I breathed a sigh of relief, even knowing my friendship with Darren was forever changed. I hoped to hell that Liv was worth it...that she wouldn't give up on us.

I took my phone out and contemplated calling her. She'd asked for space. I had to give it to her. I couldn't be another person barking at her, trying to tug at her when she wasn't ready. I wanted her to know I was still here, though. Waiting for her to be ready.

I pulled up my texts and attached the photo of the sunset with a message.

I: Sky made a beautiful canvas tonight. Made me think of you. Haven't been able to think about much else.

A minute later a reply came back.

L: It's beautiful, thank you. I'm thinking about you too.

I hesitated with what to say next. I didn't want to push her, but the smallest communication made me want more.

I: I want to see you. When you're ready...
L: Soon. Be safe tonight.

I released a frustrated sigh. If she only knew... The dangers of the city and this job had nothing on the damage she could inflict on me right now.

CHAPTER FOURTEEN

WILL

David Reilly strolled into the office. Dressed in a suit that cost more than most people made in a month, he exuded the kind of confidence that threatened a lot of people on Wall Street. He didn't affect me that way. I registered little more than disgust as he approached but knew I had to keep it to myself if I was going to get through this meeting.

I rose from my father's desk and greeted Reilly with a firm handshake. "Let's talk in the conference room."

"Sure."

His tone was clipped, and I wondered if he'd already gotten wind of my intentions. Only my father could have warned him, and I'm not sure he would have the balls to throw hindrances in my way after everything I was sacrificing.

Either way, this wasn't going to be an easy conversation. I grabbed some papers from my office and followed him into the private room, shutting the door behind us. Outside of my father's assistant, Adriana, we were alone in the office, but I didn't trust anyone with ears around this negotiation.

Reilly had chosen the seat at the head of the table—a clever move to assert his waning power in the company. Too bad I'd be the new CEO in a few minutes. I took the adjacent chair and pushed a few loose papers in front of him.

"As discussed, these are the documents to register the updated corporate filings listing me as the new CEO. They're fairly straightforward, but feel free to have your attorney review."

He picked the papers up, scanning the routine language that would strip him from his position. "Looks like everything is in order."

I pushed a pen toward him, which he used to scribble his signature on the appropriate lines. He dropped it back on the table and looked up at me, folding his hands in his lap.

"So how are things going?"

I tilted my head. "I have my work cut out for me. The investors aren't too happy."

"I understand." His voice was totally detached, as if he'd had no part in creating the challenges I now faced.

"I'm not sure that you do." I leaned back in my chair and traced the sharp lacquered edge of the table. "I have a lot of trust to earn back. No one wants to invest with a company tainted by partners accused of fraud."

His lips pulled back into a dark grin. "Allegations. Nothing's been proven."

"The indictment going public means you're guilty. Because if you get off, it's because you're a white-collar criminal and the judge feels sorry for you, not because anyone believes you're innocent."

"What are you getting at?"

"I want you to relinquish your stake in the company."

His careful demeanor broke with a laugh. He wiped at his eye with an arrogant smile. "That's rich."

"No, but our clients are. And no one wants their money tied to a crook."

"You know your father's hands aren't clean here. Why aren't you asking for his shares?"

"I don't deny he's as much to blame for the failed reputation of the company."

"Then why me? I brought in most of these investors. I have a stake in this. I'm not going to just hand it over."

"That's exactly why you should. They fucking hate you right now. If you've got any money left over after the restitution and your very pissed off ex-wife wipe you out, you can invest it with me and we'll give you a competitive rate. That can be your consolation prize."

His smile disappeared and he narrowed his eyes. "You can go to hell."

I leaned in. "Listen, fifty percent of nothing is nothing. Relationships are tenuous. I figure best-case scenario, we'll lose at least half the investors whether you're found guilty or not. They're not going to wait around to see what happens in court. They're going to wait out the lock-up period, and then they'll walk. Worst-case scenario, *I* walk and you lose the rest of them. Then this company will be worth nothing."

He was silent a moment, and I knew I was gaining ground.

"You fucked up, Reilly, and someone has to pay. Sign over your shares, or good luck finding someone else who's willing to put their reputation on the line to repair the damage you did."

He held me in a cool assessing stare. "I'm willing to walk away as a silent partner. You're Bill's son. I trust you to run the company as you see fit."

I shook my head. "If your name is anywhere on this thing, it's over. I'm already working with a handicap. Representing your name and interests in any capacity becomes me sacrificing my reputation and time for certain failure."

"What you're proposing, it's a lose-lose for me."

I shrugged. "Maybe. Maybe not. Guys like you can't seem to see any farther than your nose. Ever think about doing the right thing today and hoping it might pay off tomorrow?"

I knew Reilly wouldn't leave without taking something with him, but by offering him nothing, I wasn't giving him the benefit of a favorable starting position. Still, I'd have to bend at some point. I half expected him to double over with laughter at my proposition, but he simply stared, his discontent obvious from his stiff posture and lingering grimace.

"You seem to have a good-hearted nature, Will. But that's not what makes me money and secures a future."

"Your attitude has you facing jail time, so maybe that'll give you a minute to think about the difference between right and wrong."

He cracked a small smile then. "I'm in this business to make money. If you aren't, I'd have better luck promoting Adriana to run the company than you. The business won't turn a profit on good intentions."

"And it won't crumble under unethical business practices as long as my name is on it. I'm not trying to screw you. I just want you gone so I can do my job. And for what it's worth, I didn't want this job. Keeping this venture alive is going to take everything I've got." I turned the last few pieces of paper over to him. "The choice is yours. Get out, or I walk. I'm not going to be a martyr for the cause."

He ignored the papers and drummed his fingers on the table. "Give me a few days to think about it. I'm sure we can come up with an arrangement that we can both be happy with."

"No," I shot back firmly. "You're smart enough to have seen this coming, which means you've thought it through already. Yes or no."

He pushed up out of his chair and paced the length of the table and back again.

"Okay, Will. I see your point. I admire your tenacity. I certainly know where you get it from."

Hope flickered, but I kept my cool. I knew we weren't done yet. No doubt he still had terms, and I still had to navigate my way through them to a favorable end.

"If you're going to strip me of my shares, I can at least ask for a small concession."

"Depends on the concession."

"Obviously." He slowed and placed his hands on the table. "Jia Sumner. You know her."

"I know her well." Better than he probably realized.

"She's a hard worker. Highly intelligent. She's on the fast track with the firm she's at, but last time she tried to make a jump, she was passed over. We'd been in loose discussions to hire her on as the COO when the investigation brought things to a halt."

"I'm aware."

"Good. I still think she'd be an excellent fit. I trust you're capable, and I believe she'd be a valuable resource for you to have by your side. Secure her position here, and you and I have a deal."

His was a small concession. I didn't plan on fighting him over it, but there had to be a reason.

"Why?"

His expression was unreadable. "I owe her a favor. It's the right thing to do."

I hesitated, enjoying this last moment of watching him twist in the wind. I clicked the pen and placed it on top of the papers that would sever his last ties to the company.

"Consider it done."

OLIVIA

I stepped through the doors of the gym, which still smelled new. Regret mixed with pride. Today could have been different, but dwelling on the past wasn't getting me anywhere. We needed to move forward. All of us.

I hadn't heard from Darren since the ribbon-cutting, and despite Maya's efforts to keep tabs on my delicate emotional state, Cameron had managed to carefully avoid running into me.

For me, the initial shock of them knowing the truth about my relationship with Will and Ian had worn off. The spontaneous bouts of crying had stopped. The future seemed manageable, if a bit messier than I would have ideally wished for. But I felt secure in my choice. Both Ian and Will had secured a place in my heart. Nothing could change that.

I'd lived my whole life with convenient, proper, and socially acceptable behavior. I'd never burned the way these two men made me burn. I wasn't ready to give up.

Having a break from their intensity, however, had given me the clarity I needed to feel secure in that choice. Too easily I became a slave to their passion and possessiveness. Owning my choice was more important than the comfort they would have given me after falling out of favor with my brothers.

I held my head high as I approached the front desk. Tori, the college-aged girl who normally manned the front of the gym, waved when she noticed me. Other patrons meandered in, sliding their passes through the scanner that confirmed their membership with a pleasant beep.

"How's it going?"

She beamed. "It's going great. Still getting things organized here and there, but so far no glitches. Everyone's happy."

"Has it been busy?"

"Swamped. Local members seem psyched about the extra location, and the marketing push you organized for the new member promotion seems to have worked. We've had a bunch of new sign-ups since the opening."

"That's awesome. Have you seen Cam?"

She glanced over her shoulder. "Yeah, he's been around. Maya was here earlier, harassing him to talk to new members and schmooze a bit, so he's either in the gym following instructions or hiding out in the office."

I laughed and thanked her.

I found Cameron talking to a member I didn't recognize. I approached slowly so I didn't interrupt them, but Cameron noticed me immediately.

"Hi," he said, but the greeting seemed awkward and forced.

The guy he was with stopped talking and fixed his gaze to me. He was good-looking, heavily muscled. Definitely a gym rat. Another time I might have given him a second glance, but my brothers were always around, giving guys the death glare if they got too chatty with me at the gym. Today didn't seem to be any different. Beyond that, I wasn't interested.

Cameron seemed to notice the man's attention on me. The corded muscles in his neck stiffened. "Let me know if you have any more questions. All right?"

The man tore his gaze from me and nodded to Cameron

quickly. "Cool, thanks."

"Sorry for interrupting," I said. "Do you have a minute to talk?"

He hesitated a moment. "Sure. Let's head back to the office."

I followed him to the back where a much newer and larger office was situated. Unlike the pokey office at our other location, this one allowed desks for Cameron, Darren, and me. Prior to the ribbon-cutting, we'd moved most of our files and set this place up to be our future headquarters.

"Looks good in here," I said.

"Thanks to you. Maya's been helping me get things organized, but the layout and everything you set us up with is working well so far."

I knew I could decorate a room like a boss, but I warmed at the compliment because it came from Cameron. I wanted him to be happy with the contributions I made to the business.

He leaned against the edge of his desk, powerful arms folded across his chest and legs crossed at the ankle. He wore his signature black mesh gym shorts and an athletic T-shirt with the Bridge Fitness logo on it. Unexpected pride swelled inside me again. While he cleaned up great in a suit, this is where he was supposed to be. Not at a desk job. Nothing could persuade me to think he'd chosen the wrong path for his life.

He stared down at the floor, his countenance impassive. Slowly, sadness began to permeate the pride I had for my brother. I'd come here to make amends. I could only pray he was capable of seeing past his disappointment.

"Cam, I don't want you to be angry with me," I said, my voice brittle and small. Already fresh emotion was welling up, tightening my throat. Damnit.

He didn't meet my eyes. "I'm not angry," he said, but the words were flat and lifeless.

"I can tell that you are." I fidgeted with my bracelet, pressing the cool metal pendant between my thumb and forefinger. The little diamonds abraded my thumb, but the memento felt like a lifeline right now.

"What do you expect me to say?" He finally met my gaze and lifted the dark wing of his eyebrow.

"Darren's already said most everything I expected either of you to say if you ever found out. But right now, I'd love it if you said that you just want me to be happy. That I have your support."

"To date two men at once?"

I canted my head with a sigh. "To love whom I want to love."

He exhaled through his clenched teeth. "You're asking too much, Liv."

"I'm not asking you to agree with my choices, but you're my family, Cam. You can't get rid of me. Even if you wanted me to, I'm not going anywhere. So just stop this. Give up the fight because you're going to drive a wedge between us that doesn't belong there. I made that mistake once. I'll always regret coming between you and Maya. I should have had more faith in both of you. I mean, look at you now. It breaks my heart to imagine what your life would be like without Maya in it."

I spoke quickly, my heart racing with growing anxiety that Cameron and I might never see eye to eye.

He pressed at the frown forming between his brows. "Goddamnit, Liv. You're a real pain in the ass, you know that?"

A small smile lifted my lips. "But you love me."

He shook his head. "Can't quite help it, can I?"

"Come on. Lighten up. You're about to be a daddy. Nothing's worth ruining these precious moments. Not even my totally strange love life."

He exhaled with a groan. "Fine. Whatever. Just don't expect me to smile about it."

I smiled broadly at his small attempt at acceptance and the heavy weight that had been lifted from me with it.

He stood, the tension on his body only marginally eased. It might have deterred someone else, but I didn't have his resolve. I went to him and threw my arms around him. After a second, he returned the embrace with a sigh. Relief flooded me, washing in over the unconditional love I felt for my big brother.

"Thank you," I said in a whisper.

He rested his chin atop my head. "Just be careful. Please, Liv."

I nodded, and we separated. He mussed my hair, and a ghost of a smile passed over his lips.

I pushed him away with a laugh. "Stop."

"Get out of here. We've got things under control."

"Are you saying you don't need me?" My tone was teasing, but a little part of me regretted that without an enormous design project in front of me, my usefulness had expired.

"You worked hard on this. You deserve a break. When's the last time you took a vacation?"

"You've worked hard too. And nice try getting rid of me, but I'm not leaving the city until my nephew arrives."

He widened his eyes a fraction and nodded. "Any day now. Maya's ready. I'm not sure what ready feels like, but she assures me I'm ready too."

I touched his forearm. "You're ready. You're going to be

great."

He sucked in a deep breath that seemed to be filled with uncertainty. "I hope you're right."

"I am right. In this, as with most things."

He rolled his eyes and ushered me to the door. "Out you go."

I laughed and gave him a wave as I exited the office and made my way to the front of the gym. As I approached the entrance, a familiar figure caught my eye. My heart sped up.

Will stood, dressed in a three-piece suit, head-to-toe delicious man. He turned his cobalt gaze on me. I nearly melted. The man could rock jeans and a T-shirt, but the sight of him in a suit had my toes curling.

"Olivia." My name left his lips like something sacred.

"Will Donovan. I'm not going to lie. This corporate look is starting to grow on me."

He shot me a wicked smile. "Glad to know there's at least one perk to this gig."

I glanced around briefly and then back to Will. "What are you doing walking into the lion's den?"

"I own the building. Did you forget?"

Will's suggestive gaze slid over me, reminding me how much I'd missed him. God, the way I felt about him bordered on addictive. I reminded myself that climbing him anywhere near where Cameron might see us was a terrible idea.

"I was more worried about another awkward run-in with my brothers."

"You're worth the risk." He stroked his thumb along my jawline. "And I'm done pretending like I'm not completely obsessed with you. On that note, Ian and I were hoping to see you. Tonight, if possible."

His offer was beyond tempting. I'd missed them both, but I knew we probably needed to talk, too. If we were going to keep on like this, we had to figure out what that really meant for the long-term.

"What did you have in mind?"

"Dinner. There's a place I've been wanting to take you. Then a couple surprises." He held a white bag.

"What's in the bag?"

He lifted it and rested the cloth handle in my hand. "We picked some things out for tonight. We'll pick you up at eight."

"I can meet you—"

"No, none of that. Tonight we're doing things right. No hiding. No secrets. No regret. Just the three of us."

I bit my lip and nodded. He reached out, freeing my lip from the grip of my teeth. A second later, his mouth was on me, luring me away from my worry and into the heaven I found when we were together.

"Missed your taste," he murmured.

I leaned in for more, but he eluded me.

"Tonight," he said.

Without another word, he left me alone with my longing and an unspoken promise that tonight would be one to remember.

CHAPTER FIFTEEN

OLIVIA

Butterflies flitted around in my stomach as I waited for the car to arrive. I paced circles around my apartment, my high heels clicking on the hardwood. Something felt different about tonight, like maybe we were starting over. Pausing in front of a mirror, I triple-checked my makeup and ran my fingers through my hair, which fell pin-straight down my back.

My ears sparkled with tile chandelier earrings—glittering mosaics of tiny varied blue stones. Ian's thoughtful gift had accompanied Will's, a dress I'd unwrapped with no small amount of anticipation the second I got back home. Drawing in an anxious breath, I skimmed my hands down the sides of the sleek fabric. It had come in a silver matte box donning the Alexander McQueen logo. Undoubtedly, the dress had been designed for sex appeal. The plunging neckline was edged with tiny jewels and nearly met my navel, creating a seductive V down my chest. The hem hit at my knees, but like other dresses I'd worn when seeing Will and Ian, this one featured a slit that cut high up my thigh.

I felt expensive, sexual...and cared for. Not because of the price of the gifts, which were undeniably expensive, but because I was wrapped in expressions of Will's and Ian's affection for me.

On a hunch, I took another peek out the window just as a sleek black limo pulled up. My heart beat unevenly for a few counts until two gorgeous men exited the vehicle. Then the beat pulsed in my stomach. Then lower, between my thighs. Will and Ian were both dressed in suits, Will in a dark gray and Ian in jet black. They looked untouchable, too impressive to be real.

I grabbed my clutch and left my apartment, feeling a touch less steady on my feet. Ian leaned against the car while Will climbed the steps toward me. When he met me, I ran a finger down the slick lapel of his stylish suit, a different one than I'd admired him in earlier. The black shirt beneath was open at the collar. I bit my lip and imagined kissing him there, tasting and licking up the column of his neck.

"For a minute I thought I might be overdressed," I said.

"Never. You look ravishing, as always." He thumbed above my knee and marked a trail of fire over my skin to where the fabric split at my upper thigh.

I feathered my fingertips over his. "You seem to like this feature."

He hummed an affirmation, his gaze fixed there. "I need easy access to your assets, princess."

I smirked. "Do you?"

"I demand it." He ran his tongue over his lower lip and slipped a sly feel up the inside of my thigh, shooting a sharp bullet of desire to my already pulsing clit.

Before I could catch his wandering fingers, he cuffed my wrist firmly. The slight pressure and hint of restraint made my knees weak. He pressed a hot kiss to my pulse where my bracelet hung loosely. "Are you ready?"

My breath hitched as our gazes locked. I couldn't help but

feel like he was asking me something else. Even so, I nodded. I was ready. Whatever he had in store tonight, I was confident I wanted all of it.

Without another word, he brought me down the steps.

Ian pushed off the car as we approached. Will's hand was still in mine as Ian looped an arm around my waist and hauled me against his firm body. His other hand sifted in my hair and angled my face close to his.

A small flash of panic flitted through me at the thought of Cameron catching our embrace. The panic melted under Ian's lips—warm and tender, yet firm and unmistakably possessive. Warmth hit my heart and bloomed over my skin where he touched me. I sighed against his lips, because I belonged in this moment. I wasn't willing to sacrifice another second to worry.

Tonight and tomorrow and every day we chose to be together belonged to us, only us.

"I missed you," Ian whispered, nipping gently at my lips.

"Come on, lovebirds. Dinner awaits." Will tugged lightly, his tone teasing but laced with affection.

Ian released me, and we filed into the limo. On the short drive to dinner, we sipped champagne and made small talk, but the enclosed space after our recent absence from each other seemed to thicken the air.

I registered equal measures relief and regret when we arrived at Jean-Jacques, a swanky restaurant that I'd heard good things about but never had an occasion to visit. I was already a ball of pent-up frustration, but I was also starving, and nothing hit the spot like gourmet French cuisine.

The accented maître d' didn't blink about my being escorted by two head-to-toe gorgeous men. He seated us in a roomy leather booth around a white-linen-covered table.

The subtle light of the restaurant set an intimate and romantic atmosphere. Quiet conversation hummed through the long room, and a nearby group laughed. While I couldn't help feeling like I wore my love of two men like a blinking sign on my back, no one paid us any mind. I let the thought slip away, shifting my focus to Will and Ian.

The server brought Perrier and wine for the table, and when it was time to order, Will did the honors, all in flawless French.

"Show off," Ian muttered under his breath, his arm draped along the top of the booth. The posture tested the fabric of his suit, which he filled out exceptionally well.

Will grinned. "When it's time to put out a fire, I'll let you do the honors."

I sipped my wine slowly, savoring every subtle flavor as the three of us slipped into a comfortable banter. Whenever silence fell on the table though, sexual tension rushed in, thick and electric, like a lightning storm rolling in from a distance.

I cleared my throat and set my glass down, trying to pull my thoughts away from my primal needs.

"So, gentlemen, what's the occasion? I'm feeling thoroughly spoiled by all of this."

Will twirled his glass by the base, amusement glittering in his eyes. "Can't a couple of guys treat their girlfriend to a night on the town every once in a while?"

I laughed softly, a little bubble of happiness growing inside me. "Is that what I am now?"

Will gazed at me intently. "The ribbon-cutting was a bit of an eye-opener, for all of us, I think. I know it wasn't easy for you to be truthful with your family about our relationship, but I'm glad you were. Because this isn't a passing thing anymore.

I want to be with you and only you, for the foreseeable future. Ian feels the same way. We want to see where this goes for the long-term."

I nodded slowly. The picture he painted was everything I never knew I wanted until recently. Hearing it on his lips was a thrill and a relief, as long as I knew we could make it work. I hoped that I'd endured the strain with my family for the right reasons.

"You're both comfortable with...sharing me in that way?"

"As long as you're happy, we're happy." Ian's voice seemed to vibrate through me.

I was quiet a moment. I couldn't help but pay attention to the small kernel of doubt that crept up on me more often than I would have liked.

"Neither of you are the relationship type. At least you weren't when we started all this. I'm guessing that's because you've gotten used to keeping things simple and liking it that way. Right now, this is anything but simple. The other night was proof that things can get pretty complicated. I want to see where this goes too, but I need to know that we can get through those kinds of hurdles together."

Will spoke up quickly, his tone confident and sure. "We stood by you, Olivia, and that's what we'll continue to do. We gave you the space you needed afterward, even if it was damn near torture. We were ready to be there for you. Nothing wavered for us. Nothing changed. In fact, taking heat from your brothers has only ever solidified my resolve to be with you. I'm not letting a few rash opinions get between us."

"Neither am I," Ian said.

The determined set of Ian's jaw reassured me along with the fervency of Will's words. If I hadn't already fallen so hard, I would have been on the floor with loving these two men.

If what we had was important enough to protect, I had to stand by it. We all did.

"Thank you for giving me the space I needed. Trust me, I wanted to be with you more than I wanted to be by myself, but it was important for me to think things through after everything blew up with Darren and Cameron. I've been thinking about our future too, a lot. If we're going to do this for real, I have some terms."

My gaze settled on Will.

He smirked. "Name them."

I glanced between both men. "No matter how hard it is to do at times, I don't want to have to hide or lie about how I feel. Every time I have to pretend like I'm anything but committed and in love with both of you is going to slowly break us down. I don't want to feel the way I do right now and lose it all because we feel pressured to act like we're someone we're not."

Heat and love burned in the stormy depths of Ian's eyes. "Agreed."

Will nodded. "That's fair. We need to own it. Otherwise, there's no point in going forward. What else?"

I stuttered into my next words. "The way it's been...with sex. Our time together..." I reached for my wine and took a gulp. I swallowed over my nerves and took a steadying breath. "I don't know how to say this. Do you still want me...*together*?"

Will's lips parted on a slow exhale. "There are times when I want you to myself. I'm sure Ian feels the same way. I think we both need that. And when it comes to the three of us together, I have no intention of denying you those pleasures, unless you're intent on denying yourself."

My pulse raced, and my body heated uncomfortably under

my dress. Suddenly I was stifled by the beautiful thing. My nipples ached in my bra, and my pussy throbbed for attention.

"What do you want, Liv? Do you want both of us?" Ian pressed, his tone low and seductive, his gaze molten.

I swallowed hard, unable to form words for a second. "Yes. I want you both." I slid my hands down my thighs. Even my own touch spurred an ache for theirs.

The waiter momentarily broke the tension by delivering our entrées. While mouth-watering, they couldn't measure up to what I was taking home with me.

After the waiter left, Will exhaled heavily and tossed a hand through his hair. "Now that you've made me hard at the table, let's eat dinner."

Ian smirked, and mercifully, the conversation lightened. Will talked about work and some of the trips he'd planned that would take him out of the city over the course of the next several months. London, Hong Kong, and Mexico City. I knew all too well the demands this new position would place on him, having watched my father navigate the industry for years.

Ian would be helping Will oversee a new real estate project that had been in the works before taking over the fund. Ian's involvement would lighten the management responsibilities Will typically took on. I immediately sensed the weight that put on him and the regret of having to take his focus away from his passion to fulfill new obligations. I had a sudden urge to do whatever I could to alleviate that pressure.

"You know, Will, I've always kind of worked in a marginal way on my brothers' business. Darren became a co-owner a couple months ago, but I'm not really needed in the daily operations. Now that this new location is open and running smoothly, I'll have a lot more time. Maybe I could help, if you need it."

I was good at what I did, but I didn't take for granted that Will wanted me to put my stamp and always direct opinion on any more of his properties. But the truth was I'd be climbing the walls soon without an occupation. If he'd have me, I was up for another challenge.

Will paused and gazed at me thoughtfully. "Are you sure you're up for another project already?"

"Honestly, I'd love to have something fresh to throw myself into. I'm feeling a bit useless since the opening."

"I'd love to think I can do it all myself, but at this rate, I'm certain I won't be able to. I'd love to have your input. If nothing else, I'm confident you'll keep everyone on task." He shot me a knowing grin.

I rolled my eyes and laughed. "You know it."

"I can live with that." Ian smiled over the rim of his wineglass.

We chatted through dessert, though I was getting more and more anxious to be alone with them. They split the check, refusing to let me pay, and together we left the restaurant.

"Back home?" I threaded my fingers with Ian's as we approached the car.

"Actually," he said, "we have a little surprise for you..."

WILL

The drive to the penthouse was quiet, but the energy was palpable. Sexual and otherwise. Olivia sat between us, leaning against Ian's shoulder. Her legs were draped over my thighs. I lazily caressed up and down her silken skin. She was wearing the same pair of black heels she'd worn on our first date. They'd made me want to do truly indecent things to her at the time. Tonight wasn't much different.

My eyes followed the path my hands itched to make under the expensive dress. I couldn't wait to get back inside her, claiming every inch of her, making her scream in ecstasy. If we could get through the rest of the night without incident, nothing could hold me back.

Olivia's brief absence from our lives had been fraught with worry—that she was hurting, that we might never have her again. Not knowing where her head was at had made the past few days unfathomably worse. I'd lusted after this woman from day one, but what she was doing to my heart left me breathless and at times without words.

Tonight we'd talked through it, and together, we'd decided the direction of our future. The commitment we were asking her for had one more caveat though. After everything she'd been through recently, I wasn't sure how she'd react to it. I wanted tonight to be special, meaningful, bringing her deeper into our lives than she'd ever been. I could only hope that's what she wanted too.

Times like these, I wasn't sure if having Ian by my side made it better or worse. On one hand, the extra support was useful. Two could persuade better than one. On the other hand, both of us worrying about what she'd say almost seemed to amplify the trepidation.

Ian and I were very different people, but the way we felt about Olivia Bridge was unquestionably in tune. We were consistent in the strength and possessiveness of our affections. I didn't expect that to change for a very long time.

Along with Ian, I'd already committed that Olivia would be a part of my future. Now that I had things fairly stable with the fund, I'd get her parents off my back for a while. I'd worked things out with Reilly, and in a moment of clarity, my father had agreed to transfer his shares as well. He wasn't as worried about me fucking him over, but I didn't expect handing over the asset was too much easier than it had been for Reilly.

At Reilly's request, I'd offered Jia the opportunity to work beside me, which she'd accepted graciously and professionally. I didn't ask about her ties with Reilly or why he'd vouched for her, but I planned to. All seemed to be moving in the right direction. Now I just had to get things where I wanted them to be with Olivia.

The limo driver pulled up to the curb. Beside the Bridge Fitness entrance, another door would lead us to the luxury condos above. We left the car and brought Olivia through the doors.

"You're not putting me to work already, are you?"

"Not exactly," I said in a teasing tone, enjoying her anticipation while I tried to ignore my own.

Together we took the elevator to the top floor, which opened to the penthouse. On the heels of fast-tracking the gym progress, I'd pushed my crew to get this unit further along, leaving the others to wrap up in the coming weeks.

Marble floors stretched over an empty open living area leading into a designer kitchen. Views of Manhattan at night stretched across one side of the condo. Olivia walked in slowly, her gaze darting from detail to detail.

Pride swelled when I recognized appreciation in her eyes.

As soon as I knew this would be the next place I would call home, I'd wanted to go the extra mile to make it stand out. As soon as I knew I wanted to share it with her, I'd spared no expense to make it happen.

"What do you think?"

She circled back to me, a warm smile on her lips. "I love it. You've outdone yourself."

"Good enough to call home?"

She nodded. "Definitely an upgrade from your current place, which is phenomenal too. You deserve this, though."

"So do you."

She stilled, her gaze sliding between Ian and me. "What do you mean?"

"We want you to move in. Here. With us," Ian said.

Her lips parted and her chest moved under a sharp intake of breath. "Are you serious about this?"

I took her hand and drew her closer to me.

"We're serious. We talked about it, and this is what we want. Like it or not, spending time at your place is going to make things uncomfortable for your family. They may be able to live with it, but they're not necessarily going to like it. And this place is big enough for all of us. It makes more sense for you to call this home."

"I—"

I pressed a finger to her lips, silencing her. "Don't say you have to think about it. Just say yes."

A slow smile spread across her face. "God, you're so bossy. I was going to say yes."

She nipped at my fingertip, and I groaned. Desire and relief flooded me. Everything was falling into place. Everything felt right, yet I wanted more. Before I decided to haul her to bed this instant, Ian took her hand and tugged her away.

"There's more. Let's give you the tour."

I exhaled a frustrated breath and followed behind as Ian led her room by room until we hit the master, one of the most impressive rooms in part because it was the only room totally furnished. Against one wall was a giant bed that I'd had custom made. Covered with a porcelain-blue silk duvet, the bed dominated the space while leaving plenty of room for the other furniture that I'd had purchased.

"So this is *your* room," I said.

Her jaw fell. Her hand went to her chest. "My room?"

I kept my stance casual, even though I was reveling in every second of her surprise and delight.

"We figured it made the most sense to give you the master. I'm also assuming you have the greatest need for an enormous walk-in closet. Ian and I will both have our own rooms, and we can share this space with you as much or as little as you want."

Tears glimmered in her eyes. "Will, this is too much."

"You'll have to get used to too much when it comes to us."

She ran her fingers over the bedspread as she passed, walking quickly to the master closet, disappearing inside with a little squeal. After a few minutes, Ian coaxed her out and into the master bath, which featured its own soaking tub and an enormous shower with more rain heads than I could count.

Under our feet, an elaborate herringbone pattern made of Spanish marble intersected around a custom centerpiece. Honey onyx slivers formed a shimmering design, a golden crown—neither feminine nor masculine, but regal and elegant. Ian had done exceptionally well. His work in this room alone had earned him a place in the penthouse, even if Olivia's happiness didn't demand it.

"You like it?"

I asked the question that seemed to rest on the edge of Ian's lips. He was silent, looking at Olivia like she was the last woman on earth.

She brought her hand to her mouth as she gazed down at the elaborate design. "I don't have any words. Ian, you did this?"

He stepped closer, circling his arm around her. "Will wanted something special in here. It came together this way almost like it was meant to be."

"It's beautiful...truly. I love it."

She turned into his embrace, and he wasted no time kissing her breathless.

All too eager to relish in the delights of her body, I came behind her. I traced along the zipper that would free her from the dress. She whimpered against Ian's mouth as he kissed her deeper, and I curved my hand over her ass. I leaned close so my mouth hovered over her ear.

"It's bedtime, princess."

She arched, pushing her ass against my front, driving me fucking wild in the process. I gripped her hip firmly, trying to get hold of the fantasies I was entertaining of ripping the dress clean off her body and bending her over the vanity until I found my pleasure.

Before I could consider acting on my fantasies, she turned. Her dark hair swept over Ian's forearm as she nestled easily in his arms. Her eyelashes were low. Lust glinted in her eyes as he nibbled and sucked along the column of her neck. She melted against him with a sigh, and I imagined her pussy getting wet and aching to be filled.

In that moment, I could feel her heat against me. I could revel in the small surrender of her body and her will. Seeing her with Ian reflected my own heaven, because I'd already known it. Her happiness, her pleasure, her experience—all of it multiplied when we were both here, willing to share and eager to deliver.

"We're going to claim you everywhere tonight. Are you ready for that?"

Her chest moved under quickening breaths. She nodded slightly.

"Say it."

"I'm ready."

I held out my hand and she took it. I pulled her away from Ian and into the bedroom. She followed, her hips moving sensually with the motion. I ached to touch her, to haul her against me and show her what she did to me. Instead, I spun her and pressured her forward so her chest hit the bed, her ass pushed up high, begging for my hands and my cock.

Ian began undressing, tossing his jacket and shirt onto a plush chair that sat in the corner of the room.

"Let's see how gorgeous you are under this dress."

I crouched down and slid my palms up her calves. I kissed my way up the backs of her legs and pushed her dress up over her hips as I went. Beneath it, she wore a lacy black thong. I hooked my finger under the thin strip and slid down until I got to the place where it rested against her pussy. The fabric was wet. I pulled it to the side and flicked my tongue over the slick flesh.

She cried out softly. Her hands fisted into the duvet.

I sighed. The second my tongue had met her skin, I became drunk on her scent, her taste. I was painfully hard, but my cock was still trapped in my pants, engorged and throbbing with need.

With a frustrated growl, I slapped her ass hard. Her breath hitched, but she made no other sound.

"Good girl," I murmured, licking over the pinking skin.

My palm fell again on the other cheek. She moaned into the bed but didn't flinch away. I delivered a few more blows until her pussy was weeping with her arousal. She was ripe for what we had in store for her tonight.

I stood and gazed down at her, admiring the marks I'd made. Her ass was still lifted high, inviting more punishment. She rubbed her wrists together. I bit down hard on my lip, because I could waste the night spanking her into a frenzy. She'd hate me for it now, but she'd love it later.

For now, though, I was satisfied she was in the right mind-set for what would come next. I drew the zipper down her back and maneuvered her dress to the floor. Lifting her upright again, I spun her to face me. I hooked my palm behind her neck, and she stumbled forward a step.

She licked her lips, making them glisten in the muted light of the room. Her eyes were piercing in their lust, spurring me on.

"I'm going to watch for a while. Ian's going to get you ready for me, and then you're going to do everything I say."

She had to know I was in charge tonight. Not that Ian couldn't dominate his way through a ménage, but this was the routine we'd fallen into. It worked, and Olivia needed the comfort of that order among us.

A puff of her shaky breath warmed my lips. "Whatever you want, Will. I trust you."

"Good. Things can get a little intense. If you need a break, just tell us. We can slow down, stop, whatever you want. This is about you."

Her hands were on my chest. She was trembling, from desire or fear, or maybe both. She'd be trembling soon from another sensation altogether.

"Thank you," she whispered.

I closed my eyes against the warmth that slid over my skin. Something about those two words threatened to turn me inside out. Her trust. In me. In us.

CHAPTER SIXTEEN

OLIVIA

Anticipation was alive on my skin. I wanted to be consumed. As Will backed away, I worried I'd disintegrate into a pile of lust on the floor. Judging by the severe erection that strained against his pants, he possessed far more willpower than I did.

Ian was naked and proud before me. He tossed a condom and a small bottle of liquid on the bed. Wasting no time, he released my breasts from the black lace bra I wore. Cupping them, he bent to bring each one into his mouth. I sighed and arched into the singular pleasure of his tongue tugging and teasing each sensitive point. When I thought I'd burst from the frustration of wanting more, he pushed me down onto the bed. He nearly tore my panties in his haste to remove them.

He climbed over me, and I felt all his strength as he moved me up the enormous bed. He kissed me hard for a few seconds before breaking away. The animal hunger in his eyes mingled with a flash of concern.

"How do you feel?"

I inhaled an unsteady breath. "Overwhelmed. More aroused than maybe I've ever been in my whole life."

"Good. Now just relax."

Nudging my legs wide around his hips, he trailed his finger between my thighs and through my wet folds. I arched into him. He stopped to put pressure on my anus.

"I'm going to take you here."

I swallowed over my anticipation. I'd never given that part of myself to a man. I nodded. "It's okay. I'm ready." Ready or not, I was willing to give him free rein over my body.

He turned me to my side and spooned behind me. The small pressure of his fingertip transformed when cool liquid eased his entry. The sensation wasn't painful. The only discomfort was the forbidden way it made me feel. I tried not to think about it and focused instead on the pleasure that was promised.

Ian trailed heat along my neck with his mouth, sucking and nibbling as he massaged my opening. Gradually, he stretched my tight ring of muscle to accommodate more fingers. I gasped, tensing and then accepting his ministrations.

With the slightest sign of discomfort, he whispered passionate adorations and kissed that magic spot just below my ear that made my whole body surrender. When he stopped to roll on a condom, anticipation lit up under my skin. But by the time he pressed the soft tip of his cock to my opening, I knew I was ready for him.

His entry was marked with a slow burn that morphed into pleasant friction. His movements were painstaking, his caresses undeniably tender.

"Oh, God," I gasped when he claimed me deeper.

"You okay?"

I nodded. "Feels so much better than I thought it would."

He grabbed my hip and pushed us tighter with a groan. "Thank fuck. You're so tight. I don't want to hurt you, baby, but I don't know how I'd be able to stop right now."

Heat rushed to my cheeks. My whole body was on fire

from the intensity of the sensation. Yet it wasn't only physical. My heart was definitely involved, seeing how it raced and swelled. Ian was inside me, all around me, loving me, making me his in a way I'd never experienced.

Sharing this intimate moment with him extended beyond the pleasure and the pain, because we'd never be here if I didn't love him the way I did. And knowing Will was moments from taking me... My heart could barely stand it. The anticipation, the intensity, the trust...

"Take all of me, Liv. Please, baby." Ian's gravelly voice slid over me with a shiver, pushing me deeper into my emotions.

I pushed back against him, taking him into me on the next stroke. He went deeper, stretching me even more. I whimpered, because every small thrust added to the pressure in my pussy, like a pleasure point that was just out of reach. Suddenly I ached there too.

Will was naked when he climbed onto the bed. His thick cock was fully erect and already protected by a condom. The thought of him inside me right now made me heady with desire. I craved the sensation, even as I worried it might be too much. Then Will's words echoed in my ears.

You'll have to get used to too much...

"How does Ian's cock feel inside you?"

"So good," I breathed. "I want more. I want you, Will."

Every muscle in his body grew tense, and a growl rumbled from his chest.

"Roll on top of Ian. Let me see your beautiful cunt, princess."

I didn't have to make an effort. Ian shifted so he was on his back and I lay against his powerful chest. His legs were wide, my thighs hooked over his and spread farther.

Will took the space between them, slipping a finger deep into my pussy.

"Ah." I shuddered when he grazed the place inside me that felt electric and incredibly sensitive. I tightened, registering the fullness in my ass, unable to comprehend how tight I'd be with Will inside me too.

"I'm going to try like hell to go slow. You have to tell me if it's too much."

His finger slipped from me. A second later, he lined his cock up and pushed the head of his cock to my pussy. As much as I wanted this, I worried that I couldn't accommodate them both.

Ian's voice hummed like velvet against my ear. "We're going to make you feel so good, baby."

I closed my eyes with a sigh, and Will took that moment to push into me completely.

I sucked in a sharp breath. My eyelids flew open as he forced into my tight channel.

The undercurrent of promised pleasure was so strong, my brain cells seemed to scatter almost instantly. The next stroke was less cautious, more sure now that he'd stake his claim.

"Fuck," I breathed the curse as I licked over my dry lips.

"You good?" His voice was tight with strain.

"Don't stop. Please..."

I braced myself against Will's chest and down his abs, which tightened when he shoved into me again.

The only thing that existed was the place where we joined. Ian's strokes began to match Will's rhythm. There was no slow climb, no tease of promised release. I was at the edge instantly, breathless and clawing at Will's hips as he slammed us together over and over.

"I need to come," I begged.

"Not yet, princess. Don't you dare," Will said.

"Please, it's so intense." No amount of willpower could keep the pleasure from tearing through me, I was certain.

Before I had a chance to give in to the intense pressure, Will stalled his movements and held me with a steady gaze. "Breathe, Olivia."

Sobered by his firm order, I obeyed, inhaling a breath that I hoped might stave off the fierce need to orgasm long enough to satisfy him. But the need lingered, coiling around me like the best kind of vise. "It's like I can feel everything. My whole body wants to come."

He hushed me softly, caressing a reassuring touch up and down my thigh, all the while nestled deep and still inside my pussy. "The second you come, your body's not going to want both of us in there. I don't want to hurt you. I want this to be good for you."

My lust-addled brain struggled to wrap my head around his words. I trusted him with my pleasure. So as he began to thrust again, slow strokes that gradually gained in speed and strength, I breathed through the nearly overwhelming urge to let go.

Beneath me, Ian was tense and barely moved. His touches went from calming caresses to desperate grasps.

"Will," he grunted through clenched teeth. "Now."

Will pounded fiercely, sweat on his brow, his gaze riveted to mine. His jaw clenched. His skin was tight over his flexing muscles. "Come, Olivia. Come now."

My head fell back against Ian's shoulder. All I could do was feel. Ian's rough touch, holding me tightly to him, anchoring my hips against their punishing drives. My body, overfull and overstimulated in every possible pleasurable way. Then, a third counterpoint arrived with Ian's fingers hard against my clit, adding firm circles of pressure.

When I closed my eyes, I could almost see the orgasm tearing from me—color and electricity and heat, taking me over the edge. My jaw fell open with a soundless cry. I could barely breathe, let alone form words or the vowel sounds that were clawing out with my release.

Nothing existed before this moment. Nothing mattered after. All the world revolved around the unimaginable pleasure that rocketed through me and sizzled down every limb. I seized hard, a jagged cry finally escaping from my lips.

"Liv. Fuck. Fuck!" Ian thickened and flinched inside me, punctuating his release with a long groan.

Will's grip on me tightened seconds before he let go too, mouth agape, my name on his lips. He tunneled deep, setting off another wave of pleasure and shattering the last of me.

Our cries mingled, echoing off the walls of this room that was now ours, to house our dreams and our passion.

Seconds ticked by in a blur as my two lovers moved and shifted me so I lay on the cool, clean sheets in the center of the bed. I flinched and trembled, the aftershocks of my release ricocheting through me like a dozen flashes of remembered rapture. I whimpered through them, they were so intense.

Then the tears came, an unexpected torrent of emotion spilling down my cheeks.

"Baby, what's wrong?" Ian folded his arms around me. "We're right here. Shh."

But I couldn't talk, couldn't explain. I was living in the wake of a storm so intense I didn't have words for it. I reached for Will, and he curled closer. His heartbeat, Ian's soft murmurs, and their soothing touches gentled me and brought me back down to a place where I could breathe again.

"Did we hurt you?" The concern in Will's words pulled me out of it a little more, enough to find my voice.

"No, I'm fine. I'm sorry." The sound was weak and watery. "I've just never felt this way before. It was all too much for a minute, like a dam broke or something."

Will kissed me softly. "That's okay. I just wanted it to be good for you."

I sighed and tangled our fingers together. "So good. So fucking good."

He chuckled softly, leaving me only after Ian went to the bathroom and returned with a warm cloth. Ian cleaned me, an intimate act that I was grateful for, because I wasn't certain I could walk after what we'd done. That, and I was drifting off to sleep seconds later, cocooned between their warmth, wrapped safely in their love.

IAN

I stared up at the ceiling as the day dawned. Sunlight streamed into the room through the yet uncovered windows. Everything was new, perfect. A fresh start for all of us.

Last night had been everything we'd planned and hoped for. Liv was with us, and for the first time ever, I couldn't wait to start this journey with a woman. Making the commitment to share her with Will had taken a minute to get used to, but I'm not sure I would have taken the leap without him. The depth of our love for her seemed to fuel the fire, reinforcing feelings that we weren't used to facing, forcing us to put her needs before ours.

She rustled beside me. She reached out to the emptiness beside her, laying her palm flat where Will had once slept. Concern washed over her sleepy features.

"Where's Will?"

I brought myself up on my elbow and stared down at her, in awe as always of her flawless beauty. "He had a meeting downtown this morning. He'll be back here tonight. He was hoping we could start moving your things over today."

She lifted her eyebrows. "Already?"

"I don't think he wants to give you any time to change your mind."

She smiled warmly. "I haven't. How could I? I feel like a queen here. You're spoiling me rotten, I hope you know."

I leaned down to brush my lips against hers. "We want to spoil you. The closer you are, the more we can."

When I'd spoken to Will this morning, I'd momentarily questioned his rush to get her fully moved in so soon, until now. Now I realized that I needed her in our bed as fiercely as he did, always within reach. Her recent absence had been unsettling, bordering on painful. I didn't want to go through that again. The closer we kept her, hopefully the closer she'd stay.

She stretched, showcasing her delicious body, glowing and warm from sleep. I tugged the sheet down to reveal more of it.

I nudged her legs apart, unable to refrain from savoring a few of my favorite places on her luscious body. My mouth watered as I entertained the notion of burying my face between her pretty thighs and licking her into an orgasm. Then I remembered that she'd had a very long and intense night. It had ended in tears. Thankfully, the good kind.

The emotions that had spilled over after we'd found our pleasure weren't only hers though. Last night had been intense for all of us. I'd never felt so taken under, so enraptured. And I was devoted to making sure we had more nights like that.

"How do you feel?"

"Like a very lucky girl." She twisted her fingers into her mussed hair. She was possibly the most gorgeous creature I'd ever laid eyes on.

"Are you sore?"

She blinked. "A little."

With the single-minded goal of getting her wet, I slid my fingers over her clit. I rubbed it with just the right amount of pressure to keep her wanting more, even though I knew I wouldn't take her again so soon. I had to show some restraint, even though it seemed nearly impossible to do with her this near, and this naked.

"It's not going to be easy to let you rest. I have a feeling we're going to want you around the clock."

The statement was a warning and a promise. I wasn't sure she realized what she was in for. But she only bit her lip with a small smile.

She bowed off the bed, bucking her hips into my strokes. "I guess I'll have to adjust."

Watching her writhe and slide over the sheets was making my dick hard. Fuck, I couldn't stop myself though. I dipped my finger into her velvet heat, now slick with her arousal.

"Does this hurt?"

She shook her head, desire hooding her gaze. I slipped a second finger into her and felt her clench around me. I pushed in a little deeper, wondering if she was sorer than she let on.

Will and I had attempted to go slow and gentle, but in the

heat of the moment, neither of us could hold back from fucking her hard and fast, unable to cage the beasts that hungered for primal, violent sex.

Now she was slick and primed for me. The lips of her pussy were swollen, pink, and glistening.

"Goddamnit, I want you."

"Then take me," she whispered huskily, not a shred of doubt in her voice.

I cursed as I left her to dig a condom out of my suit pants pocket. I groaned with frustration because all I wanted to do was slide into her bare and feel her wet heat hugging my cock. I came back to the bed and rolled the damn thing on in a rush.

"I'm pretty sure I speak for Will when I say I'm ready to be done fucking you with these."

Without waiting for a response, I dropped down over her and sucked a rosy nipple into my mouth. I squeezed and licked and sucked each of her perfect breasts until she whimpered and bucked her hips against me. Moving up her body, I took her mouth in a hungry kiss. My cock nestled against her pussy, like it knew exactly where it wanted to be. Now, tomorrow, always...

"You're the only one I want to be with, Liv, and I'll get every test under the sun to prove that you can be safe with me. When I come, I want it to be inside you. Do we have enough trust between us to do that?"

She brought her hands to my face and drew lines along my jaw. "I love you and I trust you, Ian. Soon, though, I promise."

Satisfied, I took her mouth again, sealing us together. The fantasy of fucking her bare was potent enough to make me forget I wasn't. I nibbled at her lips and sucked her tongue, joining us completely. I lost myself in loving her. She was so close, under my skin, and around my heart.

No one had ever felt this perfect. No one but her...

"Harder," she whispered, wrapping her legs around my hips.

The world narrowed to only her and that look of surrender awash her features. Then I was lost. Restraint left me along with my last shred of sanity. I surged into her until I felt her ripple around me.

"Anything you want. Everything you want..."

OLIVIA

I drew my brush in a grand sweep of mahogany paint across the wall, forming the outline of a great tree. The majestic oak, adorned with imperfections and knots, would be the focal point for the mural. It would become a home for fantastic creatures that lived in the little world I was drawing for my nephew. Outside the walls of this nursery, a splendid city sprawled. Here, he could live in a world of nature and fantasy.

After weeks of struggling, I'd woken up with a vision for the wall. I'd come home from another night spent at the penthouse, gathered my old paints, and went up to Cam and Maya's apartment to get started.

The smell of the paints and the ritual of preparing my palette for another section of the mural brought me to an almost Zen-like state as I worked.

When I'd begun, I didn't hesitate like I had at the studio. The fear I'd lived with for so long had seemingly vanished, leaving only a fierce desire to create in its wake. It was as if, after a quick refresher, I'd relearned a fundamental skill. I'd reconnected with my passion as if no time had passed.

I made quick progress, but my rumbling stomach nagged at me to eat. I meandered toward the kitchen for a quick snack, when I noticed Maya on the couch, hunched over.

A flash of panic quickened my heart. "Maya, are you all right?"

She nodded. I went to her, and after a few seconds passed, she looked up, her cheeks flushed.

"Contraction. I'm okay."

My eyes went wide. "Oh, God. Let me call Cam."

She shook her head. "No, I'm good. I'm timing them. We still have plenty of time before I need to go the hospital."

"Are you sure?"

Maya would know better than I would. She'd read every baby magazine on every shelf front to back. I knew she was due in a week, but beyond that, I was clueless.

She exhaled loudly and leaned back on the couch with her eyes closed. "I'm sure. I'd rather stay here and labor as long as I can before I go in."

I worried, but agreed to wait to contact Cam. No doubt he'd totally freak out as soon as he knew she was in labor.

I ate a quick snack, packed up my supplies, and spent the next two hours comforting her through every contraction until they were close enough that we could call Cam.

As expected, he was at the apartment in record time, rushing through the house for last-minute things to throw in the hospital bag. He drove all of us, and I held Maya's hand through the contractions that came and went on the journey.

Once they were settled in their own hospital room, I quietly excused myself. I could have held Maya's hand until the baby came, but I wasn't sure if I was ready to witness childbirth. Beyond that, Cameron was the one who should be with her. Until I'd fallen in love, I hadn't known two people to love each other so hard. I knew they were destined to be together. Nothing could shake that belief.

I paced around the waiting room, hoping to get an update sooner rather than later. I shot off texts to Will and Ian, letting them know I'd be staying at my apartment in case Cam and Maya needed anything. I texted Vanessa and Darren too and promised to update them when I heard anything. Darren hadn't contacted me since the ribbon-cutting, but a second after I sent the text, he sent a short reply.

Awesome! Keep us posted.

I smiled, thrilled that before the day was through, I'd likely be an aunt. The fact that Darren had acknowledged my existence after nearly two weeks of silence was icing on the cake.

After about an hour, Cameron emerged from the room. I rose and met him in the middle of the waiting room.

"How's she doing?"

"Great. She's between contractions, so I can't stay long. They're coming pretty close, but they say she's got a little bit to go. Her water hasn't broken yet. You can head back home if you want, and I can let you know when the baby comes."

I nodded quickly. "Okay, just let me know if you need anything."

He smiled. "I will. Thanks."

I hugged him tight before he could leave and then shooed him off two seconds later. "Okay, go back to her."

He rushed back to their room with a jog, and my heart twisted for the love they had.

I took the train back home, feeling jittery and high with anticipation. Back at my apartment, I considered finishing the baby's mural, but my brain was all over the place. I was too excited, too anxious to stay focused. I needed a more mindless occupation while I waited for news from Cameron, so I started packing up some more things to take over to the penthouse.

Even though most of my nights were spent there, I'd resolved to keep the apartment furnished for another month, just in case.

The life we were building together seemed almost too good to be true, and that was what made it overwhelming at times. Day by day, our bonds grew deeper. I was happy and so ready to start living again. Because for so long, I hadn't been. I hadn't been especially unhappy, but something was always missing. Until Will and Ian had come into my life, I couldn't clearly see it.

Having love in my life had reignited a passion long lost. Now I had a future to look forward to, and I was determined not to let anything or anyone get in the way of that.

I was in the middle of sorting through my staggering shoe collection when the phone rang. My doctor's office number showed up on the screen.

I'd paid them a visit following Ian's request so they could run the gamut on labs. I'd never had unprotected sex, but if he and Will were going to submit clean bills of health, I wanted something official to offer too. More importantly, I needed to get on the pill. My love life had been uneventful enough over the past year to justify skipping the daily ritual, but I didn't want anything between us anymore either.

My doctor's voice greeted me. "So we got your labs back. Good news, everything came back fine. Everything's normal, except for one thing."

I dropped a red-soled nude pump into the box I'd been filling.

"What's that?"

"Well." She cleared her throat. "You're pregnant."

My jaw fell. I wasn't sure how many seconds passed before she spoke again.

"I can't say exactly how far along you are, but based on your HCG levels, I'd say you could see us again in a couple weeks for an ultrasound, and we can get you going from there."

"I don't understand." I forced the words out, because nothing made sense in this moment.

"You're pregnant, Olivia."

I shook my head. "That's not possible."

"The blood work doesn't lie. It's not like a home pregnancy test, where there's room for error."

I hung up without another word.

CHAPTER SEVENTEEN

WILL

I went straight to the penthouse from work. I'd spent the day bringing Jia up to speed on all the investors and game planning for the upcoming months. We had our work cut out for us, but she seemed eager and up for the task. But after a full day, all I'd wanted to do was have Olivia in my arms. She made a rough day melt away, and the more days that passed, the more the penthouse was feeling like a home.

I'd bounced around places since I was a kid, never getting too personally attached to any one living situation. Something about this place made me want to stay awhile. Of course, Olivia had everything to do with that.

I walked through the door and put my briefcase on one of the expensive upholstered chairs that adorned the foyer. I entered the kitchen, and Olivia was sitting at a stool staring down. Her hands were threaded through her dark-brown hair that fell loose over her shoulders. She didn't look up when I entered, and an uneasy feeling slid over me.

"Hey, beautiful."

When she didn't look up, I went to her. I caught her chin and lifted her gaze to me. Her eyes were glossy and red, and something seized in my gut.

"What's wrong?"

She didn't speak, only tucked her hair behind her ear with a trembling hand.

"Jesus Christ, you're shaking like a leaf. What's going on?"

"Will...I don't know what I'm going to do." Her voice was broken and watery.

"About what?"

She shook her head and a single tear fell down her cheek. I caught her shoulders, spinning her on the stool so she faced me.

"Olivia, talk to me." My tone was firmer now. She was scaring the hell out of me.

"I'm pregnant," she whispered.

My breath lodged painfully in my chest. I replayed those two words a few more times, absorbing their meaning.

"Wait... What?"

She continued shaking her head, wiping at her eyes. She was trembling harder, and now I knew why.

"I've been safe. I've always been safe. I don't know how this could have happened. Did a condom break or something?"

My thoughts whizzed a million miles an hour. Then they paused on one moment in time. Fuck.

My hands fell from her shoulders. "You weren't on the pill?"

She swallowed and another tear fell. "No. I haven't been on it for a long time. That's why I said you needed to use protection, always."

I ran a palm down my face. "Fuck."

"What?"

I paced away from her.

"Will..."

I turned back and held her in my gaze. "This is my fault."

"What do you mean this your fault?"

"I—I just assumed you were on the pill and the condoms were an extra precaution."

She widened her reddened eyes, and her swollen lips parted. "You had sex with me without a condom?"

I swallowed hard and yanked through my hair. "One night. It was the middle of the night. I had this fucked-up nightmare. All I could think about was being inside you. I had to have you. I woke you up, and you said yes. I thought you knew."

"*You* did this?"

The tears fell unbidden down her cheeks. I felt like I was drowning in them. How could I have done this to her...

"Olivia, I swear I didn't know this would happen."

"I trusted you!" Her cry was full of despair.

She slid off the stool and closed the space between us, her fists two tight balls at her sides. When she leveled them against my chest, I didn't bother stopping her. I deserved the pain. I deserved every ounce of her anger.

She beat her fists against me until the sobs overtook her. Her knees gave out, and she sank to the ground. I caught her and lowered down with her. When I dragged her into my lap, she was boneless and didn't fight me. I wrapped my arms around her, holding her tight through her tears.

Her tears were worse than her blows. They lanced through me.

Every instinct told me to protect her, to find a way to make this all right. But if I held the blame, how could I protect her? How could I possibly make this right?

OLIVIA

I wasn't sure how much time I spent cocooned in Will's arms. I hated him right now, but there was no place I'd have rather been. He'd done this to me, and somehow I knew he was the only one who would bring me through it. I nuzzled into his shirt, letting his woodsy scent comfort me as I caught my breath.

He didn't speak, which worried me. He was always so quick to take control of a situation, to make up my mind for me.

I looked up at him. "You're not saying anything."

"I'm trying not to make it worse," he muttered softly.

"Try to make it better."

He sighed, and I rested against his exhaling chest.

"I'm sorry, Olivia. I'm so sorry. I made a mistake. I know it's not enough right now, but you have to believe that I would never try to hurt you."

Fresh tears fell, but my body didn't have any more sobs to give. I pressed my face into his chest, not caring how my mascara stained the perfectly starched shirt.

"Take me to bed. I can't..." A sob broke free.

His arms came around me tighter and lifted us up. "I have a better idea."

He carried me through the bedroom and into the master bath and stood me in front of the claw-foot tub. He turned on the faucet. While he checked the temperature, I stared down at the floor. Dozens of golden tiles were cool under my feet. Ian's beautiful crown.

How would I tell him? I squeezed my eyes closed and pretended for the moment that I wouldn't have to. Nothing would have to change. Tomorrow I'd wake up, and I wouldn't be facing this unexpected situation. Everything could go on the way it had been.

I thought once the outside world agreed to mind its own business, we'd be safe inside our circle. I never thought something like this could happen. That my trust in Will could be so utterly shattered.

While the bath filled, Will turned his attention to me. With gentle care, he undressed me. His movements were slow and methodical, as if I were a child. There was nothing suggestive or sexual about it.

He held my hand and helped me into the bath. The warm water soothed my tense muscles, but it wasn't enough of the comfort I needed. I wrapped my arms around my knees and held on tight through another wave of disbelief and regret.

"Do you want me to come in with you?" Will's forearms rested on the lip of the tub. His cobalt gaze was soft and serious at once.

I nodded, and he undressed. He stepped into the water behind me, sat, and gently ushered me back so I rested against his chest. His legs framed mine. He slid his palms down my arms and gently cuffed my wrists.

I sighed as a little more of my tension melted away. At least he was here...with me. Suddenly it occurred to me that I shouldn't take that for granted. Being in a relationship didn't guarantee that he'd be on board for fatherhood. He could have bailed the second he found out I was pregnant. He still could.

"Are you going to stay with me?" I didn't recognize my voice, so small and raw.

His grasp tightened. "Yes," he said, his tone steadfast. He pressed his nose against my hair and inhaled. "It's going to be okay, I promise," he whispered. "Whatever happens, I'm with you. I'm not letting you go."

★ ★ ★

I woke early and managed to slip out of bed and leave the penthouse without rousing Will. Ian would be due back from his night shift soon, and I wasn't nearly ready to face him. The numbing shock of learning that I was pregnant had settled into a reality I was gradually getting used to.

I didn't have much choice but to accept it. Will had been careless, and here we were. He'd accepted the blame, but I should have been more vigilant too. I'd been so wrapped up in his bubble of sex and sharing and kinky fuckery that I'd gotten too comfortable.

Nothing about life was going to plan lately, and becoming pregnant by one of my two boyfriends certainly fell right in line with that.

I grabbed a coffee and a muffin at my favorite café and made my way to the hospital.

Cameron had texted me a couple of hours earlier with a photo of my newborn nephew. Aidan Jacob had been welcomed into the world at a healthy six pounds, ten ounces. He was a beautiful little red-faced angel wrapped up tight in a hospital blanket, and I couldn't wait to meet him.

I could have used another day or two to come to terms with being pregnant myself, but nothing was going to keep me from seeing my family today.

The bright sun marking a new day filtered through the hospital windows as I passed doors on my way to their room. I knocked and entered on the sound of Maya's voice. She greeted me with a smile, and I went to hug her. She looked a little pale but beamed with happiness.

"How are you?"

"Good. So relieved to have him here finally," she said.

"I bet."

Cameron's eyes were bright too, considering he probably hadn't slept a wink all night. He sat in a chair beside her hospital bed. My nephew's small body was tucked into the nook of his elbow. I peered over, eager to get a look. He was perfectly still, snoozing contentedly in my brother's arms.

Instantly, tears stung my eyes and emotion clogged my throat. "He's so beautiful."

"Do you want to hold him?" Cameron's voice was quiet.

I nodded, and he gingerly passed the precious bundle to me.

The baby made a little grunty noise, but quieted as soon as I brought him to my chest. I sat in the chair beside Cameron and looked down in wonder.

The baby opened his eyes and stared up at me. In an instant, my heart felt like it had been carried away, high into the clouds.

"Hi, baby Aidan," I whispered, feathering a light touch down his cheek.

I pretended to listen while Maya and Cameron relived the highlights of the delivery, but I was more captivated by my perfect nephew. Between his wide-eyed stares and my whispers of adoration, we were having a big talk. Somewhere in it, I made him a silent promise that only he could hear. He would have a cousin very soon.

WILL

I stared out the window of my office. The view of New York stretched from floor to ceiling. Hundreds of cars and people milled around below. Life went on, day after day. Nothing ever made this city slow down.

But yesterday's news had stopped me dead in my tracks. Olivia was carrying my child. Barring something tragic, our lives would be forever changed. She'd been pregnant for weeks, and we never knew it. I'd committed everything to her since then. I'd professed my love to her, and I'd meant it with all my heart.

Had I known somehow, deep down, that she would be forever tied to me after that night?

I'd held her all night, until the tears slowed and she clung to me like I was the only one who could bring her peace. She'd fallen asleep against me, and as I stared into the darkness, I contemplated how dramatically life could change. In the blink of an eye, everything had taken on new meaning and purpose. Olivia needed me, and in nine months, so would our child.

Waking up to an empty bed filled me with a kind of anxiety I'd never experienced. I heard Ian's voice in my head, telling me to give her time and space. Seeking that might have been her first instinct, but I wasn't accepting it. I'd created this situation, but I wasn't letting her go. From this moment forward, she was mine to care for in every way, and I'd be damned if I was going to let anything get in my way.

I pulled my phone from my pocket and dialed her number. She picked up after the first ring.

"I got worried when you weren't home this morning," I said.

"I woke up early and didn't want to disturb you."

"Is that the truth?"

She was silent a moment. "Not entirely. I wasn't ready to face Ian. And Cam and Maya had their baby last night. Seeing them was more important than dealing with any of my own drama this morning."

"How are they doing?"

"Really good. The baby is beautiful."

I couldn't miss the irony that we would be facing the same situation in nine short months. The thought didn't make me as uncomfortable as maybe it should have. With anyone else, I'd be freaking the fuck out. Even though the prospect of imminent fatherhood was filled with unknowns and a litany of fears, knowing that I'd be going into that part of my life with Olivia filled me with an unexpected calm.

"That's great. I'm really happy for them," I said, truly meaning it.

"Me too. They'll all be home in a couple days. I'm going to do some things around their apartment today to help them out."

"Okay, but I want you to stay at the penthouse tonight."

"Are you beckoning me?"

Her tone was even, not sweet and teasing the way it might have been under different circumstances.

"You're goddamn right. I'm beckoning you."

"Will—"

"The thought of you going through what you went through last night alone is unacceptable to me. I love you. I'm here for you. Whatever you're working through, I want to be there to help you work through it. Not to mention, I'm trying to figure out a few things out too."

She sighed softly. "Fine. I'll take care of what I need to here first though."

"Whatever you need to do. Also, I'm going to hire movers this week to help you get the rest of your things to the penthouse. I want you with me. Every night."

"What about Ian?"

What about Ian... God, we had to tell him sometime, and I wasn't looking forward to it one bit. I'd barely had a chance to wrap my head around her being pregnant myself. I was so busy getting her to calm down last night, I hadn't spent much time thinking about how Ian would receive the news.

"We have to tell him. The sooner the better, I imagine. He won't like to think he was kept in the dark for very long."

"You're right." She exhaled heavily. "Maybe tonight. If I can work up the courage." I heard her mutter a curse.

"We'll tell him together. It'll be okay."

As I reassured her, I worried that Ian might not adjust to the news as well as I hoped he would. I tried to imagine if our positions were reversed. Imagining it, however briefly, reinforced how grateful I was that I'd been the one who fucked up.

"Olivia."

"What?"

"Last night, when I told you I was sorry... I *am* sorry that I violated your trust. You didn't want or ask for this. But now that we're here, I want you to know that I'm not sorry about it. It's not what either of us expected, but I'm glad it's with you. I'm ready to take this journey with you."

She sniffed and sighed quietly on the other end of the phone. "I'm feeling more ready too. Meeting the baby today put things into perspective for me. I think I'm more ready for this than I thought."

I closed my eyes and tightened my grip on the phone. I wanted to hold her, kiss her, and remind her how much I loved her.

"I love you, Olivia."

"I love you too."

CHAPTER EIGHTEEN

IAN

I checked the empanadas in the oven and set the table for dinner. Will was at work all day, and Liv was busy at her place, prepping meals and getting things tidy for when her brother and sister-in-law came home with the baby in a couple of days.

I wanted to surprise her with a dinner at home. Even though my schedule was a bit erratic, we'd settled into a routine that seemed to give each of us the time we needed. I had no idea how it worked, but it did. Seeing her and spending a little time with her every day made the world feel right, no matter what shit I had to face at work.

Liv came through the door first. Her eyes were tired, and her body seemed to tense a little when she saw me.

"Hey, baby. Everything okay?" I went to her and pressed a chaste kiss to her lips.

She kissed me back, taking our kiss from chaste to passionate quickly.

"Hello to you too," I teased in a velvet tone when we broke apart.

With a small smile, she softened in my arms. "You made dinner?"

I glanced back to the mess I'd made in the kitchen. "Yeah, it'll be ready in a few minutes. Should be good by the time Will gets home."

She tensed a little again. Then she stepped out of my embrace and began cleaning up. Even though I'd grown used to our easy silences, something felt uncomfortable about this one. I'd expected her to be all smiles and energy about her brother's baby, but maybe something else had happened today that was throwing her off.

I didn't push her about it, but when Will walked through the door, they shared a look that gave me pause.

Will masked it quickly, carrying himself into the room casually. "Smells great. Thanks, Ian."

"No problem," I said, trying to shake off the edgy feeling.

Dinner carried on fine. I talked a little about work, as did Will. Business as usual, and things were going well with the fund for the most part. Thank goodness, since Will had committed himself to it so completely.

But when the conversation shifted to Liv's new nephew, she began to tear up. Normal, I told myself. Babies inspired emotions in women that I'd likely never understand.

Then she looked to Will, and a fresh wave of worry came over me. Something wasn't right.

She swallowed hard and dropped her fork on the table. "We need to talk to you, Ian."

The worry grew, spreading cold down my limbs.

"What's going on?"

She chewed relentlessly on her lip and stared silently at the table.

"Liv, talk to me. What is it?"

Finally, she lifted her tearful gaze to mine. "Ian, I'm pregnant. Please don't be angry."

Time seemed to stand still while my brain stuttered,

struggling to catch up with what that truly meant.

Pregnant? She'd been with both of us. But I'd always been safe. I'd never been with a woman without protection. It wasn't worth the risk, and I sure as hell wasn't ready for fatherhood.

"How?"

Will spoke up, his expression rigid, like he was bracing himself. "It's my fault."

All I could hear was my heart beating furiously. The breath seemed to squeeze out of my chest as I absorbed his admission. I stared at him in disbelief.

"You did this?"

Suddenly, every overprotective and insanely possessive thought I'd ever had about sharing Liv with another man forced into the forefront of my mind.

I'd been willing to fight for her at every turn, but ultimately, I'd bought into the notion that we could, truly, both be in her life in a healthy way. How could I have been so fucking wrong?

Will avoided my gaze, betraying his discomfort. "I was careless. She didn't know."

She didn't know... That meant he'd fucked her bare without thinking of the consequences. She'd told me she wasn't on birth control. Had he known? Had he taken her the way he wanted to anyway? Suddenly I wanted to fucking throttle him.

I pushed up from the table and came to him. "You couldn't have her to yourself so you had to knock her up?"

He rose to stand, his stance and his shoulders wide and defensive. "That's not what happened."

A fierce jealousy tore through me, and I tightened my fists. "How could you do this to her? To us?"

"I wasn't thinking straight. It's no excuse, but that's how

it happened."

"You weren't thinking? You think I believe that for one second? You could get your dick hard, but you couldn't think about covering it up to protect her?"

"It was the middle of the night—"

"Bullshit!" I shoved my finger at him. "You're a fucking cheat, like your father."

He narrowed his eyes. Rage and a searing pain sent a rush of adrenaline to my muscles. Before I could talk myself out of it, I lunged for him, grabbing fistfuls of his shirt. I pushed him across the room and slammed him against the wall.

"How could you do this to her?" I seethed through gritted teeth.

His face twisted into a grimace, and he shoved me back hard. I came back, ready to wind up and knock the living shit out of him, when Liv's voice rang out.

"Ian, don't!" She was suddenly beside me, a dangerous place to be. She circled my wrist, halting my advance on Will.

She wasn't strong enough to hold me back, but she had the power to pull me out of my emotions long enough to consider what I was doing. I looked over to her, feeling wild with rage.

Slowly, she moved between us. Placing her hands on my chest, she stilled me. But my heart wouldn't slow, and nothing she could say would lessen the hatred I felt for Will right now.

"Please don't fight. I know it's a lot to take in. It's going to be okay though," she whispered in a watery voice, pressing her forehead against my chest.

Her touch hurt. Everything fucking ached inside me right now.

I took a step away, sparing Will the physical punishment he sorely deserved.

I didn't know what to say. My hands wanted to do the talking. The urge to dole out justice was fierce. I had to get away from everyone before I did something truly stupid.

Without another word, I left the room and headed toward mine. I sat on the bed and let my head fall into my shaking hands.

She was pregnant. With Will's baby.

The pain was so raw, lancing through me. The anger singed like fire through my veins.

Liv was there a moment later, standing before me. She stroked my cheek and squeezed my shoulder, as if she could ease what had my body strung tight like a bow.

When I looked up, I saw my pain reflected in her vibrant eyes—two blue diamonds. Priceless, perfect, and slowly slipping out of reach.

"Why, Liv?"

I knew she didn't have the answer, but I couldn't stop myself from asking for it.

Why now, when I'd fallen so hard? I'd allowed Will into my social life as an assurance that any relationship would be impossible. Then stupidly, I'd fallen in love, and here we were. We wouldn't get past this. I couldn't.

"It was an accident. This is my fault too."

I shook my head, unwilling to believe it. "It's not."

"I know you're angry, but it's not the end of the world. I was devastated when I found out, yes. But I'm coming to terms, and you will too. We can get through this. I know we can."

I rose, stepped away from her painful touch, and paced the room.

"Do you have any idea how hard it's been to share you? To let him have any part of you when I want you for myself?"

"This hasn't been easy for any of us."

"That's because we're trying to make something work that's impossible!" I shouted, overwhelmed with the reality I was now facing.

More tears rimmed her eyes. "I can't let myself believe that," she said quietly.

The fire of my rage dulled enough to go to her. I caged her against me, willing my heart to slow down. Willing the anger and resentment away, knowing ultimately it was tearing us both apart.

Slowly I caressed down her arms and over her silken skin. She was as soft and intoxicating as the first time I'd touched her. But so much had changed. I grazed my hand over her flat belly, where Will's child was growing. Now we'd never be the same.

I fought back an albatross of emotion. I'd spent half my life taking every measure to ensure I never became a father. I didn't know what came over me now to change that, but if given the choice, I would have traded places with Will in a heartbeat. I would have given anything in that moment to be the one she was bound to, to know she was carrying that life for me.

She sighed against me and held me back, a mirror of deep love and trust. I held her tighter, overwhelmed with what I felt for this woman.

"I wish it were me, Liv. I wish I'd been the selfish one." I didn't recognize my own voice. But in that moment, I knew I'd never hold her again this way...

I pulled away. The physical separation cut through me like a hot blade. I went to my closet to retrieve the large duffle and started throwing clothes into it. I hadn't ever planned to stay with Will long, so my belongings here were few. The rest were with my family until I found a place to land. This would be over quickly. Had to be, because I could scarcely breathe. Had to get out of here.

"Ian, don't leave."

Liv was frozen where I'd left her. Her tears gutted me, as did the pain in her voice. I hated Will for what this was doing to her, but I couldn't sit here and watch this play out.

I swallowed over the knot in my throat. "I can't stay here."

I threw the last of my things into the bag and zipped it up. Then I went to her, knowing I had to say good-bye.

"Please, Ian. You don't have to do this." Her voice wavered, and she came to me, fisting her hands into my shirt.

Still, I fought the urge to drop the bag and give her everything she wanted. Acceptance, forgiveness for what Will had done, a promise that we'd find a way through this mess. Instead, I fell deeper into my pain, a journey I'd grown used to over time.

"I should have never stayed, Liv. Your first night at Will's should have been my last. This was a mistake."

The words fell cold between us. I forced myself to believe it. If I hadn't stayed and become so entangled with her, I could have saved us both the pain we were feeling now.

She shook her head against me. "Don't say that."

I lifted her chin and touched my lips gently to hers. She brought her arms around my neck and kissed me hard. I fell into it, returning her passion with all of mine. I was obsessed with her taste, the way she seemed to live inside me when we were this close. She moaned, and I almost lost all control. But I couldn't.

I broke away and gazed into her eyes. Pain lingered, but love and desire washed across her beautiful features.

"I love you, Liv." My fingers slipped away. "But I have to go."

She wasn't mine anymore.

OLIVIA

I knocked before entering Maya's and Cameron's upstairs apartment. I found Maya and Vanessa in the living room sitting beside each other on the couch. Aidan was nestled against Maya's chest.

Vanessa brightened when I joined them. "Hey, lady. I haven't seen you in a while."

"Yeah, I've been staying with Will. He's in the penthouse above the new gym. I'm probably going to be there full time in another week or two."

"Wow, that's great. I'm jealous."

I laughed lightly. She wouldn't be jealous if she knew what a mess my life was right now. I dropped onto the adjacent couch, my limbs heavy with grief. I was perpetually exhausted, likely from the hormones that were taking over my body. But no doubt too from endlessly wondering how I could have done things differently.

Ian had given up on us, and it weighed on me like nothing ever had. I called him every day, sometimes more than once. I left voice mails and sent texts, but his silence was crushing. Nothing felt right.

I wasn't alone, but my heart had broken on the fault line between the love I had for Will and Ian. I didn't feel whole. And until he changed his mind, I worried that nothing would ever be the same for me.

"You want to hold him?" Maya passed the baby into

Vanessa's eager arms before standing. "Now that you're both here, I'm going to take a quick shower if you don't mind."

Maya left us, and Vanessa cooed and clucked at the baby, seemingly as enamored with him as I had been. "Can you believe how fast our family is growing?"

In another year, our family would be even bigger. Little did she know...

"It's hard to believe," I said. "A couple years ago, I would have never imagined Cameron being a dad, but now I can't imagine it any other way. He's a natural."

"Darren's so ready."

The Darren I'd once known had seemed about as interested in parenthood as he had been in marriage. Then everything changed. He was nearly unrecognizable now. Some people really could change. Then I thought about Ian, and my heart broke a little more.

"I know he'll be a great dad when the time comes." I rose and sat beside her to admire the baby too.

Vanessa took the hint and passed him to me. My heart did a little happy dance having him in my arms again.

She leaned back with a sigh. "We won't have to wait too much longer to find out."

I turned and caught the glimmer of excitement in her green-eyed gaze. She lifted her shoulders slightly.

"We're expecting," she whispered with a smile.

"You're kidding me."

She shook her head. "I just found out this week. I was trying to wait, but of course Darren wasn't. We weren't being super careful about *not* getting pregnant, so I guess that meant it was time."

"Does Maya know?"

"I haven't told her. I don't want to distract her right now. She's got another nine months to be excited for me."

"That's so amazing." I stared back down into Aidan's perfect little face with a smile. "You're going to have some good company soon, little man."

The quick succession of sucks on his pacifier seemed acknowledgement enough. I couldn't help the happiness I felt for Vanessa and my brother. This was incredible news.

Vanessa's reasons for not sharing her news right now made sense. But when would *I* find the courage to tell my family? Then I remembered that I'd made a vow not so long ago. No hiding, no regrets.

Maybe Vanessa would be a good person to hear it first.

"This is probably going to sound crazy, but I am too."

Her hand went to her mouth. "Oh my God, you're pregnant?"

I nodded with a tentative smile. "I guess we weren't being too careful either. I just found out."

Then her lips moved, but no words came, and somehow I knew what she was trying to ask.

"It's Will's."

"Oh." She blinked a few times and clipped her bottom lip between her teeth. "How's Ian taking it?"

I sighed as a new wave of sadness settled over me like a dark cloud. "Not very well. He left. I haven't heard from him since."

I smoothed my hand over Aidan's fuzzy head and kissed him lightly on the nose. Because he brightened everything up. And when I held my own baby in my arms, hopefully he or she would chase away the sorrow that was heavy in my heart now.

"I'm sure he'll come around," Vanessa offered, touching

my arm gently.

I didn't reply because I didn't really believe he would. I'd keep trying, but the way he'd said good-bye, the pain in his eyes... I was certain we were over.

CHAPTER NINETEEN

WILL

I hunched over my desk, sifting through papers that Adriana had left for me to review. Trying to work ahead had me feeling like I was falling behind. I had a trip to London coming up soon to discuss a promising investment, but leaving Olivia alone right now seemed impossible. Fucking Ian.

I tried to temper my anger, but I found it harder to do as the days went on. Olivia put on a strong front, but I could see right through it. Ian had left her reeling. She was wrapped in a kind of sadness that I felt powerless to lift away. She was in love with him, and no matter how hard I tried to fill that empty place in her heart, I knew I couldn't.

I had argued with her about whether it was the right time to get her involved with a new building I'd purchased a few blocks from the office. She was tired and edgy, and the last thing I wanted to do was tax her more with work. In the end, of course, she'd won.

With my blessing, she'd launched herself into the early details of another remodel. In the space of a week, she'd met with the interior architect and was sketching out plans for the commercial and residential spaces that would ultimately transform the outdated structure.

With Ian out of the picture, I couldn't deny the extra help

was needed, but I worried constantly that she was overexerting herself.

A knock on my office door interrupted my troubled thoughts.

"Have a minute?" Jia sauntered in before I could invite her.

She was dressed head to toe in white. The sleek and smart blouse and skirt combo radiated against her naturally olive skin. The way she carried herself, it was no wonder she'd had new investors eating out of her palm.

As Reilly had promised, Jia more than pulled her weight. While I worried about keeping the investors we already had, she'd hustled up several new accounts. She was killing it, and for the first time since I inherited this billion-dollar problem, I actually felt like we had a fighting chance to turn it into an opportunity that could pay off.

She took a seat across from my desk and crossed her legs. "I wanted to chat about our fees."

I leaned back in my chair and stared at her over my desk. "What about them?"

"Waiving the management fee to attract new investors was a bold move, and I get why you did it. We're trying to extricate ourselves from all the controversy, and we're doing it. But I think you should reconsider waiving the fee."

My cell phone vibrated, but I ignored it.

"We're trying to win back confidence. Nothing says confidence like, 'I get paid when you get paid.'"

"I just think we're leaving money on the table. Prospective clients expect the fees. Why undercut ourselves?"

I drummed my fingers on the desk. "Need I remind you we're working from a disadvantage?"

She held my gaze a moment. "I need to be bringing in more money. I thought this would be a way to do that without cutting into the company's revenue."

I paused, trying to get a read on where she was taking this. "You're getting a salary and a share of the performance fee. What more do you want?"

"I want you to set up a management fee so we can split it."

I laughed and leaned forward. "You've been here a few weeks, and you're already trying to squeeze me for more money?"

"That's not what this is."

Adriana's voice sounded on the office phone's speaker a moment. "Will, you have a call."

"Not now," I snapped. "Jia, we already negotiated your pay, and you seemed more than satisfied. Explain why you're bringing this to me now."

She shrugged, but her shoulders and the muscles in her face were tense. "Circumstances changed. That's all. I didn't think you'd be so against the suggestion."

"I'm less concerned about the money than about why your circumstances changed so suddenly. I need to trust you, Jia. What's going on?"

"We're friends, Will. Of course you can trust me."

I frowned, because nothing about this conversation or her demeanor made me want to trust her. "You don't have friends. You have colleagues. Superiors, inferiors. You have fuck buddies and family. Don't bullshit me about friendship, Jia. I know you better."

Her expression went taut. She squeezed her eyes closed and exhaled heavily. "Maybe you're right. I don't know what to tell you. This opportunity is my whole life right now, Will.

Please, just consider it."

Something wasn't right. I could feel it in my gut.

"What the hell is going on?"

She shook her head, avoiding my imploring gaze. "I just need some extra funds. I thought what we agreed on would be enough, but it's not going to be."

"Tell me why, and I'll do what I can to help you."

She glanced up, her eyes glossy with emotion. "We're not friends, right? If it's all business, why would you want to help me?"

Her voice had taken on a desperate tone that worried me. I'd never seen her get emotional like this. Suddenly I regretted my harsh words earlier.

"I'm sorry, Jia. I'm dealing with a lot right now, but you have to know that you *can* talk to me. If we can't trust each other with the truth, I don't know how we're supposed to make this work."

Any semblance of control she'd held onto crumbled. Her face fell, and she brought her shaking hands to her mouth. "I can't. I can't... They're going to ruin me, Will," she whispered. "Everything... I'll lose everything I've worked for."

Mascara ran down her face before she could stop the tears. I stood and circled my desk. "Jia, who's they? Who are you talking about?"

She shook her head like she didn't want to say it. She stood and paced a circle around the office. When she met my determined gaze again, she finally spoke. "Dermott. And Reilly... He doesn't lose, Will. I don't know why I believed he'd just walk away. I should have known better, but it was too late. I'd already left the firm. He waited to come to me until I was already committed to you and had no place else to go. There's no going back. I'm trapped."

I tried to piece together Jia's rambling sentences. Reilly had no stake, and I had no idea why Dermott would be after her for anything.

"What do they want from you?"

"A cut." She lifted her tense shoulders up and swallowed over the tears that had slowed. "They're at risk of losing their shirts now that these charges have come down. No one trusts them. They can't make money on their old relationships anymore, so now they're coming after me."

"You don't have to give them anything, Jia. They have no power over you. You're with me now. We're running this show, and they've been cut out clean."

She shook her head, and her eyes shone with fresh tears. "They have videos."

"Videos?"

She drew in a shuddery breath. "Back when I worked under Dermott, before he decided to climb the ladder without me...there were a few late nights. I guess he thought it would be fun to capture the moment. Reilly came to me after I'd accepted your offer and told me about the videos. He said I had to cut him in or they'd leak them."

My body tensed as I cursed inwardly. "How much is he asking you for?"

"A lot more than I'm making."

"Say they decided to leak it. Wouldn't that look bad for Dermott?"

She shrugged. "I'm not sure. The clip he showed me hid Dermott's face. They're going to ruin me, Will. If that video gets out, I'm done on Wall Street. This is my whole life." Tears began to fall again, and she wiped at them. "I pushed too hard.

I climbed too fast, and now I'm going to lose everything."

I pulled her to me, holding her tight through the sobs.

White rage flew through me. I'd be damned if my father's cronies were going to get their hands on any of the money we earned. And Jia didn't deserve this. I didn't care how many finance guys she blew. No one deserved to watch their entire career get flushed this way.

"I'm going to fix this, okay?" I murmured, stroking down her back. I had no idea how, but I'd do what I had to.

She circled her arms around my torso, her breathing evening out. "Will, I need you." She gazed up at me, her dark eyes wet and puffy from her tears. "Please, I need to feel something other than what I'm feeling right now. Just one night."

I wiped away the wet streaks on her cheek. "I can't, Jia. I'm with Olivia now. She's it for me. The days of you and me getting together, they're over. I'm sorry."

A sad smile curved her lips. "Lucky her."

"Will?" Before I'd even seen Olivia's face, the confusion in her voice had my heart in my throat.

Jia pulled away quickly, wiping at her eyes. "I'm sorry. I'll go." She slipped past Olivia, leaving nothing but a lot of explaining to do.

"Maybe I should go too." Olivia looked pale.

Fuck.

I came up to her quickly, shutting the door before she could leave. "No, it's not what it looks like."

"No? Are you sleeping with her?"

I winced. "Fuck, no, I'm not sleeping with her."

She stared at me. "*Have* you slept with her?"

I shoved a hand through my hair and released an

exasperated sigh. Today was turning out to be a real piece of shit day.

"Don't tell me what you think I want to hear, Will. We promised each other honesty. Just tell me, damnit." Her brows were knit together, and her fists were tight.

I remembered a time when I used to love riling her up, but now I just wanted to see her smile. I had a long way to go...

"Before I met you, yes, I had slept with her."

Her jaw went tight. "How did I know? And now you see her and share an office with her every day. That's great."

"She's a coworker, Olivia. Nothing more."

She reached for the door handle, but I covered her hand with mine, halting her escape.

"Olivia, stop this."

"You had your hands all over her. Let me guess. It was strictly professional."

"She was upset. You saw her."

She pulled away from my touch and avoided my eyes. She was thinking the worst of me, and the only way out of it was the truth. I dragged my hands over my face. Everything was so fucked up right now.

"Listen, Reilly is blackmailing her to get cut in on what he gave up. He's got video of her fucking her old boss in his office. He's threatening to leak it if she can't figure out a way to line his pockets. I don't know yet if Dermott is trying to get in on it too, but I'm going to find out."

She blinked a few times and then softened a bit. "That's horrible."

I skimmed my hands up and down her arms, breathing out a sigh of relief. "Try not to think the worst of me, if you can help it."

She closed her eyes. "I'm sorry."

"Me too. It's a fucked-up situation, but we're going to figure it out."

She looked up at me. "What are you going to do?"

"I'm going to go to Dermott and get that fucking video."

"But you're leaving in a few days."

I cursed inwardly. This fucking trip. I'd have to get a meeting with Dermott before I left. I couldn't let the situation fester, and I didn't trust Jia not to do anything stupid while I was gone. Her career was hanging in the balance.

The idea of leaving Olivia alone still burned me too. Thank God Jia wasn't going with me on the trip. Olivia would lose her mind, no matter what I said. Then a thought struck me.

"I'll figure this out with Dermott before I go. In the meantime, you're going to start packing your bags. You're coming with me to London."

IAN

I walked through the door of my mother's house after a twenty-four-hour shift. I felt like I was leaving one kind of chaos and entering another. Sunday meant another family dinner—or a house full of nosy women, loud cousins, and amazing food.

Ever since I'd started crashing at my mom's after leaving Will's place, my mother and sisters had been all in my shit, wondering what was going on that had brought me back home so suddenly. I had to find a new place soon.

My youngest sister, Mia, lifted her head, tearing her attention away from some garbage television show. "What's up, loser?"

I dropped my bag by the couch and sank down beside her.

"Not much, brat."

She smirked. "How was work?"

I shrugged. "Same as usual."

Two panic attacks, a cardiac arrest, and an overdose. Nothing that stood out from the norm. Nothing that could touch the pain I'd endured after leaving Liv.

"Bring anyone back to life?"

"Couple people, yeah. Where is everyone?"

"In the backyard."

We shared a knowing look. Mia had just turned sixteen and wasn't overly fond of family gatherings either. We were a generation apart, but somehow we were both equally committed to sulky antisocial behavior as of late.

My oldest sister, Gabrielle, popped her head through the doorway of the kitchen. "Ian! You're here. Come out back. Everyone's here. Shawn too." She lifted her eyebrows, like in a house full of women, the presence of one male would entice me into a social mood.

"I'll be out in a sec."

She left, and I rose, fatigue heavy in my muscles.

"Sucker," Mia muttered.

I turned away from her with a tired chuckle and made my way to join the others.

As promised, the rest of my sisters and their kids and partners were congregated in the yard that we shared with the tenants above us. The autumn air was cool, but the sun shone into the private little outdoor area, making for a beautiful day.

I grabbed a beer from a nearby cooler and took a seat around the patio table where a few serving dishes had already been set out.

Gabrielle's husband was manning the grill, turning

vegetables and steaks over methodically while Ella tugged at his shirt, begging him to play. Shawn wasn't my niece's biological father. Her real father worked on a merchant ship, which meant he only spent a few months a year in the city. He and Gabrielle had had a quick romance that had resulted in Ella, but they'd quickly grown apart. A year later she met Shawn, and they'd been together ever since.

After a few minutes of determined pestering, Ella managed to coax Shawn away from the grill. He lifted her up in a dramatic sweep and turned her upside down until she squealed with laughter. He tickled her until she was breathless, laughing the whole time like he was enjoying teasing her as much as she enjoyed the torture.

Their affection toward each other wasn't qualified by their blood. He was as much her father, if not more, than the man who saw her a few times a year.

Gabrielle sauntered into the courtyard. "Come on, Ella. Let Daddy cook."

Shawn set her down after planting a big kiss on her cheek. My sister coaxed Ella back to where the other cousins played, leaving Shawn to his cooking duties.

Even though it pained me, I imagined Liv and Will's child then, a brown-haired and blue-eyed angel, playing and jumping between them. I wasn't in the picture, but I couldn't help but wonder. Did I have it in me to love Liv's child like Shawn loved Ella?

I took a deep pull off my beer and banished the thought.

Didn't matter. I wasn't going back. I couldn't. I'd left the penthouse and never looked back. It was the only thing I could do.

Since then, Will had been silent. I ignored Liv's calls,

which had been nonstop right after I left and had since tapered off to a daily attempt. Seeing her face cross my screen sliced through me like a hot blade every time.

What would I say? I couldn't hear her cry. I wouldn't listen to her pleas to bring me back, even if those last desperate words from the day I left echoed in my ears every time my head hit the pillow. Even when I could sleep, she haunted me. The memory of her...the feel of her.

I closed my eyes and rubbed the back of my neck, noting the tension that hadn't been there until the past few weeks.

"Cariño, que pasa?"

My mother's soothing voice broke me out of my thoughts for a second.

"Nothing, I'm fine."

"Dónde está tu sonrisa? Papa no le hubiera gustado verte así."

My whole body tensed. "I said, I'm fine," I bit out.

I didn't want to smile, and if my father didn't want to see me this way, he wouldn't have let the cancer kill him. Anger and resentment settled into my tired muscles, giving me something to hang on to.

I'd made a place for Liv in my heart. Now that she was gone, only anger lived there. Fresh resentment that my family had been ripped apart.

"Me partes el corazón cuando te veo así."

"Mama, English." My sister Cara gestured to her boyfriend, Nick, who was the only one in our party who didn't understand a word my mother was saying.

My mother shook her head and went back into the house, muttering Spanish as she went. She fussed more than she used to.

My phone vibrated in my pocket. I withdrew it and saw Will's name. I'd almost gotten used to ignoring Liv's calls, but seeing Will's attempt alarmed me. What if something was really wrong? With Liv, or the baby?

Without thinking, I answered the call.

"Will." I rose from the table and made my way back into the apartment to get some privacy.

"Thanks for picking up." Veiled sarcasm was evident in Will's tone.

"Is there something wrong?" I inhaled a calming breath, but a burst of adrenaline had already shot through my veins, making me alert and ready to snap into action.

"What the hell do you think? You being gone. That's what's wrong. Liv's really upset, and the fact that you won't even answer her calls is ripping her heart out. Do you have any idea how hard it is for me to watch her go through this?"

Damnit. I shouldn't have picked up.

"I did what I had to do."

"No, you reacted and didn't give one thought to how it would break her. You wanted to be in this relationship, and then you just fucking left without another word."

I clenched my teeth. I wanted to yell right back at Will because this was his fault, ultimately. That he was turning it around on me was beyond unfair.

His next words were less forceful. "She warned you this wasn't going to be simple, trying to make things work. Shit's going to get messy sometimes."

I shook my head. "Not like this."

"You never thought somewhere down the road, she'd want a family? We'd be in the same situation. Until modern science can figure out a way to make a baby out of two sperm and an egg, it would have to be you or me."

"Then we could have had a conversation and figured it out. Instead, you made the decision without consulting anyone, not even her."

That shut him up for a second.

"I know we're dealing with this because of me. But we're here now. We can figure this out." He sighed. "Ian, she's eight weeks pregnant. We got the ultrasound this week, saw the heartbeat and everything."

Jealousy and love and rage fought for dominance in my thoughts, a toxic cocktail of emotion.

"Thanks for letting me know, Will. Fucking magical. What can I say?"

"Listen, asshole, I'm telling you that so far everything looks good. She's healthy and so is the baby. Sorry, I thought you might want to know."

"Thanks."

My tone was full of spite, but deep down, I was grateful to know. I couldn't imagine what I'd do if something happened to Liv. I couldn't live with it.

"I don't know why I bothered calling. I just... Whatever."

He hung up, and I nearly threw the phone against the wall.

I shouldn't have picked up the phone. I should have never fallen in love.

WILL

Kevin Dermott had long been fired from his senior position at a prominent firm on Wall Street. As soon as word got around that an investigation was brewing, he'd been escorted out. While his humiliation was likely still ripe, he got to lick his wounds at his multimillion-dollar home on the Upper East Side.

I rang the doorbell, and he answered.

"Will Donovan, hey."

"I reached out by phone a few times." When I hadn't heard back, I decided to pay him a surprise visit. I was determined to squash this situation before the trip to London.

"Sorry, I've been screening calls. What can I do for you?"

"I want to talk to you about Jia Sumner."

He glanced over his shoulder and back to me. "I don't really do business with her anymore."

"That's not what I've heard."

He frowned. "What *have* you heard?"

"I heard that you're blackmailing her to get cut into the Reilly Donovan Capital profits."

He shook his head. "No, that's not true. I don't know what she's telling you, but I haven't talked to her in months."

"I know about the video."

He took a step back. "I have to go."

I put my hand on the door before he could close it. "Listen, Kevin. I need you to think really hard about this. I know it's been a rough few months. Your career has taken a major hit, no doubt about it. But you've still got your family. Your wife, your kids. That's what really matters at the end of the day."

He stared at me, his eyes cold and still. There was no question in my mind that he'd caught the meaning behind my veiled threat. I wasn't above making his life hell in every possible way if he compromised Jia's career or my company.

He stepped through the doorway toward me and shut the door behind him. "What about the video?"

"I want to make sure it never sees the light of day."

His breaths came shorter, and I could tell his adrenaline was spiking. "I don't want it to either. I'm in the fucking video too. It was a mistake. I should never have made it."

"Then why are you threatening Jia with it?"

He flinched. "I'm not. I told you I haven't talked to her in months. I didn't bring her up with me when I got promoted earlier in the year. I don't think she's uttered a word to me since. I do know she's calculating as hell, though. So I want to know what she's saying to you."

"Reilly gave up his shares at the fund. Did you know that?"

He shook his head. "No, it hasn't come up. We've had a few other things on our plate."

"He's threatening to leak the videos if she doesn't cut him in. She's seen them, so that means he has them."

Dermott swallowed and rubbed his forehead with the heel of his hand. "Goddamnit."

"Why does he have these videos?"

"We got drunk one night, and I made the mistake of sending them to him. I had no idea he'd ever use them against me, let alone her."

"I don't care what's gone on between you and Jia, but I need you to make these videos disappear, once and for all."

He nodded. "I will. Consider it done."

CHAPTER TWENTY

IAN

I chugged down a bottle of water, replenishing all the fluids I'd lost in the heat of the fire. Darren dropped down beside me on the length of street curb I'd claimed for my recovery. More crews had come onto the scene, and the fire was under control now. Everyone was safe. The building was damaged but not completely destroyed. Another day on the job.

"That was a bitch, huh?"

I unscrewed the cap to another bottle and drank from it. "Yeah."

"How are things going with you anyway?"

"Fine. Same old." The truth was I was a goddamn mess, but Darren was the last person I was going to talk to about it.

"I don't think I told you, but a spot opened up on Ladder 201. They offered it to me."

"Good for you, I guess," I muttered, sucking down some more water.

I wasn't sure why he was bothering to tell me. We hadn't spoken much since we'd come to blows over me dating Liv. The tension had settled into a manageable discontent for each other. And when I'd left Liv, I hadn't noticed it at all. I was too numb to notice or care.

"I thought about it, but I don't think I'm going to take it."

I shot him a tentative look. "Why not?"

He shrugged and twisted his mouth up. "I don't know. Didn't feel like getting to know a whole new crew. I've had a good run here. Why mess up a good thing?"

I shrugged and stared down at the dirty ground, contemplating why he'd tell me all this. Did he want *me* to go? Maybe he'd never be able to forgive me for being in a relationship with his sister, but it wasn't something he had to worry about for the future. Liv and I were over. I wasn't going back. As much as it killed me, I knew it was for the best. Maybe Darren didn't know that yet.

"Maybe staying won't be so bad. Things aren't as complicated as they used to be. Liv and I... We're not together anymore."

His lips formed a grim line. "Yeah, I know."

I stared at him in disbelief. I expected him to be smiling ear to ear about it. Instead, he seemed...thoughtful. I had no idea what that meant.

"Listen, Darren. I'm sorry that it messed things up between us. I really am. Hopefully we can all move on now."

He shook his head. "I'll live. But I don't think Liv's moving on very well."

Fresh pain worked its way through my chest at the thought of her hurting. After Will's call, I knew she was, but I didn't have to see it or hear it, so I could talk myself into thinking she was happy with Will and the promise of their future together.

"Is she okay?" I forced the words out, bracing myself for his reply.

"We had a family dinner the other night. Will came." He shrugged and made a face that I recognized as unimpressed.

If I weren't so emotionally fucked up over the whole

271

situation, I might have laughed.

"And..."

"I don't know. Vanessa told me you left, and I guess I didn't realize I was rooting for you this whole time. You know, between fantasies of drowning you in the East River."

I cracked a smile. "I'm touched. Truly."

He exhaled a loud sigh. "I don't know. She doesn't seem as happy as she was, you know, before..."

"It's complicated."

My relationship with Liv had been complicated from day one. I was certain Darren couldn't disagree, but I wasn't sure yet if he knew about the pregnancy. I sure as hell wasn't going to bring it up.

"Tell me the truth. Do you really love her? Like, are you sure you even know what that means?"

"Of course I love her. And yes, I know what it fucking means. Doesn't change the fact that it's not going to work out. It's over."

He drew his lips tight together. "Goddamnit, Ian."

I frowned. "What?"

Why was he pressing me about this? This was a hot-button topic that we both knew to steer clear of if we had any hope of repairing our friendship down the road.

He brought his hand to his forehead and rubbed back and forth. "I can't believe I'm going to say this. But I think you should reconsider."

"Reconsider what?"

He threw his hands up. "She's in love with you, man. I don't get this whole fucked-up thing you guys started, but I can't see that look in her eyes week after week. Whatever you did, you have to fix it. I don't care what you have to do, but you've got to make this right."

I looked away, unwilling to believe I had the power to change this path we were on. A path that was taking Liv and me in two different directions. Day by day, we got farther apart.

The street was busy with other firefighters, police, and a couple of news trucks. Above it all, a sunset washed over the sky like a watercolor made of pinks and violets.

I shook my head. "I can't fix this, Darren. I wish I could. I just can't."

OLIVIA

We had planned to stay in London for a little over a week, but after only a few days, Will concluded his business and let me in on a surprise. We'd be spending the remainder of the trip in Paris, a city I had fallen in love with long ago.

I'd never experienced Paris in the fall. The city was as beautiful as I remembered, but cozier and infinitely more romantic now that I was sharing it with Will.

Our hotel had a view of the Sacré-Cœur, and every morning, Will would wake me up with a tray of hot cocoa and chocolate croissants. The pregnancy nausea I'd experienced had been manageable thus far, and I was determined that nothing would keep me from French pastries on this trip. Life was too short for that.

On our second night, we had dinner with Will's mother. She was a petite blonde. Fashionable but not pretentious. She was warm, and the love she had for her son was infectious and heartwarming. She begged us more than once to leave New York and start our family in Paris. At the end of one of the most incredible meals of my life, I almost considered it.

Afterward, Will and I went for a walk around the Champ de Mars. The sun had set and the air was cool, but Will's hand was warm in mine.

"What do you think? Should we relinquish our citizenship and stay here forever?"

"I wish."

He lifted an eyebrow. "Do you? You know I'll give you whatever you want."

I laughed, but I knew he was serious. "Might be hard to manage your empire from here."

"No doubt it would." He sighed. "Maybe one day, when I can step away from all of it, we'll go expat and get a place on the Riviera or something. We can make love and drink wine and eat all the food, every day."

"Sounds like heaven. I think I should start brushing up on my French now."

He pecked a kiss on my cheek. "We'll have you fluent in no time, princess."

The night was growing dark, and we found a bench along the path that offered an unobstructed view of the Eiffel Tower. I pulled my coat tighter. Will immediately put his arm around me to keep the chill away. I leaned into his warmth.

Before us, the tower lit up against the navy sky. People milled around on the vast lawn that surrounded it. Happiness expanded out from my heart, and for the first time, it hit me that I hadn't been truly happy in a long time. Not since Ian had left. I had tried to smile more, for Will's sake. Most days, seeing Aidan or immersing myself in work was enough to keep my emotions above water. Other days were harder, drowned in regret and heartache.

Good or bad, every day that passed, I lost a little more

hope that we'd be able to make amends. I had no idea if I'd ever see Ian again, let alone love him. With his absence and his silence, I forced myself to accept that I'd failed. The grand dream I'd had for us was only that—a dream.

Being with Will had to be enough. I loved him deeply, and we were going to be a family. He alone was a dream come true.

A part of me wished I'd never let myself love Ian, because then his leaving would be something I could bear.

I closed my eyes and tried to forget. This moment was too perfect to color it with sadness and regret.

"I love you," I uttered quietly.

"I love you too. More than anything." Will tipped my chin up and held me with his penetrating cobalt gaze. "I have a question for you."

"What is that?"

"I feel like I'm at the risk of totally messing up a solid Hallmark moment by asking it."

I smiled. "Shoot."

"Do you want to get married?"

The question stole my breath. I hesitated, trying to gauge where this was coming from so suddenly. He wasn't on one knee, proposing. He was asking me an honest question.

"I thought you weren't husband material. Did something change?"

"Everything's changed, not the least of which is you carrying our child."

"Do *you* want to get married?"

Amusement glittered in his eyes. "I asked you first."

I laughed softly. "Seriously, Will."

He sighed and stared up at the tower lights. "I don't know. I think marriage has different connotations for different people. My parents split up when I was young, and it wasn't easy going through that as an only child so I've never put much stock in the idea of marriage. But at the end of the day, I want to do whatever you're comfortable with."

I frowned. "I don't want to get married to be comfortable."

"Okay. How about this? Let's say, in an incredibly cliché romantic gesture, I proposed to you right here at the foot of the Eiffel Tower, in the city of romance. If I got down on one knee, presented you with the biggest diamond Wall Street money could buy, and asked you to be my wife...what would you say?"

He was trying to be funny, but I understood that underneath it all, we were having a very serious conversation about our future and how we were going to define it. I tried to visualize the scenario he painted. For all I knew, he could have a ring in his pocket. What would I say?

My nerves rioted, and my breathing became shallow. Suddenly the thought of him proposing and me having to give him an answer terrified me. I swallowed hard and looked up at the twinkling lights that stretched high into the night sky.

I searched for calm, and then I remembered, whatever life threw at us, Will could handle the truth. He relied on it. After a moment, I met his gaze.

"If you asked me right now, I'd want to say yes, because I love you and I want to give you everything you want."

He blinked once, his expression calm. "But you wouldn't."

"I'm not sure I could say yes right now. Not because I don't want to be your wife, but because I already feel tied to you in all the ways that matter. We're going to have a baby. We share a home and a life. I believe in our future, and I don't need a piece of paper or a huge social event to make me feel like it's any more real or secure."

I fidgeted with my bracelet and waited for him to speak. I hoped he wasn't upset or hurt. I couldn't bear it, but I wanted him to know how I really felt.

"We've already broken all the rules, Will. Trying to follow them at this point for the sake of tradition feels a bit backward, don't you think?"

"Yeah," he said with a small nod, his gaze drifting away from me.

Guilt rushed in over my earlier panic. Maybe I'd misread him completely and I'd totally ruined a moment. "I'm sorry."

"You have nothing to be sorry for. I completely agree with you. I just was hoping I wasn't crushing your hopes and dreams by totally botching a potential proposal. I figure this is every girl's dream, right? Really good-looking rich guy offering jewels and a big white wedding."

His humor filled me with relief. "Were you prepared if I'd said yes?"

His smile softened and his eyes glimmered with emotion. "I was. I'm always going to be ready to give you whatever you need, whatever you want."

My heart stopped and my smile faded. "Will..."

He reached into his pocket and withdrew a thick white ribbon. It was tied around a delicate diamond ring. He untied the bow and held the ring between his fingers.

"It's my mom's. Used to be my grandmother's before my dad proposed. I want you to have it. And if you change your mind, you tell me, and we'll put a band next to it. We'll say all the right words in front of God and our families and all the New York City elite. In the meantime, this just means I love you, and I plan on loving you for the rest of my life."

My lips parted, and tears formed at the corners of my eyes.

"What do you say, Olivia? Do you solemnly swear to be mine...forever?"

I nodded, breathless and overwhelmed by love—the love I had for him, the love he radiated back to me. "I do."

He slipped the ring onto my finger and kissed me tenderly. "I have one more surprise for you."

I smiled against his lips. "You are full of them lately. I can't wait."

"This is the best one."

He turned his head and narrowed his eyes, like he was looking for something in the distance. I followed his gaze, searching for the surprise that already had my heart beating fast.

Then, on the walking path, illuminated with light, I saw him.

But it couldn't be him. In a split second, I convinced myself it was his French doppelgänger. Until I glanced back at Will, who was smiling down at me.

"You didn't think I was going to let you leave Paris with a broken heart, did you?"

"Will." I brought my hand to my mouth. My whole body trembled with emotion.

Ian's figure grew larger as he approached. I could see his face clearly, removing all doubt that it was truly him.

He was smiling, hands in his jean pockets, wearing a gray-brown sweater that did little to obscure the muscular chest beneath it. I pushed off the bench and went to him. Slowly at first. Then I couldn't wait. I didn't think about whether he still loved me or any of the things I'd wanted to say to him since he'd left. I just ran to him and threw myself into his arms.

He lifted me, and I wrapped my legs around his waist. I

clung to him, and he held me so tight I could scarcely breathe. We stayed that way for what seemed like forever. If it had been forever, I would have happily accepted an endless fate in his arms after our agonizing separation.

"I can't believe you're here," I whispered, nuzzling his neck. His scent filled me and brought me back to memories I had tried so hard to let go of. My chest was tight, but I couldn't find the tears. I'd cried too many. I was too full of happiness right now to drown them with a drop of sadness.

When I pulled back, my breath caught. Every instinct told me to kiss him. I ached to feel his lips on me, to communicate without words that I still loved him desperately.

"Kiss me," I whispered.

His gaze was dark, storming with emotion and drifting down to my mouth. But he didn't kiss me. Instead, he loosened his grasp so I slid down the front of his body. My feet found the ground, but his arms around me held my weight.

My mouth was dry and my throat was tight as I considered the worst. What if he didn't love me anymore? What if too much time had passed? He'd broken my heart, but I knew he'd been hurting too. Maybe it was too much to bear.

Didn't matter. I had to tell him because I might not get another chance.

"Ian, I love you...so much." My eyes brimmed with tears. "No matter what, I want you to know that. I wanted to tell you so many times—"

He hushed me and brought his hands to my face, keeping us connected, like we were tied together by some invisible force.

"I've never stopped loving you, Liv, and I'm never going to stop." He swallowed, and his lips parted gently. "I know I've put you through hell. This has been the worst kind of agony for me. I only hope that one day you can forgive me."

My heart twisted painfully in my chest. I squeezed my eyes closed, and a single tear flowed down my cheek and into his hand. Brushing it away, he brought his lips to mine with a kiss so soft and tender, I could only sigh into it.

"Take me back," he whispered.

I opened my eyes, and in an instant, the weeks of missing him dissipated. The heartache was overrun with a love so powerful, it took my breath away. What was left was only us, here, together again. The fault line in my heart healed, because I knew now what I'd known all along. Ian belonged there beside Will, in my heart, in my future.

"I never let you go..."

EPILOGUE

WILL

I checked my watch again as the flight attendant came closer. She paused when I caught her attention.

"Can I get you anything, sir?"

"Another coffee would be great. And when are we due to land?"

"The pilot has us arriving a little ahead of schedule, so we should be landing in about an hour."

"Perfect, thanks."

"I'll be right back with your coffee."

I nodded with a smile, but I was still uneasy. With the time difference and the long flight, I hadn't talked to Olivia or Ian in over a day. She was still two weeks from her due date, and all I could do was pray nothing happened while I was in the air.

Beside me, Jia stared out the window at the endless sea of clouds as we made our way back to New York from Hong Kong.

I tapped my foot, revved up from the coffee and nervous energy from being awake too long.

She glanced over at me. "Wired much?"

I laughed softly. "I'm anxious to get home, that's all."

She smiled and gazed down at the obscene diamond that shimmered on her finger. "Me too."

Not long after my Paris getaway with Olivia, Jia had gotten involved with a prospective client. Allen Easton was about ten years her senior, flush with cash, and a far cry from the usual cocky finance guys who seemed to swarm around her at social events.

After our affair had ended and Jia's reputation had been on the line, something had changed in her. She still loved the game and the challenges of the industry. She still exuded the same sexy confidence that had drawn me to her. She wasn't above using her charm to close a client, but as far as I could tell, she'd held a firm line between her personal life and professional life. Until Allen.

From day one, he was different, and she'd told me as much. Instead of trying to figure out the fastest avenue to get her into bed, he'd taken his time to win her trust. From what I could tell, he respected her well beyond her beauty and treated her as an equal. He gave her everything she'd worked so hard for, everything she deserved.

I was happy for Jia. I was even happier for Olivia. The pregnancy hormones weren't doing me any favors, but Jia having a committed partner had noticeably calmed Olivia's nerves, especially when it came to trips like this one. Leaving her for the airport at the start of this journey was possibly one of the most stressful experiences of my life. She didn't want to let me go, and I would have given anything to stay.

But duty called, and this time it was closing a whale of an investor, a connection that Frank Bridge had facilitated. It was an opportunity that we couldn't pass up.

The past six months at the fund, newly named Donovan Capital, had been anything but smooth sailing. While Jia and I continued to pull our weight, doing it against the periodic setbacks was taxing. Always two steps forward, then one step back.

I'd done what I'd agreed to do. I instilled confidence, drummed up fresh opportunities, and made healthy profits. Despite our best efforts, when the charges came down on my father and the others, many clients who were no longer obligated to stay with us left.

My father was charged and sentenced with twelve months in jail, what some thought was a paltry measure of justice. As the primary orchestrators and perpetrators of the fraud, Dermott and Reilly got hit the hardest, both being sentenced with five years.

While those charged paid restitution and had time to serve, we all knew the real justice was served when it came to their reputations. Their careers were over. Their lives would never be the same.

As the news died down, life returned to some semblance of normal. Jia and I continued to work hard and distinguish ourselves from the fund's troubled past. The days were long, but the future was bright.

With Olivia to come home to and our baby on the way, I couldn't ask for anything more. Life was as close to perfect as I could have ever imagined.

IAN

Olivia cursed Will all the way to the hospital.

"I can't believe he took this trip. I told him not to. Goddamn him." She gripped the handle on the door and hissed out a long breath.

I took her hand and held it tight while I steered with the

other. "I know, baby. He'll make it. Just breathe."

"Drive faster," she whispered as the contraction tapered out.

I hit the gas and silently cursed Will too.

Olivia was two weeks from her due date. The doctor had said with this being her first child, she was unlikely to go into labor before he got back. But Hong Kong was a long way away. Even though he was due back today, it would probably take a miracle to get him to the hospital in time.

"You called him?" Olivia had pain and worry written all over her beautiful face.

"I called him about twenty times and left as many voice mails. I'm sure I'll hear back really soon. Don't worry, okay?"

She nodded quickly, like she had too much on her mind to devote all her worry to Will's absence. Then she squeezed my hand tightly. So tightly I thought she might break something, but she was the one in labor. We'd been timing contractions for hours, since the early morning. Then her water broke, and I prayed to everything holy that Will was somewhere in this country, getting off a plane, checking his fucking messages.

We got the suite at the hospital that Will had reserved for the inevitable time. Moments later, Liv's heavily pregnant body was submerged into a deep tub designed for this very moment. She breathed through every contraction, clinging to my hand like she'd die if I let her go.

"You're doing great," I murmured.

But she only glared at me before another contraction took her focus completely away. I'd seen babies delivered before, but watching Liv go through this was way outside of my comfort zone. I couldn't comprehend her pain or her determination to endure it without meds.

I was checking my watch again when my phone rang. "Hang on a minute. I'll be right back."

She glared again. "You can't leave me."

"Nope, not leaving. I'm right here." I answered the call while she crushed my hand through another wave of pain. "Hey." I didn't dare say his name.

"What's going on?" Will's voice sounded like a distant echo.

"She's in labor. Seven centimeters dilated. Where the fuck are you?" I said lightly, trying to keep my tone friendly even if my words weren't.

"I'm at the airport. Just landed. How long do I have?"

I glanced up at the nurse and tapped my watch. "How long?"

"Maybe an hour or so. She's progressing quickly."

"You've got an hour. Book it."

"I'm on my way," he said gruffly before hanging up.

Olivia's eyes were wide and glossy like she might cry. "Is he going to make it?"

"Yeah, baby. He's almost here. You just concentrate on your breathing."

She nodded again and took a series of short breaths that seemed to give her some relief until the next contraction arrived.

"Oh, fuck. Oh, no. Ow, ow, ow, ow."

I hushed her and held her through the longest contraction yet. The next few were consistently intense, and I got the strong sense that we were running out of time.

Then Liv's eyes took on a wild look. "Ian, I have to push. I think I have to push."

The nurse rushed over, and together we lifted her from

the tub, dried her off, and brought her to the bed.

The nursed quickly checked her. "Oh, yeah. She's ready. I'll go get the doctor."

"What about Will?" Her voice was frantic.

"He'll be here. I promise." Lies, because I had no idea if he'd make it, but I had to try to make her happy one minute to the next. Thank God I was here.

The doctor strolled in like there was all the time in the world, all the while Liv was groaning. All the blood had been crushed from my hand, and the nurse was showing me the baby's head crowning. Dark-brown hair.

Liv's baby. Will's baby. Our baby. He or she was nearly here, and my stomach was about to drop out.

The doctor got comfortable where the action was about to happen, and the nurse talked Liv through the first push.

One contraction seemed to blend into the others, but the nurse assured us progress was being made. Just as I was about to give up hope that Will would make it, he slid in the door, out of breath and grinning from ear to ear.

"Olivia!" He rushed over to her other side.

"I hate you," she snapped, grabbing his hand and squeezing through the next contraction.

He winced, but then his broad smile returned. "That's okay, because I love you. You're beautiful and amazing, and we're about to have a baby."

I winked at him. "Don't worry. She's been telling me the same thing since we got here."

"Hate you both." She breathed out and into the next push that brought the baby's head farther into view.

Two more pushes and the baby came. A girl.

They placed her on Liv's chest and cleaned her. Liv held

her, tears in her eyes and an exhausted, contented smile on her face. My heart exploded with happiness and more love than I knew I was capable of. Somehow, the love I'd carried for Liv these many months had instantly multiplied and spread to include the incredible little human she'd just given birth to.

Will cut the cord, and the nurses took the baby to weigh her and check her vitals. Liv wilted back into the bed, glowing with energy and happiness.

Leaning down, I kissed the beautiful warrior woman who'd given us the greatest gift.

"I'm so proud of you," I whispered.

OLIVIA

The second my parents walked into the penthouse, my mother's countenance tightened with concern. While Will greeted my dad, my mother walked over to where I sat on the couch and put her hand on my cheek.

"Olivia, you look exhausted. Are you getting enough sleep?"

I laughed and leaned in to hug her. "I have a newborn, Mom. Sleep isn't really happening a lot right now."

"Are the boys helping you?"

I smiled because she routinely referred to the two men in my life as boys. The term made Ian roll his eyes. If Will cared, he didn't show it, but he had more experience schooling his features in mixed company. Neither would complain though, as both my parents had mercifully avoided discussing our relationship or living arrangements since Darren had taken the opportunity to explain it to them, in no uncertain terms.

"Yes, they're definitely helping," I reassured her, "but I'm the one nursing, so they can only do so much."

A small cry came from the nursery.

"Oh! There she is. She must know I'm here." My mom's eyes lit up. I'd never seen her so happy as when she held Amelia.

Not long after she'd learned about the pregnancy, she and my father had rented an apartment in the city so she could be closer. She'd been staying there for the past two weeks since Amelia was born, on call whenever I needed her or invited her over to visit.

Before I could go check the nursery, Ian appeared. Amelia's little body was swaddled and nestled securely against his broad chest. She looked like a little pink peanut, nearly swallowed up by Ian's strong arms. He rocked her and clucked quietly as she fussed. Her tiny feet kicked at the blanket that held her.

"I changed her, but I think she's hungry, Liv."

"Bring her here."

I held out my arms, and he lowered her into them with care. She was so small, her skin still pink and so velvety smooth. She began rooting, and I pulled down the top of my tank to give her my breast. She latched on instantly, as she had from the day she was born. Overachiever for sure.

"Olivia." My mother spoke in a tight hushed voice.

"What?" I looked up, mystified by her reaction.

She glanced to where my father stood in the kitchen chatting with Will and then back to me. She shook her head and opened her mouth, but shut it again. "Sorry. I'm out of practice with things, I guess."

I sighed, only mildly concerned about my lack of modesty and the discomfort it might have caused her or my dad. I was too tired and too in love to care. Instead, I stared down at my daughter, riveted with every precious noise and movement.

I hadn't known true love until Will and Ian had come into my life. But the explosion of adoration that hit my heart when Amelia came into the world was unmatched. Her perfect little feet stretched, and I marveled at her delicate toes and fingers.

She was the greatest gift I'd ever been given.

All the moments of fear and regret and worry disappeared the minute they laid her against my chest. The world as I knew it had stopped, and everything recalibrated to orbit around her—her needs, her comfort, her future.

While my mother had been relatively detached throughout Maya's pregnancy, something had shifted when she became a grandmother. Maybe after years of my brothers and me defying her best wishes, we'd finally broken her. Where I'd grown used to fielding pressure and expectation at every turn, I now found resignation and acceptance. We didn't discuss wedding plans or why Ian shared our home. They knew, and if avoidance meant acceptance, I could handle that.

My dad's demeanor had changed over time too. Some of the tension that seemed to follow him around eased. He smiled more, worked less. Our growing family provided the perfect excuse. They were grandparents now, and as soon as Vanessa gave birth, which would be any day, they'd have three little people to dote on.

For the first time since we'd been children, I felt like we were a family again.

As Amelia nursed contentedly, my mother leaned close and brushed a loving caress over her soft brown baby hair.

"She's perfect," Mom whispered. Tears glistened in her eyes, and then she tucked a tendril of hair behind my ear with a smile. "Just like you, my princess."

BONUS SCENE

From Darren & Vanessa

DARREN

"You'd better run faster than that."

Vanessa giggled and scurried across the apartment toward our bedroom. I could have caught up to her on the way up the stairs but decided to make the chase a little fun and give her a head start.

She flew into the bedroom and attempted to shut the door, but I put my hand on it before she could. No match for my strength, she gave up quickly and spun for the bathroom. Two more paces and I caught her by the waist before she could escape. She squealed when I pulled her tight against me and nuzzled her neck.

"Got you, baby."

I wiggled my fingertips against her ribs and down her sides.

"Don't!" She laughed and tried to squirm away.

The chase was over, so I took us down to the bed. I crawled over her, eating her up with my gaze the way I had all night at Cam and Maya's after dinner. Her auburn hair fanned out on the bed, and her light blue eyes were bright with mirth.

Some days—most days—I couldn't think of much else but tearing up the sheets with my new bride. Today was no exception. I couldn't get enough of the woman.

I dipped down to take her lips. She tasted like apples and wine. I groaned and reveled at the way she melted under me. Made me want to spend hours winding her up and watching her let go. I'd never get tired of it.

I settled between her thighs and ground against her. I pressed my growing erection to the seam of her jeans to ensure pressure to her clit. She gasped and lifted her hips into the contact. Now that she was in the right frame of mind...

I caught her breast in my hand and squeezed. I kissed along her jaw and nipped at her ear. "Let's make a baby."

When I rounded back to her mouth, she smiled under our kiss.

"You know you want to," I teased, nibbling gently at her lips.

"We need to talk about this some more."

"Do we?" Goddamn, when was she going to give up the fight? I went for the button on her jeans and deftly unfastened and unzipped the denim barrier. "Let me get inside you, and we won't need to talk about anything."

"This is a big deal."

She was trying to be serious, but I could tell she was struggling not to smile.

This was how I got my way. If I could just keep her laughing or coming, she couldn't dig her heels in too much.

I lifted off of her, pretending like I wanted to talk, but swiftly took advantage of my position to slip my hand into her jeans and tease her through her panties.

"You got off the pill. I thought that was the green light." I glanced down between us, harnessing all my willpower not to push the fabric aside and sink my fingers into her pussy.

"You threw my pills out half way through my cycle, so I

didn't bother getting a new prescription. Not quite the same."
She circled my wrist but didn't slow my strokes. Instead, she
slid her hand over mine, joining me as I rubbed her.

I smirked. "You didn't argue."

"Much," she muttered, arching into my touch.

All I could think about was claiming her, reaching the
deepest part of her, and binding us together in every way
possible. The thought of trying for a baby had always been
attractive. After all, fucking her was no hardship. But making
love to her was so much more than the physical act. I wanted
to look deep into her eyes when I let go and know she wanted
exactly what I wanted—a family, a future made up of the two of
us and our children.

But if she wasn't ready, she wasn't ready.

I drew in a sobering breath, withdrew my touch, and rolled
off of her onto my back. I scrubbed my fingers through my hair
and tried to get my libido under control. Then she straddled
across my hips. That wasn't really helping matters.

"I thought you said you wanted to talk," I grumbled.

"I do," she said softly. "I want to do a lot more than talk,
but...I'm scared that we're moving too fast, Darren. Everything
has been so rushed. With us, and then the wedding. I know I
want this with you, but I don't want to overwhelm either of us."

I sighed and held her by the hips, ignoring the
suggestiveness of her position over me. "Vanessa, I want to be
overwhelmed. Especially by you and with you."

"You say that now..." She lifted her shoulder and looked
down to where her fingers tangled in my shirt.

She was being too cautious and careful, as usual. When
we'd talked about it before, she'd seemed ready, but then
something spooked her. Maybe it was seeing Maya go through
these past couple months of late pregnancy. Maybe her work

at Youth Arts was picking up speed and legitimately stressing her out enough to want to take a step back.

But if we waited until we were ready, we never would be. The thought of being a parent scared the shit out of me too, but the love that burned inside me for Vanessa was stronger than my fear. I was determined to have every experience with her, and if Cameron was brave enough to take the plunge, so was I.

I flipped her to her back again, but instead of stripping her down and ravaging her the way I wanted to, I simply stared into her eyes.

"I know you think I'm being my usual crazy impulsive self." I hesitated, hoping she would truly believe what I was about to say. "I love you, Vanessa. More than my own life, and I know I'm going to love our children the same way. It's going to be intense, more than we can even imagine right now. But I'm ready for that kind of love."

Her expression softened with a sigh. "Darren..."

"I want a family with you, baby. I know it's not obvious with the way my parents are, but Cam, Liv, and I had some good times. Being around them all the time makes me miss it. I had no idea if I would ever settle down, but I figured if I did, Cam's and my kids would grow up together. I'll wait as long as you want to, but—"

She pressed her fingers to my lips. "Darren, trust me, I've got baby fever. Like really bad. The second Maya told me she was pregnant, I started living vicariously through every milestone with her. But it's a really big decision. I want to be sure you're really ready too."

She didn't have to say it, but I could guess at the source of her hesitation. I feathered my fingertips over the freckles that danced across her nose and cheekbone.

"Red, I'm not like your dad. I'm not going anywhere. You

and I, we're partners for life. I'm going to be here, always, for you and for our family when we decide to have one."

Her eyes glimmered with emotion. She sifted her fingers through my hair and pulled me down into a kiss. "Thank you."

I lifted away a fraction, gazing into her eyes. "Do you believe me?"

She nodded. "I know you're not like him. I'm sorry."

"You don't have to be sorry. You just tell me when you're ready."

She opened her mouth to speak, but I swallowed whatever she might have wanted to say with another deep kiss. I roved my hands over her, tugging at her clothes and discarding mine. Ready or not, I was having her tonight. We could argue about the baby thing later. In the meantime, she was my wife and I had every intention of making her come until we were both completely wasted.

The second I had her naked, I was sinking into her. My love... my whole life. She was everything to me, and this was where I belonged—in her arms, every day of our lives.

I caressed her everywhere, kissing her, whispering in her ear. I loved her so damn much...

My body was on fire for her, responsive to every small touch and reaction between us as I made love to her. I was close and sensed she was too.

"Darren." Her voice was breathless as she tightened around me.

"Right here, baby."

I expected her to tell me to go faster or slower or mutter something deliciously dirty.

Instead, she caught my face in her palms. "I'm ready."

I blinked, trying to get my brain to work. Then my heart started racing faster when I caught her meaning. "Are you serious?"

She nodded, her chest heaving under soft breaths. "I'm ready. Let's make a baby."

I closed my eyes and went deeper on my next thrust. "Vanessa..." Her name on my lips was a question and a prayer.

Was she sure? I hoped to God she was, because I wasn't sure I could stop myself. I wasn't thinking clearly. I couldn't when we were this close, when she was wrapped all around me. Goddamn, but I wanted her to be ready.

I was about to ask her again when she brushed her lips over mine.

"Come inside me."

That was it. I groaned and pumped harder, but I didn't rush. I held on steady, gazing into her eyes, sensing her climb and waiting for the right time.

Our eyes locked, we shared each breath, and in a moment of perfect harmony, we came together. Instinct drove me to stay nestled deep inside of her.

I smiled as I caught my breath. "That was fun."

She laughed softly. "It was. We should do it again sometime."

"Definitely. At least a few more times tonight."

"You're a man on a mission, I can tell," she teased.

I shook my head. "Ever since I met you, Vanessa, I've been on a mission to make you mine. Never going to stop, so you might as well get used to it."

I melded my mouth to hers with a gentle kiss, determined to make good on every promise I'd ever made to her. Tonight and every day of our future.

ACKNOWLEDGEMENTS

Olivia's story has been kicking around in my head for almost two years, so having the chance to finally sit down and pen it was a relief and a thrill. Some stories just flow. Even when people got a little wide-eyed when I described the premise, deep down I knew that my characters would pull through and help me get it done.

Mia Michelle, thank you yet again for being an amazing cheerleader and helping make writing fun again. I'm not sure the words would have flowed so well without our little side project (wink wink). Our late-night chats and inappropriate banter kept me sane, yet again!

Dave Grishman, thanks for your Wall Street insights and keeping the operation running smoothly while I disappeared into the writing cave for weeks. And to all my Waterhouse Press peeps, Kurt, Yvonne, Dave Mac, Amber, and Jonathan.

Big thanks to Shayla Fereshetian for your late-night writing sprints, caffeine deliveries, and endless support. I'm lucky to call you a friend!

Thanks, Mom, for always being there for me...

Special thanks to Angel Payne and my sprint group buddies for making the many writing pushes much less lonely.

My betas, thank you for your amazing feedback! Hearing your thoughts after I cross the finish line is one of my favorite parts of this process.

As always, thanks to my amazeballs editor, Helen Hardt, for helping me get another manuscript ready for the masses in record time.

Last but not least, Team Wild, your unfailing support and enthusiasm give me purpose! Every time I sit down to write, I'm writing a story I hope you'll love and remember. When I started our little group over two years ago, I could have never imagined the friendships that would be forged. I am so grateful for each and every one of you!

ABOUT THE AUTHOR

Meredith Wild is a #1 *New York Times, USA Today,* and international bestselling author of romance. Living on Florida's Gulf Coast with her husband and three children, she refers to herself as a techie, whiskey-appreciator, and hopeless romantic. When she isn't living in the fantasy world of her characters, she can usually be found at www.facebook.com/meredithwild.

You can find out more about her writing projects at www.meredithwild.com